Advance Acclaim for *Crater*

"Long-haul trucking on the Moon . . . with raiders, romance and a secret mission . . . High adventure on the space frontier."

—*Kirkus*

"*Crater* shows what it would be like to live on the Moon: to work there, to struggle and to triumph. A fine piece of work by Homer Hickam."

—Ben Bova, Author of *Leviathans of Jupiter*

"Readers will be caught up in Homer Hickam's thrilling novel of life on the moon! Plenty of twists and an admirable, spirited hero in Crater who takes us on an adventure filled with intrigue and excitement that leaves us wanting more."

—Donna VanLiere, *New York Times* & *USA Today* Best-selling Author of *The Good Dream* and *The Christmas Shoes*

CRATER

CRATER

A HELIUM-3 NOVEL

HOMER HICKAM

THOMAS NELSON

Since 1798

NASHVILLE DALLAS MEXICO CITY RIO DE JANEIRO

Published in Nashville, Tennessee, by Thomas Nelson. Thomas Nelson is a registered trademark of Thomas Nelson, Inc.

Thomas Nelson, Inc., books may be purchased in bulk for educational, business, fundraising, or sales promotional use. For information, please e-mail SpecialMarkets@ ThomasNelson.com.

Scriptures taken from the Holy Bible, New International Version®, NIV®. Copyright © 1973, 1978, 1984, 2011 by Biblica, Inc.™ Used by permission of Zondervan. All rights reserved worldwide. www.zondervan.com

Publisher's Note: This novel is a work of fiction. Names, characters, places, and incidents are either products of the author's imagination or used fictitiously. All characters are fictional, and any similarity to people living or dead is purely coincidental.

Library of Congress Cataloging-in-Publication Data

Hickam, Homer H., 1943–
 Crater : a Helium-3 novel / Homer Hickam.
  p. cm.
 Summary: In the twenty-second century, sixteen-year-old Crater Trueblood, who mines the moon for Helium-3 to produce energy for a desperate, war-towrn Earth, undertakes a deadly mission that could mean the difference between life and death for every inhabitant on the moon.
 ISBN 978-1-59554-664-7 (hardcover)
 [1. Moon—Fiction. 2. Science fiction.] I. Title.
 PZ7.H5244Cr 2012
 [Fic]—dc23   2011051931

Printed in the United States of America

12 13 14 15 16 QG 5 4 3 2

TO AMI McCONNELL

Part One

MOONTOWN

The little mining village of Moontown, set deep within the lunar Alpine Valley, was bathed in the bluish glow of a vast and sinuous river of stars flooding across a black velvet sky. On the Helium-3 scrapes to the west of the settlement, the miners of the Medaris Mining Company's third shift trudged toward the dustlocks, their bobbing and weaving helmet lights shooting bright spokes across the gray dust, silicate flakes caught in the beams sparkling like diamonds.

Two miners remained behind on the slope of the scrape designated eleven north. Clad in the red coveralls of explosives experts, they were working feverishly to prepare the next section for blasting before the shift was over. Nitro Ned, the leader of the team, smacked the black box he was holding and took a long second to control his anger. It had been a frustrating day. Even though the blue banger foreman had made several mistakes, including a failure to move the belt line in a timely fashion, the shift had worked twelve sections when the average was eight. Everyone was worn-out, including Nitro Ned. He just wanted to get to the dustlock and go home to his sweet wife and two daughters.

"What's wrong, Ned?" the assistant asked. She was a puter-bride turned miner who called herself Unlisted Sally, thus following the tradition of many citizens of Moontown who adopted nicknames, sometimes to hide their past but often to simply renounce all ties with Earth, their lives begun anew at the gritty mining outpost in the wayback of the moon.

Ned smacked the box again and said, "I told the blue banger we didn't have time to check this section before the end of the shift. Now this scrag pulsor's gone belly-up."

The pulsor was an ultrawide band unit, designed to let its operator peer through the dust to see what lay below, especially basalt boulders called rollers. Rollers, if blown up by a detpak—as the explosives packages were called—could turn into what their names implied, rolling boulders that careened down the slopes, some big enough to crush machines and miners.

"I'll get another pulsor," Sally said.

Ned shook his head. "Naw, you'd have to drive all the way to the maintenance shed. By the time you got back, the first shift would be coming through the dustlock and we'd have to wait until they were all through before we could get inside. We'll have to use the sticks."

"The sticks" were six-foot-long lunasteel rods designed to penetrate the dust with a hard thrust. Sally followed Ned to their truck to retrieve them and drop off the dead pulsor. She examined one of the pointed rods. "Do these things really work?"

"Use 'em right, they're better than pulsors," Ned grunted,

and demonstrated by plunging a stick into the dust. "Rollers aren't usually more than a few inches deep. If they're here, we'll find 'em."

Sally tested her stick. It entered the top of the dust easily, then jammed. "You got to push harder," Ned said. "Give it all you got. See? I penetrated five, six inches that time."

Sally tried it again, this time pushing the stick in deeper. "I guess it should work," she said, though her voice betrayed her uncertainty.

"Sure it will. Come on."

Ned led Sally back to the section and the pair began jabbing the dust. Ten futile minutes later, Ned, breathing hard, stopped. Pushing the stick into the dust again and again was not easy. He looked around and saw the last of the miners from his shift entering the dustlock. The miners for the next shift were probably already lining up to enter the other side. Ned made a decision. "There's nothing here but dust," he announced. "Let's call it a day."

Sally wasn't certain they'd done a thorough job, but Ned was her boss. Not only that, her back and her head hurt. She longed to get out of the sticky gluelike biolastic material that coated her body. Her helmet also had a bad air delivery valve. All day she'd felt like she was half suffocating. Still, she felt compelled to ask, "Are you sure, Ned? We clear it, they'll blow this section without checking again."

Nitro Ned was already halfway back to the truck. "I know these slopes like the back of my hand. This ain't roller geology. We're done." He called up the foreman's frequency on his helmet communicator. "Bossman, our last section's ready for detpaks. We're coming in."

The section foreman came back. "Hurry up. The next shift needs this dustlock clear."

The blue banger didn't have to tell Nitro Ned and Unlisted Sally twice. They tossed the dusty sticks in the back of their truck, stirred up its fuel cells, and raced, headlights blazing, down the slope and across the dust-laden flats.

::: ONE

rater Trueblood was right where he wanted to be, and Petro Mountbatten-Windsor-Jones was right where he didn't want to be—although neither opinion mattered because both of them were right where they were. That was in converging lines of first-shift Helium-3 miners making their way through the busy corridors of Moontown toward the dustlocks that led to the scrapes. There was a hint of butterscotch in the air, the fragrance of the day. There was also piped-in martial music, appropriate to soldiers marching off to war, or, in this case, heel-3 miners off to do battle with the dust.

Like the other miners in the line, Crater and Petro were dressed in standard tube clothes of tunics, leggings, and plaston boots. Crater's tunic was a careful gray, his leggings the standard black, his boots an ordinary beige. Petro's tunic was an exceptional red, his leggings a unique diamond-patterned blue and white, and his boots a rare purple. Crater—at sixteen going on seventeen—was small for his age, just over six feet tall, while Petro, just turned nineteen, had topped out at six feet, five inches, an inch taller than the average adult born and raised on the moon. Lunar gravity did not compress the human backbone like the heavier pull of the Earth.

Fifteen minutes, the gillie on Crater's shoulder said while watching Petro with an amused expression, difficult since the gillie had no eyes.

"Your gillie is making faces at me," Petro accused.

"It has no face," Crater replied.

"It is also illegal."

"It knows that."

There were signs and arrows in the corridor pointing this way and that to the various hatches that led to the neighborhoods, dustlocks, foundries, tank farms, warehouses, depots, maintenance sheds, and company offices of the town. Crater and Petro didn't need directions to anywhere. They intimately knew every tube and hatch, having explored them all at one time or another while growing up in the tiny town beneath the dust.

Unlike Petro, who was scowling at anybody and everybody, Crater smiled and nodded to every miner he encountered as well as the tubewives and tubehusbands, many with their children out and about on their errands at the company store or the company doctor or the company dentist or the company chapel. Crater, by his very nature, was friendly to the core of his being. He had gentle eyes that saw things always in the best possible light and a sweet, round face, unmarred by worry lines. When people saw him, he made them feel better just for being who he was, an orphan who never complained and who worked hard at his job on the scrapes.

Petro, slogging along behind as if every step he took was

a great inconvenience, saw life a little differently. He saw Moontown as gray and uninspiring. He saw the work outside as hard and boring and the pay far too low. He saw Crater differently too. Crater was a sweet kid, that was true, but if he was ever going to get anywhere in life, he needed to toughen up and recognize that not everyone was as nice as he was. As his friend and sort of older brother, Petro took Crater's education in the realities of life as one of his main goals. Accordingly, he called out to Crater's back, "We are better than this, Crater. We should turn around this instant, pack our bags, and be off to secure our fortunes in Armstrong City, perhaps even on Earth. And—will you please stop and listen? What are you now—sixteen?"

Crater sighed and turned around. "Almost seventeen. Come on, Petro. We're gonna be late."

"So what? Think of all the times we've been early. You've been working on the scrapes for three years, right?"

"I started on my thirteenth birthday so it's almost four."

"Almost four and you're still a scragline picker, the lowest of the low!"

Crater never knew what to say to Petro when he was in one of his "get out of town" moods, which seemed lately to be more and more often. Although they weren't related, he and Petro had been raised together and he thought of the older boy as his big brother. He didn't like disappointing Petro but just couldn't help it. "I don't want to leave Moontown," he said. "Anyway, what's wrong with being a scragline picker? Somebody's got to do it."

Petro lowered his head in mock despair. "Why I even bother to talk to you is a mystery. Look, Crater, don't you get it? The deck's stacked against us! You're an orphan and what am I? Yes, yes, I'm the Prince of Wales and all that, but no one will make me King of England anytime soon."

"If you left, wouldn't Q-Bess miss you?" Crater asked, referring to Petro's mother, who was also Crater's guardian and the manager of the Dust Palace Hotel.

Petro allowed a sigh. "This is not about my dear royal *mater*. Yes, of course, she'd miss me. Who wouldn't? But look, brother, this is about me and you. I am quite simply the best poker player on the moon, and I aspire to take my talent elsewhere and empty the pockets of those who should know better. You speak a dozen or more languages, you know math to the doctorate level, nobody can beat you in physics and chemistry, and you're an ace mechanic. Yet, with all that knowledge packed into your little brain, all you want to be is a heel-3 miner."

Crater couldn't disagree with the truth. "A heel-3 miner is a fine profession," he said. "I'm proud to be one."

"Stay here and rot, then!" Petro spat. "Just as soon as I save enough johncredits, I'm heading to Armstrong City where I will board a Cycler, play cards on the game deck, and win some big money off those rich tourists who fly here to see hicks like you."

The bank account as of three point two seconds ago of Philip Earl Thomas Reginald Osgood Mountbatten-Windsor-Jones aka the Prince of Wales aka Petro Jones amounts to thirty-three johncredits and seventy-two bits, the gillie said.

"I have a cash flow problem," Petro confessed, then glared at the gillie. "What are you doing crawling around in my bank account, you ugly blob of slime mold?"

"It is a bad gillie," Crater said, then spoke to it. "Don't ever hack into Petro's account again."

The gillie shrugged or would have if it had shoulders, which it didn't. "Into your holster," Crater commanded.

The gillie did as it was told, sliding into the holster on Crater's left arm, but first it said, *In ten minutes, you will be late for work.*

Crater, glad to end the unsettling conversation with Petro, turned and hurried through the tubes, pulling the older boy along as if caught in his wake.

To go outside onto the scrapes, Crater and Petro first entered a dustlock that contained rows of gray lunasteel lockers. Inside each were hooks and hangers for their tube clothes and also a helmet and a bio-girdle, sanitized and placed there by the dust-lock crew. Petro came in, flung open his locker, stared with distaste, allowed a contemptuous sigh, then stripped bare, tossing his tube clothes on the deck, and began to strap on the bio-girdle, which provided him another chance to gripe. "Putting on this nasty thing every shift is yet another affront to my royal dignity."

"It is not nasty at all," Crater calmly replied. "It's a wonder of design and function that takes care of waste products throughout the day. As for your royal dignity, if you had any, you'd pick up your clothes off the deck and hang them in your locker. Recall the Colonel's rules on neatness."

Petro didn't like the Colonel's rules on neatness nor, for that matter, any of the Colonel's rules. As far as he was concerned, Colonel John High Eagle Medaris, the high and mighty owner of the mine and everything else in Moontown, made up his rules as he went along, every one of them meant to wring the life out of life and eliminate all possibility of fun. Recently, the Colonel had decided to remove all electronic games from the Earthrise Bar & Grill because a single miner—just *one!*— had been late to work and was found playing at one of the machines. Still, the old man couldn't stop the card games Petro organized. A deck of paper cards was the one unstoppable force in the universe.

Petro picked up his tunic and leggings and hung them in his locker, tossed in his boots, then slumped down on a bench and contemplated his toes, which he despondently wiggled. "If history were fair, I would be sitting on a throne, not a lunasteel bench in a smelly dustlock in the wayback of the moon."

"Count yourself lucky," Crater offered, hoping to cheer Petro up. "People here like you for what you are, not what your title is or was."

Petro snickered. "Since they would be bowing and kowtowing to my every wish, I would prefer that they like me for my title."

Crater decided to stop responding to Petro. There simply was no more time for meaningless talk. He finished strapping on his bio-girdle, then made certain Petro's was also properly affixed. A misaligned bio-girdle meant an awkward, uncomfortable day. Petro had managed to accomplish that feat a few weeks back, which meant not only a mess for the dusties but also that he got to quit early. Crater still wasn't certain if Petro had done it deliberately.

A scraper driver named Lonesome Larry came through the hatch and spotted Petro. "I have twenty johncredits riding on you in the race tomorrow, your royal dopiness," he said. "I hope your noble duff is ready to plunk down in a fastbug and race."

The fastbug race was held during the annual celebration known as Arrival Day. Petro had won the race twice before in machines Crater had fashioned out of junk and old parts. "Oh, I'm quite ready, Larry, my man," Petro said. "I'll win it again too."

"You probably will," Lonesome Larry replied, hanging up his tube clothes. "That's why nobody makes much money betting on you."

Petro took on a thoughtful expression. "What're the odds on my competitors?"

"Only one is given any chance against you at all. The Neroburg entry at ten to one."

"Ten to one? One johncredit wins ten? So if a fellow bets on the Neroburg entry and it wins, said fellow would make a pile, would he not?"

"That's the way it works, your lowness," Lonesome Larry said with a shrug, then began to buckle on his bio-girdle. "Say, you're not thinking of throwing the race, are you?"

Petro took on a righteous frown. "I'm a prince, Larry, not a charlatan! Shame on you for even thinking such a thing!"

Most of the other miners on the shift were already outside, so Crater grabbed Petro by his arm and hurried him along. The next dustlock contained the showers that applied the biolastic sheath that acted as a pressure suit and also provided warmth and cooling as required. The acronym used to describe it was BCP, for Biolastic Counter Pressure suit. Before BCPs were used, Moontown miners had worn ECPs, or Elastic Counter Pressure suits, made out of an elastic fabric that could wear blisters on a miner after a long day on the scrapes.

Crater and Petro drew on silken hoods that covered their faces and necks, then placed their helmets in a preparation unit. Crater unstrapped the gillie's holster and put it on a lunasteel table, then entered one of the showers. Holding out his arms, he said, "Crater Trueblood. Scrape number eleven north."

The dustlock puter confirmed Crater's size and shape, then turned on the biolastic spray that came out of the nozzles in a silvery mist. The spray had a sharp odor and felt clammy and creepy on his bare skin. It took all of Crater's will every time it was performed to stand without movement and be coated by what was a cloud of busy microbes, genetically designed to form a pressure film on anything they covered, providing the equivalent of one Earthian atmosphere of pressure, or Moontown standard. They also threw off heat or absorbed it, keeping the body warm or cool, depending on whether the sun beat down on the scrapes or it was the two weeks of the long shadow. The mist finally coalesced into a shimmering film that covered his body up to his neck.

When the nozzles stopped spraying, Crater stayed very still while the macro lasers did their work, looking for even a molecule-sized hole in the biolastic sheath. Finding none, a green light came on, and Crater stepped out, donned his coveralls and gloves, then pulled on a backpack containing a microbial soup that provided oxygen to a mixture of nitrogen to approximate Earthian atmosphere. He next retrieved his helmet from the prep unit, which had supplied a biolastic ring around its base. Always hungry to join their mates, the microbes in the ring sealed Crater's helmet to their brethren, thus creating an impermeable joint. The lasers checked the seam and the green light flared again. After clicking the air supply hose to the port on his helmet and latching shut his helmet faceplate, Crater was ready for the next stage required to go into the big suck, as heel-3 miners called outside in the near-vacuum of the moon. He strapped the gillie back to his arm, then pushed Petro, clad also in a helmet, backpack, BCP suit, coveralls, and gloves, into the final airlock chamber.

Crater pulled the inner hatch of the airlock closed and punched in the proper code on the keypad by the outer hatch. An unseen valve opened, and the air inside the airlock was slowly expelled until the pressure reached zero to the third decimal place. A green light came on beside the hatch, and Crater turned the hatch wheel and pushed it open, then stepped outside, followed by Petro.

"That's one small step for a prince, one giant leap for a bunch of fools," Petro said as he made a boot print in the dust atop a thousand others.

Crater glanced upward, then drew his awed gaze across the river of stars. "Look, Petro. Aren't they glorious?"

"They're just a bunch of stars," Petro groused, not even bothering to look up.

"More than can be counted."

"So what? Lots of things can't be counted, like the dust in a scrape or the days you've got left in your life. You can't waste the stars or the dust, Crater, but you can surely waste the days."

Crater reluctantly dragged his eyes away from the magnificent stars. "You forgot to close the airlock hatch."

"I don't see why it doesn't close automatically."

Crater walked past Petro and pushed the airlock hatch closed. Since it had built-in resistance springs, it took an effort.

"You know why," he said. "We have to use our muscles or lunar gravity will kill us. We may have been born on the moon, but our bodies are still designed for Earth."

"As if I don't use enough muscles with a shovel and pry bar every shift," Petro retorted.

Petro's foul mood was even wearing on Crater, who always tried to see the best in everyone. "Are you done complaining, your graceless?" he demanded.

"I've just started."

Any fool can complain, the gillie said, turning a pleasant blue, *and most do*.

"Hush now," Crater said. "You're not the least bit funny."

"I wish you'd get rid of that thing," Petro said. "It's an artifact that belongs in a museum."

"Maybe I'll save up enough for a modern do4u someday," Crater answered. "But right now, it works well enough as a communicator. *Which*," he said with emphasis, "is all I want you to do, gillie. Do you understand?"

"It is cheeky," Petro said when the gillie did not reply.

"It is only a biological machine," Crater answered. "With neither feelings nor intelligence." He felt the gillie stir within its holster. "Don't argue with me!"

Crater and Petro walked to the scrape, where they stood in front of the foreman who silently read the notes from the previous shift. The foreman, or blue banger as such were called, was Mrs. Liu Sho Hook, former puter-order bride and now widow of a heel-3 miner who'd gotten run over by a shuttle. She looked up from her reader and briefly pondered her crew. They looked tired, but who wasn't? It had been three shifts a day, six days a week for months, and the company was still behind on its orders. Besides Crater and Petro in their gray coveralls—gray designating scragline pickers—there were the scraper, loader, and shuttle operators in their navy blues, the red suits of the explosives experts (called devils), orange suits for the mechanics (called orangutans), and yellow suits for the solar furnace operators (called sundancers). Blue bangers such as herself wore navy blue coveralls with broad white stripes on the sleeves. Although there were none in attendance, white suits were for the managers and engineers, and green were for the medics. One glance on the scrapes and it was easy to figure out who did what.

Mrs. Hook took a final head count, then went over the plan for the shift including the number of heel-3 canisters to be filled. A short safety briefing followed. The week before, she reported, a shuttle driver on another scrape had neglected to depressurize the pneumatics before getting out and removing a chunk of rock from the shovel lift. As soon as she'd levered the rock free with a pry bar, the lift had slammed down on top of her. Her dust was now scattered in a crater north of town, which had been set aside for the remains of the good people of Moontown. "Let's make sure none of us end up there anytime soon," she said. "Wait for the pickers if you've got rocks stuck in your machines." She nodded toward the two boys. "Petro and Crater have the tools to get those rocks out, so let them do it. That's why they make all those johncredits."

This earned a laugh from the assembly, including Crater but not Petro. "Sure, laugh at the pickers, why don't you?" he griped.

"Safety, safety, safety, people," Mrs. Hook said.

The desire for safety stands against every great and noble enterprise, the gillie said, then added, *Tacitus*.

"Oh, well said, gillie!" Petro hooted.

Mrs. Hook looked at the gillie, which looked back at her— or would have if it had eyes, which it didn't. "Gillies are illegal," she said.

"It knows that," Crater answered.

Mrs. Hook had a brief staring match with the gillie, if staring at a thing with no eyes can be called such, then shrugged and nodded to Montana Bill, the oldest miner on the shift. According to Moontown tradition, it was the oldest miner who was always tasked to say the traditional heel-3 mining prayer. He stepped out in front of the others and prayed:

> For those of us who go into the dust,
> Our lives and limbs to Thee we trust.
> But if the scrapes shall kill us today,
> Take our souls, oh Lord, we pray.

"Amen. Thank you, Bill, and let's move some dirt," Mrs. Hook said, then she and her shift walked onto their scrape where two murderous giants—asleep for four billion years— were patiently waiting to kill them.

::: TWO

The sheriff of Moontown was not a handsome man. He was, in fact, a rough cobb. He had a round, red face, a nose so repeatedly broken it was squashed like a cauliflower, tiny brown eyes better suited for an Earthian mole, and an unkempt brush of a moustache that did not hide that he was missing his upper lip, shot off in some long ago and unfortunate brawl. His ominous appearance, however, was pleasing enough for a puter-order bride from Patagonia to fly down to the moon to marry him and present him two children, a boy and a girl, both of whom—and he thanked heaven every day for this—looked more like his wife than him. The sheriff counted himself blessed and, the way he saw it, those blessings had all flowed from Colonel Medaris, which made him very loyal to the great man, indeed.

The sheriff's job consisted principally of maintaining order in the little mining town, a job that was not always easy considering the felons who turned up there begging for work. Since there was a severe labor shortage across the moon, Colonel Medaris didn't much care what a man or woman had done on Earth, only what he or she might do for him and his company on the moon. Usually, they were promptly hired, sent to the Dust Palace to secure a bunk, and put to work on the scragline. It was the sheriff's sad responsibility to occasionally have to bust the heads of noogies—as new arrivals were called—who got out of line. Surprisingly, this included very few of them, since most were grateful to have escaped whatever crimes they had perpetrated on Earth, or whatever crimes had been perpetrated on them. Usually they quickly settled down, found a spouse, had some kids, and, just like the sheriff, made a whole new life for themselves in Moontown.

There were, however, always those few miscreants who were still thieves in a place that had little worth stealing, or killers in a place where no one ever did much that deserved killing. It was just their nature and they couldn't shake it off, even on the moon. The sheriff had two big deputies to help him take into custody those men—and they were nearly always men—who strayed across the border of common decency. There was no jail in Moontown, although the sheriff had a big closet attached to his office that he used when necessary. Criminals were usually tried, convicted, and sentenced by a jury of their peers, meaning the sheriff himself, and the sentence was either bread and water until the sheriff got tired of hearing their chains clink in his closet or, in the worst cases, the sentence was exile: being crammed inside an old-fashioned pressure suit and put outside where they might beg their way aboard a heel-3 convoy or wander down the valley until their suits failed or they fell into an old lava tube. Resources were scarce on the moon and there was nothing to be wasted on thieves and killers.

Another part of the sheriff's unwritten job description was solving the Colonel's problems, whatever they were, and that was why the sheriff—dressed in his finest uniform tunic and polished boots—sat outside the Colonel's grand office, waiting to be invited in to hear what the latest problem was. It was always pleasant to wait in the Colonel's reception room. Soft music played, and the perfume of fresh-cut grass was piped into the room. The sheriff also enjoyed the view of the Colonel's new Earthian assistant, a young, copper-haired lass, pretty as punch, named Diana. The Colonel was a widower, and if he wanted to bring sweet young girls to Moontown, the sheriff surely didn't mind. Most of them were courted and married off to bachelor miners fairly quickly anyway.

After he'd cooled his polished boots for a pleasant hour, the assistant turned to the sheriff and said, "You may go in now." The sheriff rose, made a small bow in her direction, and, hat in hand, entered the Colonel's sanctum by passing through a massive wooden door with carvings of lunar miners accomplishing their work. The only one like it anywhere on the moon, it had cost a fortune to bring it in from a Brazilian art house but, fortunately, the Colonel had fortunes enough. The Medaris Mining Company was but one of his enterprises, most of them exceedingly profitable.

The Colonel was at his desk, studying his puter. The sheriff did not approach, waiting to be called. While he had a moment, he studied the Colonel. Though well into his sixties, he was still a handsome fellow, his silver hair and moustache making him more distinguished as the years went by.

There was also something in his posture, standing or sitting, that informed the sheriff that here was a very tough man, one who was capable of almost any means to reach his ends. That included getting rid of the sheriff if such proved necessary for any reason. The sheriff always tried to keep that in mind.

"Ah, Sheriff," the Colonel said at last, turning in his direction and allowing a brief smile.

The sheriff squared his shoulders and lowered his chin in respect. When the Colonel beckoned, he approached. The Colonel didn't ask him to sit down in any of the chairs that faced the desk, which wasn't surprising. Whatever was on the Colonel's mind wouldn't take long. He would have already studied it from every angle, turned it over and looked at it from the bottom, the top, every which way, before calling the sheriff in to fix whatever it was that needed fixing. "I'm looking for a specific kind of man," the Colonel said without preamble. "You see them all as they come in here, know their records, and so forth. I'd like you to find him for me."

"Of course, sir," the sheriff said, listening carefully and intently as the Colonel explained the kind of man he wanted to find. Unfortunately, as the Colonel listed the attributes of the man, the sheriff knew it was of the type that was in extremely short supply in Moontown. The Colonel wanted an honest man who was above suspicion and also easily manipulated.

"Most of the men who come up here are refugees from wars," the sheriff said, "combat vets or refugees of some sort, from prisons and concentration camps and such. Now, a woman, perhaps . . ."

"No women," the Colonel declared. "A man is always what he appears to be. A woman can be one thing today, another tomorrow. No, Sheriff, make it a man with the attributes described."

It never paid to bandy words with the Colonel. "Yes, sir," he said. "I'll start looking today. When do you need him?"

"The sooner the better. But, Sheriff, are you certain you don't already know a man who fits the bill?"

"I honestly don't, sir. I'm sorry."

The Colonel pondered the sheriff's answer while the sheriff felt a bead of sweat form on his forehead. It was enough to trickle down his forehead on Earth, but in the moon's light gravity, it just swelled until it hung there, an embarrassing display of the sheriff's unease.

For his part, the Colonel was thinking back to the time he'd hired the sheriff. Moontown was growing and was showing it by an increase in petty crime. There were too many fights over at the Earthrise Bar & Grill, miners accusing others of theft, that kind of thing. The sheriff had shown up to work as a miner on the scrapes, but the Colonel saw that he had spent most of his life in law enforcement—although it had been in prison, on the other side of that enforcement. No matter. The Colonel was a savvy judge of a man and offered him the job. He'd been a good sheriff too, doing what he was told, overlooking things when the Colonel wanted them overlooked, taking care of company business while knocking in the occasional head to let miscreants know there was law and order in Moontown.

The Colonel said, "I'm disappointed you don't know of at least one man in my employ who is honest, naive, and easily manipulated. Although in a way, I suppose it's good we have such a tough lot."

The sheriff wiped the bead of sweat off his forehead with the back of his hand. "Indeed, sir. One has to be tough to work the scrapes."

"One has to be tough just to get here, Sheriff."

"You are correct, sir."

"Still, I'm confident you'll find the man I need. On your way, now, and get back to me as soon as you can."

The sheriff quickly exited the ornate office, nodded again to the pretty secretary who ignored him, and headed for his office, which was set along the common corridor next to the company store. Tubewives and tubehusbands out shopping greeted him as he passed but he made no response, his mind elsewhere. He'd never failed the Colonel before on any assignment, large or small, and he wasn't going to fail this one. He was on a manhunt, though where to start looking, he had not a clue. After reflection, he supposed the personnel records might be the place to begin.

He passed the deputy sitting in a chair outside his office and sat down at his desk. Hearing the clink of chains from behind the closet door, he recalled his sad prisoner, a miner who'd ordered a puter bride, only to be rejected by her once she'd seen him. Another miner had come along and married her, and that had resulted in a back stabbing. The man locked in the closet was the stabber, but since it appeared the new groom would recover, the sheriff had decided to let his prisoner go in a few more days, probably after knocking him around a little so the bruises would remind him to leave the happy couple alone.

The sheriff, putting the prisoner and everything else out of his mind to focus on the Colonel's demand, called up the personnel records on his puter. The first thing he did was reject all married men. Married men had wives who asked too many questions. Besides, what the Colonel had in mind, he suspected, might cause the chosen man to be killed, and widows tended to ask even more questions than wives. A bachelor was therefore required. There were plenty of them, of course, and all of them lived in one place, the Dust Palace run by Q-Bess Mountbatten-Windsor-Jones or whatever her real name was.

"Dust Palace register," he said, and the puter called up the denizens of that place. As each flipped by, he became depressed. Never had there been a group of more rough, gruff, and potentially murderous men, all now supposedly reformed but still quite capable of general mayhem. With this lot, how was he supposed to find the honest and simple man the Colonel required? "They don't exist here in Moontown," the sheriff moaned to himself. "Innocent men don't come here—they're all on the run for a reason."

The sheriff asked the puter to keep looking, but all it found were felons, gunrunners, and university presidents, sly and wily, and not an innocent among any of them.

"No, no, and no again," the sheriff kept saying as each name and bio flitted by. After a while, the sheriff gave up and leaned back in his squeaky chair, the squawk causing the deputy outside to scrunch up his face in sonic pain and the prisoner in the closet to rattle his chains. There was, the sheriff confessed to himself, no such man in Moontown as the Colonel had requested him to find. That meant the sheriff, as the Moontown miners on the scrapes oft said of themselves, was in some deep scrag.

THREE

When the Apollo astronauts, the first Earthly visitors to the moon, brought back a ton or so of rock samples, it didn't take long before it was discovered moon dust was saturated with a product of the solar wind, the isotope known as Helium-3. A hundred years later, fusion reactors, using the same principles that powered the sun, were perfected, and Helium-3 proved to be the perfect fuel. The technology had come just in time for a wounded, war-weary, and overpopulated Earth, desperate for clean, pure energy and willing to pay handsomely for it.

Since an atmosphere and a magnetic field kept the solar wind away from Earth, the moon was the best and nearest place to get Helium-3. Entrepreneurs and risk-takers began to climb onto rockets to fly across cislunar space to the gray sphere, there to explore for not only the magical isotope but scarce industrial metals such as titanium and platinum. This was all done in a place where there was no law, the moon wilder than even the old American Wild West. There was not only no central government, there was no government at all, just independent mining companies prospecting in the most extreme environment any people had ever known. Many of the early pioneers died on the way to the moon, many more after they got there, sometimes in pitched battles over claims, but the tough men and women who survived gradually prospered.

While most of the early Helium-3 towns were built close to the original Apollo landing sites, Moontown was located in the far northern reaches of the Alpine Valley of the moon. The valley was a major feature of the gray planetoid, an eighteen-mile-wide trench nearly three hundred miles long. Some lunar geologists thought it was a lava-flooded rift from an ancient volcano. Others said an asteroid must have struck at a shallow angle and smashed out a channel. The people of Moontown didn't much care how their valley had been formed. All they cared about was the Helium-3 in its dust. On both sides of the valley were corrugated cliffs with slumped steps that held the richest saturations yet known of the wondrous isotope.

Mining on the scrapes of Moontown was a sequential, orderly process: blast down the dust from the cliff faces of the valley, push the dust with a big machine called a scraper to pile it into mounds called tents, load the tents onto shuttles, run the shuttles to conveyor belts called scraglines, and offload. From there, the belt carried the dust to the shakers and solar collectors where the isotope—the miners called it heel-3—was shaken off and secondarily boiled off, the dust left behind called scrag. After that, it was a matter of venting the Helium-3 into an initial holding chamber, then compressing it into lunasteel canisters. Trucks were used to transport the canisters across the moon in convoys to Armstrong City where it was taken up the lunar elevator and moved to the industrial Cyclers for transfer to Earth.

Though it might be orderly and well understood, heel-3 mining was still a dangerous enterprise. Suit failure meant the horrific results of exposure to a vacuum—boiling blood, skin turned purple from bursting capillaries, eyes reduced to mushy blots, lungs starved and collapsed. When the sun rose, it stayed up for two weeks and the temperatures in which the miners worked was greater than the boiling temperature of water. In the two-week darkness that followed—miners called it the long shadow—a cold far below the Earth's polar regions froze the scrapes. Failure of the suits to maintain a moderate temperature caused many of the early miners to either freeze to death or die from heatstroke before they could crawl to safety.

Moon dust, formed by ancient volcanoes and the sledge-hammer pounding of meteors and comets over billions of years, was a complex structure of interlocking glass shards and fragments that could rip lung tissue and grind down the toughest steel. Rocks and pebbles also got hung up in the gears, levers, and axles of the scrapers, loaders, shuttles, and belts, turning them into immobile hulks. Dust was the prize but it was also the problem.

When Crater and Petro reached the beltway, even Crater couldn't hold back a groan at what they found. The previous shift had left them a lot of work. Before the first shuttle arrived, he and Petro had to shovel hard and fast to put loose dust back on the belt and dig out small pebbles in the rollers. Belt stoppage was common when the pickers didn't do their job of keeping the rollers clean. "That third shift is worthless," Petro crabbed as he popped out a big rock with a lunasteel pry bar.

Although Crater agreed, he didn't say anything. What good did griping do, after all? If it made you happy, Petro should have been the happiest person on the moon.

Before long, the first shuttle loaded with dust arrived, and within an hour a lot of things on the shift turned scrag. A scraper blew a wheel bearing, a fuel cell on a shuttle kept shorting out, and the conveyor belt motor broke down, forcing Crater and Petro to use fastbugs with trailers to haul the dust up to the sundancers while the belt was being repaired. Then the blue banger was called away to help open up a new scrape to the south. "Call me if you need me," Mrs. Hook said to each of the leaders of her various teams and then drove away. Crater watched her go and felt a bit uneasy. He didn't like it when the blue banger was off the scrape. What if something happened on the scragline and they needed her to make a decision? It might be a decision he would have to make, and he didn't trust himself to make the right one.

Lunch was a welcome fifteen minutes of being allowed to sit down and suck out a protein-rich soup through a straw stuck in a helmet port. After the soup, which he barely tasted, Crater leaned back against a big rock and admired the steep dun-colored cliffs soaring above the brown, gray, and white rock fragments and dust that flowed like a river down the valley.

Petro rested his back against a boulder. As he did, the Earth began to peek out from the horizon. "Mother Earth," he said in a wistful voice, and added, "puffy white clouds, blue seas, and green forests. Glorious."

Crater watched the bulbous blue and white orb making its appearance, so colorful compared to his drab little planet.

By strict definition, of course, the moon wasn't a planet, but the people who lived there tended to call it that, good as anybody else's. And although Crater marveled at the world, he did not envy the people on it. He had heard too many stories of war, death, destruction, cruelty, and starvation. Still, despite his opinion, he felt a nearly genetic longing to someday walk along its sandy beaches next to its great blue seas and lie upon its cool, green pastures, or walk amongst the trees of its great forests. He had heard there were living creatures there that were different from humans, yet caught up in the same web of life and time, creatures such as whales and cats and dogs and giraffes and insects and who knew what else? He couldn't imagine what it would be like to actually touch such a creature. He wondered if it would feel anything like touching the gillie, which didn't like to be touched. It had scurried away when he'd pressed his fingers on it once or twice. It hadn't felt that bad. Just sort of soft and dry.

It was an hour after lunch when the gillie crawled out of its holster. It said, *Roller alert.*

"What do you mean?" Crater asked.

Look and see, it said.

Crater looked and saw nothing, just the explosive devils about to blow up a detpak. When they blew it, down came a cascade of dust. Although there was no sound—sound waves can't travel in a vacuum—Crater thought the explosion was normal.

Roller alert, the gillie said again.

Petro drove up beside Crater. "What are you looking at?"

"The gillie thinks there's a roller up there."

Petro turned to look. As more rocks and dust fell away, both he and Crater could see that the devils had indeed blown loose a roller. It was slowly emerging from the steep cliff, gravity teasing it out, grain by grain. Suddenly, the roller fell free of the dust and rolled down the face of the cliff. Beneath it was a scraper, manned by an operator who called himself Thumper Tom. Crater and Petro began to bleat out warnings, but Thumper Tom was oblivious to their transmissions, probably because he was playing music in his helmet, an illegal but pervasive activity on the scrapes. When the roller hit a step, it bounded into the vacuum, then fell, clipped Tom's scraper, turned it over, then kept rolling on a downward slope, gathering velocity and momentum.

"Scrag!" Petro yelped. "It's coming right at us!"

Confirmed, the gillie said, its skin turning as red as a rocket's glare.

Crater and Petro gauged the path of the massive boulder and swerved out of its way, then watched as the roller kept rolling until it reached a rise in the terrain that stopped it. Petro peered at it, then said, "Crater, I hope you take this as a sign because that's what it is. We've got to get off these scrapes before we get killed."

Crater wasn't listening to Petro but instead to the calls going out to the blue banger from the various team leads, telling her about the unfortunate roller. There was no reply. Mrs. Hook had apparently moved into a radio shadow the helmet communicators couldn't penetrate. "Gillie, call the blue banger," Crater said and the gillie, being vastly more powerful, quickly made the connection whereupon Crater explained to her what had happened.

"The scraper was knocked over. We can't see Thumper Tom. He could be beneath it," was his conclusion.

"How about the rest of the crew?"

"They're okay."

"Tell everybody to stay put. I'll be there in fifteen minutes."

The gillie said, *Thumper Tom is under the scraper. Thumper Tom heart rate 160. Blood pressure 180 over 100.*

Crater was relieved to hear the scraper driver was alive but then the gillie added, *Leak, right boot caused by biolastic cellular dust damage. Suit failure will occur in approximately twelve minutes.*

It was not Crater's responsibility to do anything more than what he had done, inform the team leaders of the blue banger's instructions and also about Thumper Tom's perilous situation. The replies generally fell into the category of passive acceptance that Thumper Tom was as good as dead. "No way I'm going to crawl under that scraper," the other scraper driver said.

"Poor old Tom," Petro said. "He owed me money too."

"We have to save him!" Crater blurted, surprised by his own audacity.

Petro thought perhaps he had misheard his tubemate. "What are you talking about? We don't have to do anything but wait for the blue banger."

"But, Petro, don't you understand? By the time she gets here with help, Tom's going to be dead as a hammer!"

"So? We're just scragline pickers. It's not our job to rescue anybody."

"But ... but ... I know how to rescue him," Crater said. And even as he said it, he saw in his mind a force diagram, the vectors pointing in the necessary directions, and the machines and devices needed to make the diagram come true. There was, however, a major problem that Crater couldn't get his mind around. "Oh no," he groaned. "I know how to save Tom but we can't do it."

Intrigued, Petro asked, "Why not?"

"Well, we'd have to drive the shuttles and operate their winches and we don't have permits."

This struck Petro as a profoundly *Crater* thing to say, which made him laugh. "Permits? You're worried about permits? We go out there and lift that scraper up, it'll probably fall on top of us. That's what you should be worrying about!"

The gillie, which apparently couldn't decide what color to be so was just staying a uniform gray, piped up. *Approximately eleven minutes until suit failure due to dust intrusion. Alert. Another roller.*

Crater processed the information provided by the gillie. Eleven minutes before the biolastic material in Thumper Tom's right boot failed. Although biolastic cells were capable of repairing small breaches, moon dust in the tear could disrupt the pattern, causing the rest of the sheath to unravel. As for the other roller the gillie had just reported, Crater studied the slope above the overturned scraper until he saw it. A cascade of dust and small rocks was falling around it as it slowly emerged, and it was at least four times bigger than the first one.

Petro also saw the new danger. "Crater, maybe it's best to just let old Thumper Tom go."

Crater wasn't good at making decisions—he was terrible, in fact—but he knew if Thumper Tom was to have a chance, he needed to make one now. He got off his fastbug and ran to one of the shuttles. After hesitating, Petro ran to the other one, yelling, "What's your plan?"

Crater explained the required force vectors as he and Petro

cranked the shuttles up and drove them onto the slope behind the overturned scraper. Once in position, they put their winches in neutral, got off and pulled the cables to the scraper, hooked the cables onto its lifting pintles, then ran back to their respective shuttles and wound in the cables, tilting the scraper up and off Thumper Tom. Only his helmet could be seen protruding from a big pile of dust.

Petro allowed a sigh. "I guess I'll dig him out." He climbed off the shuttle with a shovel in his hand. "Just keep your eye on that roller. Sing out if it moves an inch. Do you hear me, Crater? An *inch*!"

"I hear you, brother," Crater said, his mind swirling with worries, which for some reason made him add, "Don't worry."

"Yeah, right," Petro retorted as he loped to the scraper.

Crater looked across the valley and saw two green suits at the perimeter of the scrape. Someone had called the paramedics but they didn't seem to be in any hurry to help. Likely they had spotted that big new roller too. In the distance, he saw a spray of dust. It was probably the blue banger's fastbug but she still had a way to go before arrival. It was then the gillie announced: *Roller out.*

"Roller out, Petro!" Crater yelled, transmitted instantly by the gillie.

Down the massive roller came. It slammed into the scraper, the impact snapping the cables. Crater ducked as one of them came flying back at him like a giant whip. When he looked up, he saw that Petro had managed to pull Thumper Tom into the clear without being killed. The roller, however, careened on.

Roller will impact western maintenance shed in approximately twenty-one seconds, the gillie said. *Breach probable.*

The roller was trundling mercilessly across the scrape as if aimed at the western maintenance shed, a big mooncrete hangar that sat partially above the surface on the west side of Moontown. A breach in the shed meant the unsuited mechanics inside would die horrible deaths, their bodies swollen, their insides turned to pink mush.

Crater's instinct took over. He wound the remnant of the cable onto the shuttle winch while simultaneously pushing the accelerator pedal to the floor. He set a course at an angle to intercept the roller, catching vacuum as his shuttle leapt across a narrow, collapsed lava tube. Empty shuttles were fast. Crater had an angle on the roller so he caught up to it, did a hard steer in front, and jumped off just as it slammed into the shuttle. When Crater looked up from the dust, he saw the roller ricocheting off in a harmless direction. He also saw the shuttle was smashed. The maintenance shed was untouched.

Suit integrity confirmed, the gillie said, making an automatic report of Crater's biolastic material.

"What about Thumper Tom and Petro?"

Petro nominal. Thumper Tom fifteen seconds to suit failure.

Crater cringed. "Petro, where are you?" he called, fearful of the answer.

"At the entry hatch," Petro replied, his tone so calm it sounded as if he were about to yawn. "Paramedics are with me. Thumper Tom's going to be okay."

"You saved him!" Crater cried, then let his breath out for what seemed like the first time in hours.

"*We* saved him," Petro answered. "And you saved the orangutans and the entire maintenance shed. We're heroes, Crater!"

"No, we're not," Crater answered miserably. "We're in trouble. We drove the shuttles without permits."

Petro laughed and said, "If you could sell simple, brother, you'd be a rich man."

Crater didn't know how to respond to that, so he didn't. In any case, it was about then that the blue banger arrived. "What happened?" she demanded as the other miners climbed up the slope to where Crater was standing. They gawked at the shuttle, which lay smashed in the dust, and the gigantic roller that had finally stopped a mile away. When no team leader seemed to be able to find his or her voice, Montana Bill told the blue banger how the devils had accidentally blown loose not one but two rollers, how one of them had rolled over Thumper Tom's scraper, how Crater and Petro had taken the shuttles and pulled the scraper off Tom, how Petro had dragged the scraper driver clear, and then how Crater had knocked aside the big roller by sacrificing the shuttle, concluding with, "That dang roller would have surely killed every worker in the maintenance shed, Mrs. Hook, and that's a fact."

Mrs. Hook looked at Crater, then at the devil leader, a man who called himself Boston Blackie. "What do you have to say for yourself, Blackie?" she demanded.

Blackie wasn't about to take the blame. "Third shift probed that area, ma'am, and gave me and my team the all clear. They must have missed those blamed old things. It happens."

Mrs. Hook turned to Crater as Petro came walking up. "I told you two to stay put," she growled, but before they could reply, she waved their potential excuses away. "You two boys did a brave thing. Don't expect a medal for what you did but, just for the record, I'm grateful."

Mrs. Hook warily eyed the flock of white-suited engineers and managers emerging from the airlock and coming in her direction, then said, "All right, people, get back to work. I'll whistle up a float scraper and shuttle and we'll sort this all out later."

She subsequently did her whistling, then reported to the ghosts as the engineers and managers were called, while her miners, including Crater and Petro, went back to work. Crater tried not to think about how much trouble he and Petro were in for driving the shuttles without permission and destroying one of them too.

Astonishingly, the shift met the production schedule, but just barely; and after it was over, Montana Bill prayed, beseeching the Big Miner to look after Thumper Tom in the company clinic, and wrapped it up with, "It was a scrag shift, Lord, but we got the Colonel his heel-3 anyway. Thank you at least for that. Amen."

"Amen," the miners chorused, then headed to the showers.

::: FOUR

Every so often, a burst of deadly radiation would escape from the sun and roar across the inner solar system and scour everything in its path. If you were lucky enough to live on a nice, fat planet with an atmosphere and an intact magnetic field, it was not much of a problem. But if you lived on the Earth's moon, which had neither one, you had a big problem. To avoid the deadly results of these outbursts, Moontown's people lived in tubes made of mooncrete set twenty feet underground. Scraper's Row was the largest of the tube neighborhoods and contained seventy-three tubes of residential dimensions.

In the neighborhood called Medaris Acres, eight residence-size tubes were set aside for Colonel Medaris's personal use. Another sixteen tubes in Medaris Acres were assigned to the chief engineer, the doctor, the dentist, the sheriff, and the preacher. Three more residential tubes were set aside for Very Important Visitors.

The "downtown" or administrative tubes, a cluster of twenty business-size tubes, held the company store, the medical clinic, the sheriff's office, the chapel, the theater, the library, the art center, and the engineering and business offices. Connected to the downtown tubes were observation towers where, during the two weeks of the long shadow, the people of Moontown could see a sky so filled with stars it was as if God Himself had placed there an infinite ocean of diamonds for them to admire.

The Dust Palace Bachelor's Hotel contained a cluster of sixteen tubes. Petro's mother, known as Queen Bess or, informally, Q-Bess, ran the Dust Palace, and Crater and Petro shared one of its tubes. Single miners occupied the other tubes, sometimes with hot bunks, meaning as soon as one man got out of it, another took his place. Nearby was a tube cluster that contained the Earthrise Bar & Grill, a place where heel-3 miners were allowed to let off a little steam as long as they didn't get too drunk or too loud or try to kill each other. Petro organized his poker games there but his reputation and ability at cards was such, few Moontown gamblers would play with him anymore, a frustrating situation for the royal boy.

Extra-large tubes were placed north of town for the foundry and processing plants where titanium, platinum, silicon, and iron, byproducts of heel-3 production, were processed. There was also a tank farm where heel-3 canisters were stored and readied for shipment, and two big maintenance sheds, one each on the east side and the west side of town. Beneath the town were the grease traps and bioseptic tanks that processed the inevitable wastes of human habitation.

※

Happy to be alive, the shift that had just survived the two rollers first entered an airlock where they threw off their dust-covered coveralls and boots, and the dustlock crew—dusties as they were known—took them to be washed and cleaned. The miners next passed through a hatch where there were showers that removed the biolastic sheaths. Helmets, along with bio-girdles, were handed over to the dusties for sanitizing. After donning filter masks, the miners moved to the next dustlock and the water showers that removed all vestiges of dust and the biolastic material, and finally through a series of blowers into the changing lock where they changed into their tube clothes.

In the Dust Palace cafeteria, Crater and Petro and the other first-shift bachelors got their food trays and pushed them down the tubular rack. After a day of being enveloped within the pungent odor of bioprocessed air, the cafeteria's aroma of hot food was delicious to their noses, and their stomachs growled in anticipation. Crater took the soup, the broccoli, the beans, the cornbread, and also loaded up on the carrot cake Q-Bess was famous for. Petro chose entirely brown food: fried potatoes, fried okra, fried shrimp, and fried bread. Of course, none of it was real, being products of the biovats, but it tasted real or at least as real as Q-Bess and her cooks could make it. The spoons and forks Crater and Petro were handed by a cafeteria waiter were moontype, which meant they were six times heavier than they needed to be, giving them the same feel and heft as similar utensils on Earth. That, however, wasn't the reason for their design.

When the pioneer owners founded the heel-3 towns, they were surprised when the young, healthy miners they imported to work the scrapes became sick and feeble after only a few years. Medical examinations revealed their bones had turned brittle, their muscles flabby, and their hearts weak. Living and working in a world that had but one-sixth the gravity of Earth caused the human body to deteriorate in almost every way possible because muscles, bones, and hearts—evolved to work efficiently on Earth—tended to relax in the light gravity of the moon. The solution was to make things much heavier than necessary. Steel shot was the most prevalent material added to increase mass, but molybdenum and titanium slugs were also used because they were byproducts of heel-3 production. Every hatch in most mining towns was moontype, which meant they were designed to require a hefty pull or push. Miners and their families were also encouraged to walk, do push-ups and sit-ups, and participate in weight training. Every child born on the moon grew up lifting weights. The strategy worked. The muscles, bones, and hearts of Moonians, for the most part, were as healthy as if they'd grown up on Earth.

Q-Bess came over and sat on the bench opposite her boys, who were shoveling in their food as fast as good manners would allow. She knew everything that had happened on their scrape and allowed herself a moment of happiness that they were alive.

Crater was such a handsome youngster, and his face reflected sweetness. Petro, she had to admit to herself, was a bit fox-faced and his eyes a little shifty. Unfortunately, the royal Mountbatten-Windsor lineage had more than a few men with that particular aspect although it didn't hamper their intelligence. Or, she thought ruefully, keep them from being attractive to the ladies. Her grandfather, the last king of the United Kingdom, had been a brilliant ruler, but it was a woman who'd betrayed him and brought down the monarchy. Since then, the royal family had been on the run. Eventually, she had landed in Canadalaska where she had married Troyce Jones, a commoner and an engineer hired by the Colonel to help plan Moontown. Petro was their beloved son and, since there were no other males left in the family line, heir to the throne. When Jones had died of dust poisoning, Q-Bess, recognizing there was little or no hope of restoring the monarchy, had taken over the management of the bachelor's quarters and raised Petro as just another Moontown boy.

Asteroid Al, a longtime resident of the Dust Palace, came over and sat beside Q-Bess. He was famous on Earth for being the first human to walk on the asteroid Ceres. After his return, Al, unhappy with the government that ran his country, made his way to the moon, and thence to Moontown and finally the Dust Palace. "You boys keep the scragline picked up today?" he asked.

"I guess we did," Crater said, surprised that Asteroid Al hadn't heard about what he and Petro had done. The gossips in Moontown were slipping.

"I guess we could save the whole moon and this bunch wouldn't care," Petro grumbled.

"What did you say, Petro?" Q-Bess asked.

Petro stared at his plate. "Nothing, Mum."

Doom and Headsplitter, both refugees from the Indian subcontinent, walked by, nodding to the boys. The pair had taught Crater and Petro their version of the martial arts, which meant they'd taught them to fight dirty and with the utmost of violence.

"What's wrong, noogie?" someone called from one of the back tables. "You gonna start crying now?"

"Uh-oh," Q-Bess said, "here we go. I thought it was too quiet."

Crater looked up from his meal and saw a fellow at one of the back tables lumber to his feet. He was a big man, blond hair braided into pigtails, an elk sticker taken up from the holster on his leg. A lot of the combat vets carried the vicious knife, which was a favorite of commandos. "Don't call me noogie again!" he raged at the miner sitting across from him, a fellow with heavy, bored eyes and a thick moustache. He was marked by a diagonal scar from his forehead to his chin.

"Blood's gonna flow," Asteroid Al said, although he didn't look particularly perturbed.

Elk stickers began appearing all over the cafeteria and were slapped down on the tables. The miners who owned them started screaming at each other, taking sides.

Crater was surprised that Q-Bess and Asteroid Al were just sitting there doing nothing to stop the coming mayhem. "Maybe you should say something," he suggested.

Q-Bess waved a hand, jangling with bracelets, and said, "Do it for me, Crater. I'm kind of tired."

Crater didn't think it was his place to tell anybody anything. He sat there, embarrassed. Petro, however, stood up and banged on the table with a spoon, shouting, "Now, look here, fellows. My mother has a clear rule about this kind of thing. No fighting in the cafeteria!"

Grim faces turned toward Petro. Q-Bess and Asteroid Al

got up and moved. "What did you say, boy?" a miner called. He was a big fellow, a veteran of some Earthian war, no doubt, muscles bulging on top of muscles and scars etched across his ugly face.

Crater slowly got to his feet. He had to back up Petro whether he liked it or not. "No fighting in the cafeteria!" he squeaked.

"No fighting in the cafeteria?" the angry miner asked. "Is that the best you can do?"

Crater's heart was racing, and he felt his face getting hot. He wished Doom and Headsplitter would come back and make everybody sit down and eat their food, but a quick glance around showed no sign of either one.

The pig-tailed miner reached below the table and came up with a pie. "Here's what I think about no fighting in the cafeteria!" he yelled and flung the pie at Crater and Petro. Before they could react, everyone in the room did the same with their own pies. As the boys were struck while dodging and weaving, a big banner was unfurled:

OUR HEROES—PETRO AND CRATER!

Crater and Petro were covered with pie crust and cream, but they started laughing as all the men and women in the cafeteria surged to congratulate them. Q-Bess kissed them both. "I am so proud of my boys!" she roared, and the applause surged over them as she smeared more cream in their hair.

A party ensued in which nearly every miner took the opportunity to insult Crater and Petro, calling them stupid scragline pickers who couldn't be trusted on a scrape, and who probably caused those rollers to come out in any case, and were sure to catch it from the Colonel for driving shuttles without a permit.

Petro took most of the credit for the rescue, saying, "So there I was, beneath that scraper that was about ready to fall on my head while Crater was just sitting there, trying to figure out what to do . . ."

Viking Val hooted at that one. "Thumper Tom owed you money, Petro. That's the only reason you went out there. Tell us what really happened, Crater!"

Crater, looking uncomfortable, replied, "Well, if that's the way Petro said it happened, I guess that's the way it did."

This earned Crater more derision and a few more thrown pies, which he successfully ducked so they hit Petro instead. In a corner, unseen, the sheriff of Moontown observed all the fun and, after enjoying it at first, began to think. The more he thought about it, the more he was convinced that fate and circumstance had solved for him a vexing problem. He'd found the kind of man the Colonel wanted him to find, although it wasn't a man.

It was a boy.

::: FIVE

The annual fastbug race at the Moontown Raceway ran along a track that wound through a series of obstacles, some natural, some man-made, and all treacherous. Crater had cobbled together sufficient parts from worn-out and wrecked company fastbugs to bolt together a machine he called Comet. Crater was certain Comet would win, because not only was it fast but Petro, the best fastbug driver on the moon, would be at its wheel. But there was a slight problem. The race was supposed to start in fifteen minutes and Petro had not shown up. Crater, who was working on Comet's gearbox, asked the gillie to call Petro again. It did and reported, *Petro has his do4u turned off.*

Crater felt his stomach sink. If Petro had his do4u turned off, then maybe he was not going to show. A fanfare of trumpets blared through the gillie and all the do4us in the crowd. It was a recording, of course, there being a serious lack of trumpeteers in Moontown. Everyone in the stands and in the racing pits turned to look toward the Colonel's box, a rectangle of mooncrete with a thick glass viewing pane. Another viewing pane, this one much larger, fronted the stands for everyone else.

The Colonel was wearing a formal tunic with only a few of his more important medals attached. There was a woman standing beside him who also wore a tunic, hers scarlet with a golden sash. She was an imposing woman, her gaze straight ahead, steady and stern. Asteroid Al, who'd put on a suit to see how Crater was doing, said with some awe, "That's Czarina Zorna."

Czarina Zorna was the leader of the family that presided over the Russian territories that included most of the Sea of Serenity. "She's glorious," Asteroid Al added. "Beautiful, brilliant, a natural leader."

On the other side of Colonel Medaris stood a man. He was short and had very black hair—an obvious hairpiece—and a thin moustache and a goatee. He was dressed in a plain gray tunic, buttoned up to the neck. "General Caesar Augustus Nero himself," Asteroid Al said, all but hissing. "A villain, Crater, of the worst stripe. He is not above theft or even murder to gain an advantage over anyone who might oppose him."

"He looks nice," Crater said.

Asteroid Al chuckled. "Only you, Crater, would think General Nero looked anything other than the rascal that he is. Your heart is too big."

Crater looked down, ashamed of his heart. He supposed it was true. He always looked for the best in everybody.

Asteroid Al said, "Chin up, boy. You've also got the courage of a dozen lions. You proved it on the scrapes yesterday."

Crater thought Asteroid Al was wrong. He had no courage

at all. That was the real reason he didn't want to ever leave Moontown. He feared what lay beyond. What he'd done saving Thumper Tom and then the fellows in the maintenance shed had just been instinct. After he thought over what had happened, he'd discovered himself barely able to breathe.

The Colonel addressed the crowd. "People of Moontown and our esteemed guests," he said, "I invite you to welcome Czarina Zorna and members of the royal party from New St. Petersburg. We are honored by their presence." He made a slight nod to General Nero. "And we also have the esteemed presence of General Caesar Augustus Nero with us today."

"Here to celebrate our victory in the fastbug race," Nero interrupted in a reedy voice.

"We will see about that," the Colonel replied in a cold, measured tone.

"We will, indeed," Nero snapped.

Asteroid Al noticed Comet's empty seat. "Where's Petro?"

"I don't know," Crater answered miserably. "If he doesn't show soon, we're going to have to default."

"You can't default," Asteroid Al said. "Nearly every manjack and womanjill in the Dust Palace has a wager on the Comet."

"I should go look for him," Crater worried. "He could be sick."

"Petro isn't sick," Asteroid Al replied with confidence. "He may be playing cards at the Earthrise, or gorging himself on Q-Bess's carrot cake, but that boy's not sick. Anyway, Crater, you're going to have to drive."

Crater reacted with a shudder. "I can't!"

Asteroid Al gripped Crater's shoulder. "Look, Crater, Colonel

Medaris is depending on you! None of these other schlubs can beat Neroburg. General Nero wants to embarrass the Colonel in front of Czarina Zorna. You can't let him get away with that!"

It was then the Colonel announced, "Drivers, you may start your engines."

Crater felt as if he might throw up. "I don't know what to do," he said, as much to himself as to Asteroid Al. Still, he climbed into the Comet, and the gillie jumped off his shoulder and positioned itself on the fastbug console. *Gillie will help*, it said. Crater cast a doubtful glance at the thing. "I can't do this," he moaned.

"You have to try, Crater." Asteroid Al said.

Crater took a deep breath and when he let it out, he knew Asteroid Al was right. He was going to have to race, but he also knew he was surely going to lose and also wreck the Comet, strewing pieces of it—and probably himself—all over the track. Still, with his heart thudding in his ears, he reached over and flicked the switch for the fuel cell stirrers that, after a few seconds of chugging, purred to life.

Asteroid Al patted Crater's back encouragingly. "Watch that Neroburg car. You see that big knobby rear end it's got?"

Crater had seen it but he didn't know what it was for, although he supposed it had some function having to do with the fuel cells. Asteroid Al soon rid him of that idea. "It's to whack you, Crater. That rear end is a hammer as sure as I'm standing here. Watch out for it."

"But that would be cheating," Crater said.

"No rule I know against it," Asteroid Al replied.

"But it's not right."

Asteroid Al smiled a sad smile. "Son, doing right to fellows like those Neroburg louts just means what they can get away with." When Crater looked confused, he added, "Not all people are as kind and honest as you are. Very few, in fact. I'm sorry about that but it doesn't change anything. Put that goodness and kindness away for just a little while and win this race!"

Crater nodded uncertainly, then drove into position. By the draw, he was on the outside of the second line, each line consisting of four fastbugs. There were ten fastbugs in all, the third line containing two racers. Six of them came from Moontown, three from the Russian territories, and Neroburg's entry named Flashinpan. Besides the odd tail, Crater had observed Flashinpan had twin fuel cells and a beefed-up lunasteel alloy transmission. It was sure to be not only fast but rugged. Flashinpan's driver, Trace Farley, also had the reputation of being a hotshot driver, a cocky win-or-burn type.

Crater gripped the steering wheel and waited for the signal for the race to begin. The Czarina counted backward from ten. The gillie, picking up her transmission, mimicked her perfectly. When she reached zero, Crater waited a split second for the fastbug in front of him to move, then jammed the accelerator to the floor, swerved through a small gap just barely large enough for him to slip through, and swept into the front rank. It was a move Petro liked to use in a crowded field, and Crater had copied it perfectly.

Racing in the moon's light gravity, and on the special courses with their ramps and turns designed to send the fastbugs into the air—or to be more accurate, the vacuum—demanded a set of skills and knowledge no Earthian race driver had ever needed to learn. One of them was a working knowledge of the physics of rotational vectors, which described how a rotating wheel created a force at right angles to the plane of the wheel. This meant by selecting a wheel on a fastbug and spinning it up during flight, drivers could cause the car to rotate while flying. Since ramps were often set up just before a turn, novice drivers often oversteered upon landing and flipped over. An experienced driver, however, could rotate his bug in the direction of the track and land in the right direction with all wheels spinning for maximum traction. It was a tricky maneuver and it didn't always work, but Crater had at least practiced it. The puters aboard the fastbugs were designed to tell drivers when and how to spin up. That would be the gillie's job for Crater.

The second turn saw one of the Moontown fastbugs plow off course and into a crater field where it flipped over, the driver quickly dragged away by the rescue crew. The first ramp loomed and Crater didn't have time to think about anything but hitting it straight on. Comet and Flashinpan reached it at the same time with two other fastbugs close behind. One of the Russian fastbugs ran off the rails of the ramp, dropped over the edge, and rolled over. Comet reached the end of the ramp and started flying.

Coming off a ramp in a fastbug at maximum acceleration was pure adrenaline. There was no turn, just a long straightaway, and when they landed, Comet and Flashinpan were neck and neck. There were only six fastbugs left, the other drivers taken away in ambulances from their badly bent racers.

Crater jammed the accelerator pedal down, aiming for the next ramp, but just as Comet reached the base of the ramp, Flashinpan turned sharply inward. Crater veered away, steering into the ramp at an angle and launching away from the track.

The gillie advised: *Spin front and rear right wheels. Now.*

Crater spun up the wheels. Comet landed hard and Crater had to dodge another fastbug coming apart in big chunks beside him, but he emerged from the dust to find himself just yards behind Flashinpan and the remaining cars. They hit the next ramp, and Crater saw Farley spin up his wheels so the tail of the Flashinpan whipped around and struck the nearest fastbug, causing it to go into a roll from which there was no recovery. It crashed, came apart, and flipped into a deep crater.

The next part of the track was a series of dips and turns. Two fastbugs crashed through the barriers, rolling end over end. Another sailed off into the dust. Only Comet and Flashinpan were left. Crater jammed down the accelerator, caught the Neroburg racer at the next ramp, and up they went side by side.

Flashinpan spinning up, the gillie warned, and Crater glanced over his shoulder and saw the deadly tail whipping in his direction.

Spin up. Left wheels both.

Crater spun up as advised and dodged Flashinpan's tail. When the two fastbugs landed, Crater zipped into the lead and streaked for the final series of turns, one of which went down into a deep crater with a collapsed rim that was a natural ramp. He kept the pedal to the floor and Comet flew up the slope of the crater.

Spin up. Right wheels both! The gillie nattered but Crater ignored it. Comet was flying straight and true so why change anything? At the apogee of the arc, he looked around and could not see Flashinpan. Crater thought he'd left it behind even though the gillie kept whining at him. *Spin up right wheels! Spin up, spin up, spin up!*

Crater finally relented and spun up, although he was certain the gillie was wrong. But the gillie wasn't wrong. The knobby tail of Flashinpan came down hard and missed Comet by inches. It had been above Crater all the time.

Since it had missed its target, Flashinpan began to tumble, and Crater spun up again to get out of its way. As the two fastbugs landed, Flashinpan hit hard and began to break apart. Comet landed hard too, and Crater nearly lost it, but he spun up all wheels, gritted his teeth, held on, and, somehow, out of a spray of dust, sped straight and true, flashing across the finish line.

It was the most amazing thing. The checkered flag was waving for him. Crater had raced the race and he had won. Nobody was more surprised than he.

::: SIX

Though Farley was alive and his biolastic suit intact, he needed to be pried out of Neroburg's mangled fastbug. Crater ran over to see if he could help but was brusquely shooed away by the Neroburg pit crew. Shaken, still not quite believing he'd won the race, he entered the dustlock to doff his BCP suit and put on his tube clothes. That was where Petro showed up. "Congratulations, brother," he said. Though he was smiling, he didn't sound entirely happy about it.

"Are you okay, Petro?" Crater asked. "When you didn't come, I thought you must be sick."

Petro shrugged. "As you can see, I'm perfectly healthy. Watched the whole thing from the stands."

"You were here? Then why didn't you drive?"

Before Petro could answer, the sheriff briefly pushed his head through the hatch into the dustlock. "Get on up to the Colonel's box," he said. "Your trophy awaits."

Crater headed for the hatch, but then a sudden truth

popped into his head. He stopped and turned back to face Petro. "You bet against me."

"Sure I did," Petro replied. "There was no way you were going to beat that Neroburg fastbug, not with that knobby hammer on its back. I figured to make a lot of money. Guess I got fooled."

Petro's bank account as of one point seven seconds ago is zero point zero zero, the gillie said.

"You see?"

"You bet against me," Crater said again in disbelief.

Summoning up a twisted smile, Petro shrugged. "Come on. It's not the end of the moon. So I bet against you. So I lost money. You should be happy."

"How can I be happy that you think so little of me?"

"What's your beef? I'm the one who lost money." He put his arm around Crater's shoulder, making the gillie dodge out of the way. "Forget it. Let's get your trophy."

"Stay away from me."

Crater pushed Petro's arm away and headed to the Colonel's box. Though he felt no sense of victory at all, it would have been impolite not to go. Petro shook his head, shrugged, then followed.

To get to the Colonel's box required going along the common corridor, down another set of tubeways, and then up a series of stairs. When Crater entered the box, the Colonel was sitting in an ornate chair with Czarina Zorna perched on a throne at his side. Standing and talking into a do4u while looking grim was General Nero. The Czarina looked up from the crystal flute glass from which she was sipping wine. Crater started to say who he was but before he could, Petro stepped up beside him. "Your majesty," Petro said and bowed, pulling Crater down. "It's royalty, you rube," he hissed.

The Colonel smiled as the boys straightened up. "Our conquering heroes," he said, snapping his fingers toward a servant. "Let's have our little ceremony, eh?"

The servant handed the Colonel the trophy, a mooncrete cup painted gold. The Colonel handed it to Petro. "Well done, my boy."

Czarina Zorna added, "You were a brave driver. I salute you."

"Crater drove," Petro said, gesturing toward Crater. "Of course, I taught him everything he knows."

"Petro has won the cup for the last two years," the Colonel said.

Petro passed the cup to Crater. He had worked up a little speech and began, "It was a hard race but—"

"Perhaps you have heard of me in a different manner, your highness," Petro interrupted. "My mum is the queen mother of the late United Kingdom. I am the Prince of Wales, Earl of Chester, Duke of Cornwall, Duke of Rothesay, Earl of Carrick, Baron of Renfrew, Lord of the Isles, and Great Steward of Scotland."

Crater began again. "It was a hard race but—"

Colonel Medaris interrupted this time. "So Q-Bess says of the boy. It could be true, for all I know."

Crater opened his mouth, then shut it, recognizing his moment had passed.

Czarina Zorna inspected Petro. "Intriguing, yet your name sounds Greek."

"It is an acronym, your majesty. My given names are Philip Earl Thomas Reginald Osgood. First letters put together, you get Petro. Coincidentally, it means rock in Greek and serves me well. As you know, royalty must oft be anonymous in these days. I am beyond pleased you are an exception."

A tall, sturdy, and stern-faced man came forward wearing a green tunic and an elk sticker on his belt. He also wore several military medals that Crater recognized were for bravery under fire. "Twice a winner of this race and a fastbug instructor, eh?" he said to Petro. "I don't care about this prince stuff, son, but if you ever want a job, I could use a fastbug scout."

"Captain Jake Teller," the Colonel introduced. "Convoy commander."

"Appreciate the offer, sir," Petro said with a disarming smile, "but I've got my eye on bigger paydays."

At the Colonel's beckon, a young woman rose from a chair and stepped forward. Crater was instantly transfixed by this slim girl with long ebony hair who wore a faux leather suit that hid scarcely a curve of her young body. His mouth went dry, his knees trembled, and his heart thudded in his ears. This was confusing, as these were the exact symptoms he had when he was scared.

"Maria," the Colonel said, "this is Petro and, um, Crater, our winning fastbug team. Boys, meet my granddaughter Maria. She's named for the *mares*, that is to say, the seas of the moon, and is as lovely as all of them put together."

Crater could not argue with the Colonel's proud introduction of his amber-eyed granddaughter. Impetuously, he stepped in front of Petro, handing off the trophy cup to the older boy as he did, and eagerly put out his hand. "G-g-good to meetcha!" he blurted, then cringed. He surely sounded like an idiot.

The girl seemed amused as she shook his hand—hers was cool and dry while he knew his had surely turned clammy—and then shook Petro's hand. "I think you ran a noble race," she said, before noticing the gillie on Crater's shoulder. "What's that?"

"It's a gillie," Crater answered, pleased that he'd done so without stuttering.

The gillie preened and tried on a number of colors, settling on a soft green. Crater said, "Stop it," and the gillie shifted back to being gray. "It gets above itself sometimes," he apologized.

"Personally, I'm enchanted," Maria replied, then reached out to touch the gillie, which shied away.

"It doesn't like to be touched," Crater said.

"Gillies are illegal," General Nero said, snapping shut his do4u.

"It knows that, sir," Crater answered.

"Illegal everywhere in the world, it's true," the Colonel said, "but I decided to let Crater keep his gillie. It was the only artifact of his biological parents."

"He is an orphan?" the Czarina clucked. "We do not allow orphans in New St. Petersburg. They are not productive."

Colonel Medaris shrugged, then waved Petro and Crater away. "Toddle off, boys. And thanks again for maintaining the honor of Moontown over those Neroburg ruffians." General Nero, back on his do4u, shook his fist in mock outrage. The Colonel laughed.

Crater wanted to say something else to Maria but he didn't know what, and before he could open his mouth, Petro handed the infernal trophy back to him and took her arm and steered her away. "How would you like to go to the Earthrise tonight?"

he asked her. "I have a band and we're playing there. I'll make sure you have a table up front."

"I will have to check my calendar," Maria replied, smiling.

"I'll take that as a yes," Petro said, then added out of the corner of his mouth, "Crater, tell the gillie to make it so."

Crater didn't like that Petro had taken Maria by her arm, nor did he like that he'd asked her out, nor did he like he'd called the band his. It wasn't his, not even nearly, but, as always, Crater was quick to forgive Petro.

Without Crater telling it to, the gillie made the call. Within seconds, it said, *Earthrise puter confirms table for Maria Medaris.*

"That gillie is handy," Maria said. "How much for it?"

"It's yours for a kiss," Petro grandly replied.

She peered around his shoulders at Crater. "Since it belongs to Crater, shouldn't he get the kiss?" Crater blushed and the gillie turned pink to match.

Petro chuckled. "Crater's too shy and, anyway, he's just a child—so I'll collect your kiss for him."

"Well, no kiss for you today, nor tomorrow, nor perhaps ever," she answered, her smile turning coy. "Unless I decide it should be so. Now, go away. I'm told there's to be a parade and I want to watch it."

Petro made a little bow, then ambled off while Crater stumbled along behind. Crater had won the race, yet Petro had still received the glory. And the girl too! All he'd gotten was an ugly mooncrete trophy cup. At the bottom of the steps, Petro said, "That's a great girl, Crater. I'll get her to kiss me tonight—don't think I won't."

"I was talking to her," Crater said, "and you interrupted me."

"So? You think she's ever going to kiss you?"

"Why not?"

Petro chuckled. "Crater, you know nothing about women. In the first place, they're attracted to men with a future. You're a scragline picker and that's all you're ever going to be. But you heard what I told that convoy cruiser. She heard it too. Although I've lost my throne, I'm still destined for bigger things."

"But you could see I liked her. You're my brother."

"Not really," Petro replied. "We live in the same tube and Q-Bess is my mum and your guardian. Otherwise, there's not a thing that makes us brothers."

A lump formed in Crater's throat and tears filled his eyes, but no words came to him. He turned and walked away. Petro called after him. "What's your problem, anyway?" When Crater kept walking, Petro hurried after him and put his hand on Crater's shoulder. "Hey, I was just joking."

Crater brushed Petro's hand away. "No, you weren't."

"You're too sensitive, Crater. Toughen up!"

Crater didn't reply but took his trophy cup and threw it against the tube wall, whereupon it shattered into a dozen pieces. He stared at the shards on the deck, then knelt and picked them up, lest anyone think he wasn't grateful for the honor. Carrying the mooncrete chunks and flushed with anger and embarrassment, he walked away, wishing he could keep going and never look back. Life was suddenly very dark.

Back in the viewing box, the sheriff approached the Colonel. "So that's your boy, Sheriff?" the Colonel demanded.

"Indeed, sir."

"Is he naive?"

"Completely."

"Not too dumb?"

"He's actually a brilliant lad. Knows a dozen languages and is a fair engineer."

"Brave?"

"Braver than a squad of generals."

"Loyal?"

"No one is more loyal to you than he."

"The other boy? Our royal pretender?"

"Not right, sir. It's Crater you're needing."

"Well done, Sheriff."

"Thank you, sir. Anything else?"

The Colonel turned back to his guests and waved his hand. The sheriff was dismissed. Another problem solved.

::: SEVEN

The Scragline Pickers, as the band called themselves, mostly played Lunarian Country. Crater had formed the band, scheduled all the practices, and written nearly all the songs. His instruments were the electronic guitar and the fiddle, and he also sang. Petro played bass indifferently since he rarely practiced. There were two electric guitar pluckers and a fellow who played the trumpet. One of their recordings had even gotten play over the Armstrong City station. It was called "Moon Dust Girls," and Crater was plenty proud of it. As he sang it that night, Crater discovered he was singing it for Maria, who sat up front with Captain Teller and some tough-looking truck drivers.

> *All I want is a moon dust girl,*
> *Down in a crater waitin' for love.*
> *All I want is a moon dust girl,*
> *Kissin' me 'neath the world above.*

All I need is a moon dust girl,
Makes workin' in the dust almost fun.
All I need is a moon dust girl,
Scrapes heel-3 up by the megaton.

Now I have a moon dust girl,
Puts her helmet next to mine.
Now I have a moon dust girl,
She's one-sixth gravity fine.

After their sets and some nice tips collected in an old moon boot from the regulars plus the Neroburg and Russian visitors, Crater headed for Maria's table. He'd been practicing what he was going to say. "Hello, Maria. Thank you for coming. You're looking pretty tonight." He'd said the lines over and over in his head, but before he got to the table, Petro beat him to it, bringing Maria a soft drink. Maria smiled at Petro and turned her attention to him. Crater, his boots dragging, went back to the Dust Palace, there to stare into the darkness until Petro came home. It was after midnight. Crater, pretending to be asleep, heard him whistling "Moon Dust Girls."

The next day after their shift was over, Q-Bess met Crater and Petro at the Dust Palace hatch. "Colonel wants to see you in one hour, Crater. You'll see it on your reader. And, Petro?"

"Yes, Mum?"

"That granddaughter of the Colonel's left you a message. Said to meet her at the Earthrise."

Crater gulped, but managed to say, "Have fun."

Petro grinned. "I always do!"

A few seconds later it registered in Crater's head that he

was to meet with the Colonel. He looked to Q-Bess for an explanation but she shrugged. "No clue."

Crater gulped. "I'm going to be fired for driving a shuttle without a permit!"

Q-Bess thought that over. "If that were so, Petro would be called in too. I swear, Crater, you could depress an army that just won a war. Maybe the Colonel's gonna give you a medal. Ever think of that? Now, get going."

Crater, having no other choice, got going. On his bunk, Crater found Q-Bess had laid out his best tunic, a clean pair of leggings, and tube boots polished to a gleam. Crater headed for the administrative offices. When he passed the office with the sign that said Sherrif of Moontown, the sheriff waved him inside and leaned back in his chair, which protested in a rusty squawk. "I believe you are off to see the Colonel," he said. "Do you know the topic?"

"No, sir."

The sheriff took on a melancholy aspect and leaned forward, the chair squawking in the opposite direction. "Crater, the Colonel is not an ordinary man. He thinks at different levels and in different ways than you and I. Keep that in mind."

Crater was anxious to get moving lest he be late, but the sheriff showed no interest in letting him go. "I'm not much for general conversation and I don't usually give advice but ... Bill and Annie Hawkins, your foster parents, were friends of mine. Did you know that?"

"No, sir."

"They came across on the same convoy as I did. You were in Annie's arms and Bill was so proud. They adopted you from the Armstrong City hospital. That was kind of them, taking an infant of dead parents to raise. Bill and Annie went off to the scrapes, I got into the sheriffing business, but we were friends, like I said, and I guess I should have looked after you a little more than I've done over the years. At least I can now offer you some advice, and here it is. Don't do anything unless you think you can handle it. Do you understand what I'm saying?"

Crater scratched his head. "If I think I can't handle something, I shouldn't do it?"

"Very good," the sheriff said, then added, "and it might be best if you left the gillie with me."

The sheriff's suggestion was not, of course, a suggestion, so Crater handed the gillie over in its holster and the sheriff put it in a cabinet and locked it. "You can pick it up after you're done," he said and waved Crater on his way.

Crater walked to the Colonel's office, his thoughts turning to what he knew about how he'd come to Moontown. His parents had come from Earth, he knew that much, but their lander had crashed. That was before the moon elevator had been built. When Crater had been born at the hospital in Armstrong City and his mother had subsequently died, the nurses had started looking for some foster parents and found Bill and Annie Hawkins, a couple who had a contract to work in Moontown. Crater was handed over to them with a letter testifying who he was, made official since it was signed by the head nurse. Almost seventeen years later, here he was, orphan and ward of the company, off to see the Colonel, the greatest man in Moontown and probably the entire moon.

Crater didn't know how he should feel, so he chose pride. *Pride goeth before a fall*, he recalled somebody at the Dust Palace saying, but he didn't care about that. He needed any emotion he could grab to cover up what kept exploding in his brain like a double-charged detpak: jealousy. It was awful, green-eyed, and purple-footed, and if he let it, the monster was going to overwhelm him. Somehow, even though he had only spent a few minutes in her presence, Crater had decided Maria Medaris was worthy of his complete and utter worship and adoration. That she was allowing Petro, who could not understand her perfection, the favor of her presence and probably lots of kisses was tearing him up inside.

Tamping down his jealousy as best he could at least got him to the Colonel's office, which required going past most of the company administrative offices. As Crater passed them, the employees within—the engineers, draftsmen, clerks, and such—stopped what they were doing to watch him go by. It wasn't every day a scragline picker was invited into the bureaucratic palace. In the Colonel's anteroom, Crater discovered a young woman sitting at a standard office desk. Her hair, the color of copper, flowed across her shoulders, and she was wearing an obviously very expensive amber silken tunic. When she looked up, Crater said, "I'm Crater Trueblood. I have an appointment to see the Colonel."

The receptionist provided Crater with a tilt of her head and then told him to sit. This he did on one of the hard mooncrete chairs positioned around the tube wall while the receptionist proceeded to ignore him. It was deathly quiet, save the faint whisper of the ventilation system blowing the scent of something organic and sweet—Crater couldn't identify it—through the hidden vents in the ceiling and floor, and the occasional click of the receptionist's fingers on the keyboard of her puter.

After precisely one hour, the receptionist looked his way and said, "The Colonel will see you now." She rose as Crater did, her duty apparently to open the ornate door to the great sanctum. "Colonel, he's here," she announced, followed by the Colonel's parade-ground voice booming, "At last he's arrived! Send him in, Diana, send him in!"

The receptionist stepped aside to let Crater pass, the big door swinging shut behind him with a soft click. Crater was instantly in awe of the Colonel's office. Paneled in a warm brown with patterned faux woods and a floor cushioned by a soft, green carpet, it was not like anything Crater had ever seen. Alongside a massive desk were enormous globes of the Earth and the moon, both set on stands made of what appeared to be bronze. There was also a gilded placard on the front of the Colonel's desk that said *De inimico non loquaris sed cogites* which Crater recognized as Latin and meant—if the instruction he had received from a former Latin professor turned heel-3 miner meant anything—*Do not wish ill for your enemy; plan it.*

The Colonel was seated on a stool in front of the moon globe. "Do you like maps, Crater?" he asked. "I have been contemplating the geologic map of the nearside northern hemisphere, which includes most of the present civilization of the moon. Come over here. I want you to have a better look."

Crater came closer and peered at the gray globe. It had black letters on it identifying the craters, mountains, plains, rilles, and settlements. It was so beautiful Crater wanted to touch it, but he didn't dare. "Our planet," the Colonel said. "Magnificent, isn't it?"

"Yes, sir."

"What do you know of it?"

There were many experts on the moon, and Crater had been taught by a few of them at the Dust Palace. "Well, the moon's surface is about 14.6 million square miles, a little smaller than Asia on Earth," he recited. "In terms of volume, about fifty moons could fit inside the Earth. It has a complex geologic structure including mountains, rilles, basins, all covered with a rubble of rock fragments and dust we call the regolith."

"And your namesake, the craters," the Colonel added.

"True is, sir. Craters represent the bombardment history of the inner solar system."

"Very good. Now, tell me. What kinds of rocks are on our little planet?"

"Three kinds, sir. Basalts, anorthosites, and breccia. Basalts are the lava rocks that fill our basins, anorthosites are the bright rocks that make up our highlands, and breccia are composites, mostly caused by meteor, comet, and asteroid impacts."

The Colonel's eyes warmed. "You've learned your lessons well. I will have to compliment her royal highness Q-Bess for tending to your education. But what did she and her lodgers teach you of Earth?"

"Of its geology, sir?"

"I was thinking more of the history of the people who live on it."

Crater formed his thoughts around the stories he'd been taught by various tutors over the years, then answered, "As far as what we call Western Civilization, I know the Egyptians seemed to get things started, then there were the Greeks who figured a lot of things out about math, and then the Romans who were ruthless but great organizers and engineers, and then there were the dark ages, which really weren't all that dark because a lot of wonderful cathedrals got built. All that was followed by the Renaissance where people started to throw off superstition like their belief in witches and wizards and the evil eye and stuff, and then came the rise of European countries and then the United States and Russia too. The industrial revolution happened and then all the world wars and then people started flying into space. During all that time, China, Japan, and the Asian countries were working on their civilization, and Africans and the other nation states of the Americas were trying to figure out where they fit in, and then there were all the civil wars and little wars everywhere when the old nations began to fall apart and turn themselves into smaller countries. And then a lot changed when the moon started to be mined and settled. It's complicated, isn't it, sir?"

"Oh yes, Crater. Very complicated. But history is going somewhere, that much is apparent. Past is prologue as they say, so if we know history, we might predict where it will all end up. You've never lived anywhere other than the moon, have you?"

"No, sir."

"Many people on Earth hate the way we live here amidst our ancient lava flows and rubble, Crater. Did you know that?"

"No, sir. Why would that be?"

"Jealousy, pure and simple. We live free. No one on Earth does. They are all controlled by governments, most of them with a very heavy hand. Oh, there's been some improvements with the new countries, but even they have their tax man with his hand out." He fondly studied the moon globe a little longer, then turned in Crater's direction and asked, "Do you like living in Moontown?"

"I love living in Moontown, sir." It was an honest admission.

"I believe you."

"Thank you, sir."

"Do you know why I've asked you to visit me?"

"Are you going to fire me for driving a shuttle without a permit?"

The Colonel stared at Crater for a long second, then laughed heartily. "No, no, Crater, not at all. I should give you a medal for that, and maybe I will someday when I have nothing better to do. After all, you saved me having to rebuild a maintenance shed and hire a bunch of new orangutans. No, I called you in because I want you to understand something."

The Colonel tapped his finger on the globe at Armstrong City, which was the main settlement built near the first landing of humans on the moon, then trailed his finger north-westward. "I have in mind a great project, Crater. A monorail across our storied wayback. It will begin or end at Armstrong City, depending on your point of view, then travel northerly through the Sea of Tranquility, skirt the Plinius Crater, cut across the Sea of Serenity between the Aristillus and Autolycus Craters, then proceed to a depot a few miles from Moontown. If constructed, it would be a true wonder and allow a safer and more economical delivery of Helium-3."

Crater, who knew a great deal about engineering since he had been taught by the best ones to show up at the Dust Palace, thought it would be a difficult proposition to build anything as complex as a monorail through the wayback. But he supposed if anybody could do it, it would be the Colonel.

The Colonel moved to his desk and sat, then waved Crater to a leather upholstered chair in front of it. Crater had never sat in such a fine piece of furniture. He carefully lowered himself into it, feeling its softness form around his rump.

"Unfortunately," the Colonel went on, "there are obstacles. One of them is that the monorail would cross most of the Sea of Serenity, which is Russian territory. They don't want it because they are in league with General Nero, I fear, who opposes my attempts to modernize lunar transportation. And without the Russians on board, the Earthian money men are loathe to fund it."

"Why don't the Russians want the monorail, sir?"

The Colonel took on an expression of distaste. "Because they are idiots, fools, misanthropes, vodka-swilling, nineteenth-century nincompoops! Excepting the Czarina, of course, but she's heavily influenced by the louts who purport to advise her, louts who are paid under the table by our dear General Nero."

Colonel Medaris, after a brief period of contemplating his own words, continued with what Crater considered a most peculiar question. "Crater, how are you at subterfuge, lying, being underhanded, that kind of thing?"

Crater, believing the Colonel had a good reason for everything, thought the question over. "Not very good. Q-Bess always catches me every time I try to tell a fib."

The Colonel nodded. "Not surprising since that lady's been known to tell a fib or two herself. Nobody in Moontown can cook the books quite so well as our Q-Bess." He chuckled. "I admire her majesty's audacity, though. How about any of those misbegotten denizens of the Dust Palace? Any of them ever teach you to lie, cheat, that kind of thing?"

Crater decided not to mention Petro and replied, "Doom and Headsplitter taught me how to fight dirty, sneak up on people, knock them on the head, although I've never actually done it and I don't really think it's right to fight that way."

"How about Asteroid Al?"

"As far as I know, nobody scrapes a straighter path than Asteroid Al."

The Colonel shrugged. "A straight path, Crater, can also go through an unproductive field, but that's a never mind. If someone asked you, what would you say you were good at?"

It was a hard question since Crater didn't think he was particularly good at anything. Still, he needed to answer so he said, "I guess I'm a pretty good scragline picker, and I know fourteen languages so I'm okay at that, and I can play a few musical instruments, and maybe I'm a fair mechanic too."

"I've heard you're better than fair when it comes to machines. Tell me, are you loyal to my company?"

"Why, yes, sir. I wouldn't have a home or a job without it."

The Colonel pretended to ponder Crater's answer for a moment, then pointed at a display on his desk. It was a glass dome and within it was a gray splintered rock about the size of a man's fist. "I collect artifacts of the movement into space. That is my most treasured one, an actual rock picked up by Neil Armstrong after the first moon landing and carried back to Earth. It cost me a pretty penny. What do you think of it?"

Crater peered at the rock, which looked just like any one of the thousands of such rocks he'd popped out of conveyor rollers. He considered a pleasant lie, couldn't manage it, and said, "It's a rock, sir."

The Colonel chuckled at Crater's response but then his

expression turned grave. "Crater, I have a proposal for you. It's simple, really. I would like you to take a job as scout with the Medaris Convoy Company. You'll work for Captain Teller and journey with the next heel-3 convoy to Armstrong City and, once there, go up on the Cycler and retrieve a package with a very important space artifact and bring it back to me. What do you say?"

Crater was startled by the Colonel's proposal and didn't know what to say. Seeing what he took as confusion, the Colonel said, "This artifact is more than a collectible. It has much to do with the future of Moontown or I wouldn't ask you to do this job for me. You see, Crater, if I sent someone after this thing, someone clearly dispatched to the Cycler to pick it up, there might be some bad men who'd try to stop him. So here's what I'm thinking. What if someone they didn't suspect went after it? Do you understand?"

Crater didn't understand. "I like working on the scrapes, sir," he said.

"I know, Crater, but it's a ruse. Do you understand what that is?"

"A trick or a deception," Crater replied. He felt like he'd just lost a battle in a war he didn't even know he was fighting.

"Precisely," the Colonel said. "So what do you say? Besides doing me a great favor, it might be just the adventure for a young man. Wish I was your age again. I'd be out of here and on that fastbug scouting for the captain faster than you could say the name of my great-grandmother, Penny High Eagle Medaris."

Crater, who'd read the historical accounts of the Colonel's ancestor, said, "She was a prodigious woman, wasn't she, sir?"

"Yes, she was, Crater, and she would approve of what I'm asking you to do. She loved the company she and my great-grandfather formed, out of which all of the present Medaris family companies were spawned."

The Colonel held every card. If Crater refused, he might lose his job or be kept as a scragline picker for the rest of his life. "I guess I can do it," he said slowly. "But can I come back and get my old job afterward?"

"Why of course!" The Colonel smiled tenderly at the boy. "You are a first-rate lad. I always knew that. That's why I let you stay at the Dust Palace after your parents—that is to say your foster parents—passed. I don't think you had a defender in my company. They all said you should be sent to Armstrong City to fend for yourself but I said, 'No, this lad's a survivor, that's what he is, and smart as paint. Let him stay, let Q-Bess raise him—she has but one child, the Prince of Wales or Petro or whatever he's called—and she loves children.' So I solved another problem to everyone's satisfaction."

The Colonel looked pleased with himself, then said, "Now, Crater, get thee to the company administrative office and tender your resignation. Then seek out Captain Teller who will take you on as a scout."

It was all too fast. Crater was already scared, and he hadn't done anything yet. The Colonel took no notice, saying, "There's another thing I am going to ask you to do. My granddaughter, Maria? She and I are joint owners of the convoy company. Like all Medarises, she knows the best way to run a company is to learn it from the inside. She has decided, therefore, to be a convoy scout on a few runs. I'm against it, but she has me twisted around her finger. That's true for just about anybody she meets, so watch yourself, eh? A convoy across the moon has significant dangers. Captain Teller is quite competent, but Maria is headstrong and more than a little arrogant about what she can and cannot do. Things can happen out there. You will be working alongside her and I expect you to keep her safe. That, of course, includes giving up your life for hers if necessary. Agreed?"

Crater didn't know what to say. Look after Petro's new girlfriend? He supposed he could do that, especially since Petro wouldn't be around. "Of course, sir."

"Splendid. However, presuming you don't die in defense of my granddaughter, your next most important duty is to get to the Cycler *Elon Musk* on time. If you don't, there may not be another opportunity to acquire this artifact. I've already tried twice but had to call off the show. Don't let me down, Crater, hmmm?"

"I'll do my best, sir."

"I expect you to do better. Now, the convoy leaves in two days. It will take approximately ten days—twelve at most— to get to Armstrong City. So if it's twelve, the *Elon Musk* will rendezvous with the elevator's ferry one day after that. By my calculations, um, sixteen days from today I expect you to be on the Cycler. Got it?"

"Fifteen days, sir, and I won't fail you. Maria will be protected and I will get to the Cycler on time."

"It's all set then," the Colonel said. "Off you go."

Crater rose, searched his muddled thoughts for something adequate to say, finally settling on a pallid "Thank you, sir," and left the office. To his surprise, the sheriff was in the waiting room. The gillie was with him in its holster and he handed it over. "How'd it go?" the sheriff asked.

"I'm not sure," Crater said.

"Was the Colonel smiling when you left?"

"Smiling, sir? I'm not certain. Should he have been?"

"No, of course not. A silly question. Well, on your way, lad."

After Crater left the waiting room, the sheriff went inside to see the Colonel. "Your receptionist called and said you wanted me to visit after Crater, sir."

The Colonel was still at his desk. "I was going to congratulate you for finding him. Now I don't know," he said.

"I'm sorry, sir. Did he not prove to be good, honest, naive, and loyal?"

"Perhaps too much."

"Shall I look for someone else?"

The Colonel took a deep breath and leaned back in his chair. "No. I need him. But have I done the right thing?"

The question startled the sheriff. "The right thing, sir? I don't know much about right things. Now, if you asked me about the expedient thing, that I could advise."

The Colonel allowed a small, sad smile. "Do the names George Taylor Grange and Lawrence Zummer mean anything to you?"

"Why, yes, sir," the sheriff answered. "They are employees of yours, stationed in Armstrong City, and recently deceased. Their files crossed my desk. Natural causes, I believe?"

"So we allowed everyone to believe. Both were murdered. Grange got it with an elk sticker in June. Zummer was poisoned in September. I had assigned them a particular duty. They were to go up to the Cycler and retrieve a certain artifact. The same artifact I'm sending Crater after."

The sheriff processed that information. "Who killed them?"

"I have no idea. There are many candidates but I really don't know. All I know for certain is I'm sending that fine, innocent boy on a mission that may get him killed. No, will *probably* get him killed. What say you now, Sheriff?"

"One does what one has to do, sir."

The Colonel nodded. "One does, indeed," he said, though he allowed himself a brief pang of regret, then rejected it as unworthy. What was one orphan, even one as smart and good as Crater? The Colonel allowed himself to relax. He'd done the right thing, the only thing to be done. It was for the good of his family and their various enterprises, which meant it was for the good of the moon.

When Crater arrived at the Dust Palace, he found Q-Bess with both a smile on her face and a tear in her eye. She held up her reader. "Crater, it says here you've quit the mining company and joined the convoy company. Is it true?"

When Crater said it was true and that he was to be a scout on the next heel-3 convoy, she took him into her arms for a big hug. "Oh, my darling boy," she sobbed through a proud smile. "Don't get yourself killed out there, but do good. Do real good!"

"I'll make it back, Q-Bess," Crater swore. "And I'll do good too," he added, although he had his doubts about both propositions.

::: Part Two

THE
CONVOY

::: EIGHT

cceptance of his application to be a convoy scout came instantly, and Crater test-drove the fastbug assigned to him. Thinking it a bit sluggish, he asked Captain Teller if he could work to make it faster. Teller approved as long as Crater strengthened the fastbug's frame. "Speed is good, Crater," he advised, "but I can't afford to have one of my scouts break down out there."

Crater told the captain he understood, then beefed up the fastbug's frame with lunasteel bar stock. He also installed a heavy-duty torsion beam suspension and modified the fast-bug's fuel cell with a design of his own utilizing a sling blade pump. Crater figured it would give the fastbug at least a quarter more power and speed on the dustway, as the convoy route that started in Moontown and ended in Armstrong City was called.

Petro showed up to help install the modified fuel cell. After cranking down a few bolts, he said, "Just so you know, I've quit the scrapes and joined the convoy. I'm going to drive one of Carlos Sepulveda's trucks."

Crater angrily tossed down a wrench and grabbed the one Petro was holding. "Maria's one of the scouts. Guess that's why you're going along."

Petro took the wrench back. "That's not why I'm going. Maria's a sweet girl but not my type. When I took her out, all she wanted to talk about was business and profits and, oh yeah, *you*. Kept wanting to know what you were like. I told her you worried too much about everything. Don't even think about grabbing this wrench again. I'm gonna help you whether you like it or not."

Crater reached for the wrench but Petro pulled it away. "Maybe you're right about me being a worrier. If so, you're a worry I don't need. I'm going to ask Captain Teller to kick you off the convoy."

Petro studied him. "Why would you do that? Haven't I always looked after you?"

"No, you haven't. I can't think when you ever have."

Petro frowned, then assumed a crooked grin. "You don't mean a word of that. It's Maria, right? I already told you that's not going anywhere. Anyway, the captain's already signed my papers. One of Carlos's drivers came down with kidney stones and is flat on his back. Both he and the captain were glad to have me."

Crater knew Carlos Sepulveda mostly by reputation. He was an honest trucker, quiet and reserved, although he had an eye for Q-Bess and perhaps vice versa. Whenever he was in town, she always did something with her hair.

No matter what Petro said, Crater was sure he had joined the convoy so he could chase after Maria. Petro wasn't one to let a girl get the better of him. He would figure out how to win her and kiss her beneath the stars out there on the dustway. It made Crater's stomach hurt to imagine how it would all develop. "If you're going, Petro, it's because you've got some angle, not because of me," he accused.

"Don't be silly, brother," Petro said.

"You're not my brother," Crater snapped. "We just used to live in the same tube."

Petro threw down the wrench. "Fine. If that's the way you want it, you and me—we're through. You're on your own."

"What else is new?" Crater demanded, then pretended not to care when Petro stormed out.

The night before the convoy began its journey across the wayback, Captain Teller ordered his scouts to the east maintenance shed for a briefing. Crater and Maria sat cross-legged on the mooncrete floor beside the two scout fastbugs while the captain went down on one knee. Behind him was a big, boxy truck filled with spare parts, food, water, puters, and bunk beds. It was Teller's truck, which he called the chuckwagon.

The black tunic Teller wore was severely plain, excepting a white collar. It reminded Crater of pix he'd seen of the Pilgrims who'd settled old New England. All Teller needed was an ancient, cracked Bible in one hand and a blunderbuss in the other. Based on the flurry of directives and rules that Crater had received on his reader, the convoy commander was a man who was careful, meticulous in thought and manner, and tightly wound. He had set forth how-tos on everything that had to do with a convoy: the order of march, the route, the minimum distance between trucks, even the average joules a truck solar panel should collect in an hour's soak. At the bottom of each directive, Teller had written, "You will study and understand everything in this directive or be subject to immediate employment termination."

"Hear me, scouts," Teller said. "Once we get rolling, we're pretty much on our own. Our radios are short-range, line of sight and the moon's horizon is never far away. That means you get a few miles from the convoy, I can't hear you. Or if a hill or crater rim gets in the way, same story."

Crater raised his hand. "Captain, my gillie can communicate farther than any do4u."

Teller frowned at the interruption. "Your gillie is illegal."

"It knows that, sir."

"You ever had that thing out on the dustway?"

"No, sir."

"Then you don't know what it can do, so be quiet and listen. You'll see communication antennas here and there that can connect with a relay-sat, but those have to be in your line of sight. Even then, you can't depend on them. Truckers have been known to knock one down by accident or just for the scrag of it. I've got a sat-phone for emergencies, which lets me communicate directly with the Colonel, but it's expensive. Anyway, when we get a hundred miles or more out into the wayback, there's not much the Colonel can do for us." He allowed a sigh. "Crater, I can see by your expression you have another question."

"How about a jumpcar if we need one?"

"Why would we need a jumpcar?"

"Well, it could fly in supplies if we needed them, or fly out somebody who maybe got hurt."

Teller shook his head. "Number one, too expensive. Number two, both of the company's jumpcars are broken. As a matter of fact, we're expected to bring jumpcar parts back with us on the return convoy. Just get it through your thick skull right now, Crater. It's going to be you, Maria, and me against a thousand miles of dustway and eighteen crazy drivers who'll do everything they can to drive us nuts. You're going to have to play nursemaid to them every foot of the way. That means if they break down, you help immediately, not ten minutes later, because the convoy can only go as fast as its slowest truck. We'll be averaging, if we're lucky, about fifteen miles an hour, probably less. Best case, if we're able to run twelve hours a day, which is unlikely, that's one hundred and eighty miles a day. We'll have to stop a couple of times and refit, and that'll take its toll on our time."

"Can we make it in ten days?" Crater asked, thinking again about his requirement to catch the Cycler *Elon Musk*.

"That's the plan. If we don't, we'll be caught by the long shadow, and once the sun goes down, it gets spooky out there. I don't want that to happen. Tomorrow first thing, Maria will take the point. Crater, station yourself at the Copperhead Bridge. That's the first hurdle, and it's a big one. A lot of the truckers get nervous about crossing that fool bridge, especially when they've got a full load. You may need to kick their tails to get them across. When everybody gets across the bridge, run alongside the convoy where the terrain allows it. Otherwise, squeeze into the line."

"Try not to run into any of the trucks," Maria advised with an impish grin, "or get lost. Just watch what I do and you won't mess up too much."

Crater ignored her. "When I'm on point, what do I look for?"

"Anything that will slow us down. Holes or cracks in the road, a collapsed lava tube, a wreck, or sabotage. There are some people out there who'd just as soon not see us make our delivery. For instance, the Umlaps stopped a dustway convoy and begged for money a few months ago."

Crater knew something of the Umlaps, but they were a mysterious bunch. He'd met three of their peculiar citizens when they'd lived at the Dust Palace. One was named Runs Away Again, a young Umlap who'd done just that. The other two were Walks On Dust and Tells No One, both kicked out of the Umlap town of Baikal for unknown reasons. They'd come to Moontown seeking jobs, which the Colonel had given them despite the objection of some parents who were worried that their children would be traumatized just by seeing one walk by.

The history of the Umlaps was a pathetic one. A genetic experiment in a remote compound in Siberia, they had been created for a Russo-Chinese company to work their scrapes after their first miners had been struck down by the effects of low lunar gravity. Developed in secret and carried to the moon as cargo, the Umlaps were put to work on scrapes near the Piton crater field. They proved to be well adapted for the work because they were very strong, required 30 percent less oxygen than standard humans, and had an IQ of something south of average. After a disgruntled miner who'd lost his job to the Umlaps blew the whistle on the experiment, the company was forced to show both Moonians and Earthians their gene-tweaked slaves.

It was a shock to the two worlds upon seeing pix of the Umlaps for the first time. They had big hands, short legs, robust chests, lantern jaws, and no ears—just holes. Even on war-torn Earth, countries and organizations condemned their creation. The compound where the Umlaps were created was burned to the ground, the scientists who'd done the work imprisoned, and the Russo-Chinese heel-3 company put out of business.

This, however, left around sixty Umlaps on a thousand square miles of lunar regolith where, ever since, they had been spectacularly unsuccessful. Now, after decades of defaulting on loans and losing their land put up for collateral, the Umlaps had but a small area left. The dustway ran through a corner of it, and though, by common consent of the companies, the route was treated much as the oceans were on Earth—that is, it belonged to no one and everyone—the Umlaps apparently now had a different opinion.

"What will we do if they try to stop us?" Crater asked.

"They will be dealt with," Teller said in a grim tone. "Let me worry about that. Now, let's get some sleep while we can. We'll not likely get much until we get to Armstrong City."

Crater didn't want to go back to the Dust Palace since he'd already said good-bye to Q-Bess, Asteroid Al, and the others, so he bedded down beside the fastbugs. Maria left to stay in town, although where she was going, she didn't say. Crater suspected it was somewhere dark where probably she and Petro could meet and hold each other. He fought back jealous outrage before finally dipping into a shallow, fitful sleep.

::: **NINE**

Beside the east maintenance shed, the convoy trucks sat with their rooftop solar panels tilted toward the sun, the panels turning rainbow colors as they soaked energy into the bio-driven fuel cells. Before the convoy could roll, the panels would be lowered and a cover deployed to keep them free of dust.

Teller sent Maria to count the trucks. When she came back, she said, "Eighteen trucks, sir. No drivers yet. They're in the maintenance shed."

Teller nodded. "All right, let's go roust them out. We need to be on the road in thirty minutes."

Teller, Maria, and Crater went into the shed to find the drivers lounging around, some talking, others sitting in huddles, and a few stretched out on the mooncrete, apparently asleep. Crater noted they wore a variety of old fabric ECPs— Elastic Counter Pressure suits.

"They don't look like much," Teller said, "but most of these fellows have made the dustway trek at least a dozen times."

Some of the drivers were singing, their voices echoing in the cavernous shed.

> *Pretty little girl wearin' a wedding ring,*
> *Waitin' for me like I was a king,*
> *Singin' Dustway Trucker, why do you roam?*
> *Dustway Trucker, ain't you ever stayin' home?*
>
> *Honey, I'm on the dustway pushin' east,*
> *Steerin' my way 'cross the Lunar beast.*
> *Heel-3 to deliver, off to roam,*
> *It'll be more'n awhile before I get home.*

Petro got up from the floor and came over. "Even though you're mad at me for no good reason, I bid you greetings, moon scout," he said to Crater, then winked at Maria. A jealous tide flooded Crater's brain.

Crater didn't see if Maria had winked back but she said, "We're leaving in thirty minutes."

"You will find me and my truck ready, my lady," Petro said with a mock gallant bow that set Crater's teeth on edge, especially when Maria smiled.

The drivers kept singing.

> *Pretty little girl wearin' a wedding gown,*
> *Got the best lovin' in old Moontown.*
> *Singin' Dustway Trucker, why do you roam?*
> *Dustway Trucker, ain't you ever stayin' home?*

Teller got on the loudspeaker. "The water trucks have arrived, people, and they were all that was holding us up. Get to your trucks, get behind the wheel, and prepare to move out. We leave in thirty—that's three zero—minutes. Any driver and truck not ready will be left behind and you can answer to the Colonel. He won't allow you to stay at the Dust Palace, he won't sell you food at the company store, and any water you drink will be what you brought with you. It's up to you."

The response from the drivers was a variety of smirks, ugly hand signals, and more singing.

> *Honey, you know I got to be free,*
> *Got a truck to drive, craters to see,*
> *Heel-3 to deliver, off to roam,*
> *It'll be more'n awhile before I get home.*

Although Crater was certain Captain Teller was going to yell at the drivers, he pretended not to notice their gestures and waited them out. After they'd established their independence, they zipped up their suits, plunked on their helmets, and trudged through the combo locks out on the dust to their trucks. Crater heard Petro call out, "Good-bye Moontown, hello Armstrong City!"

"A thousand miles to go, noogie!" a driver called back at him. "If you make it."

"You'll be sor-r-r-r-ry!" another driver sang.

After the drivers all got into their trucks, Teller called up the convoy frequency and gave them their first orders. "Comm silence, people, and listen up. I will now read the official rules.

"The lineup has been arranged by the convoy commander. Do not change it.

"Fastbug scouts have authority over all drivers. You will follow their orders as if they were mine.

"All communications will be across the convoy frequency. No talking on private freqs. An hourly test of comm will be made by the convoy commander.

"In the event of a mechanical failure, drivers will immediately notify the commander either by comm units or by signaling and pulling over. The entire convoy will pull off the dustway to a safe location until the failure is corrected.

"Passing other convoy trucks is prohibited.

"Don't separate from the convoy. If you get lost, immediately stop and communicate with the commander or the scouts. Bottom line: don't get lost.

"Questions?" Teller barked. When none of the drivers said anything, he said, "Take down and secure your solars."

Petro went through the procedure on the control panel to stow the solar panels, then got out to make certain they were locked in place. He climbed back into the cab, closed the door, and heaved over the latching lever. His side view mirrors showed Crater on one side and Maria on the other, running down the convoy, making their checks. He was proud of Crater for making such a big decision, quitting the scrapes and all, though it wasn't much like the boy. He wondered if Crater's visit with the Colonel might have had something to do with it, but his mum wouldn't talk about it so he didn't know. And, after all, it didn't really matter. What mattered to Petro was getting himself out of Moontown and on to his destiny, whatever it was. As for

Maria, she wasn't his kind of woman. Too young, just sixteen, for one thing, and she had a bit of mouth on her. Besides that, she had sometimes wanted to talk about Crater. If there was one thing Petro couldn't stand, it was a woman who wanted to talk about somebody else other than him. No, Crater could have her if he could handle her—which, of course, he probably couldn't.

"Truckers are authorized to pressurize their cabins and take off their suits," Teller said over the comm loop.

Petro told the truck puter to attend to the pressurization, and the hiss of air into the driver compartment told him it had begun. He watched the gauge that measured air pressure. When it reached Moontown standard, he unlatched his helmet faceplate. The air from the truck supply smelled a bit oily but it would do.

"Drivers, mix your cells."

The truck's fuel cells thrummed when Petro started their mixers. The digital readouts blinked the numbers, and Petro was gratified to see all his numbers in the green. He heard two truckers report one or more of their cells were dead, and Teller didn't hesitate to kick them off the convoy. Another driver called to report he was too sick to drive. Before the convoy had moved a foot, three trucks were out.

Maria drove to the truck that had the sick driver. When she called him, he lifted his head, his expression one of sheer wretchedness. "I need a doctor," he said.

"And you'll get one," Maria answered, "but not until you're in the maintenance shed."

The driver presented a disrespectful hand signal, then allowed his head to droop.

"Alcohol," she said to Crater on their private channel as he drove up.

"Maybe he's really sick," Crater said.

"He's not sick, just drunk."

"How do you know?"

Maria responded curtly, "You can't be soft, Crater, or the drivers will have you wrapped around their axles. Never believe a word they say."

Before Crater could answer, not that he had an answer, Teller called. "Crater, you still here? Stop dawdling and head for the bridge and wait for us there like I told you!"

"You ever cross the bridge?" Maria asked. When he shook his head, she said, "Prepare to be impressed. Now, get going."

Crater turned his fastbug around, ran along the line of trucks, then went ahead, following the worn tracks of the dustway. When he reached a small rise in the road, he stopped and looked over his shoulder. Already, Moontown was out of sight. "Well, here we go, gillie," he said, forgetting gillies weren't for conversation, then pressed hard on the accelerator, wheels spinning and dust flying. They were on their way.

::: TEN

The bridge that crossed the Copperhead Rille was five years old. On the Colonel's first trek to the Alpine Valley, he'd picked his way through the rugged hills to the northeast and skirted the rille to cross into the main valley. Once he'd established his scrapes, his pioneering route proved to be a difficult track for fully loaded heel-3 trucks, so he authorized the construction of a bridge across the half-mile-wide and five-hundred-foot-deep abyss. The engineer he chose to design and build the bridge was a Japanese refugee who also had an artistic flair. His design was a suspension bridge of spaghetti-thin lunasteel cable and soaring mooncrete towers on opposing abutments. It was an elegant bridge—constructed to take advantage of the low gravity—but it was also one nearly everyone was afraid to cross. The problem wasn't its design or structural integrity. The problem was that most humans didn't trust a bridge, however elegantly designed, that looked so wispy and weak. Even if born on the moon, their minds still conceptualized things as if they were within the deeper gravity well of Earth.

Crater admired the bridge from a small hill a mile away, then ran his fastbug up to its approach. He got out, summoned up his courage, then walked out on it. He thought he felt it sway under his tread, but he knew that was impossible. He didn't weigh nearly enough to affect the bridge, not even in his fastbug. He'd heard of the swaying phenomena. Nearly all truck drivers thought the bridge was moving beneath them even when instruments proved it wasn't moving at all. It was a trick of the mind.

What wasn't a trick was the sympathetic resonance that a convoy of trucks could apply to a suspension bridge, especially one so finely constructed. As the trucks crossed, they sometimes built up a cascade of vibrations that had the bridge resonating like a tuning fork, threatening to demolish the entire structure. That was something the Japanese designer had forgotten to include in his calculations. To diminish the problem, no more than three trucks were allowed on the bridge at any time with a full minute after to give the bridge time to settle down. This was Crater's job, to keep the number of trucks on the bridge to the magic three and the equally magic one minute between them.

Before long, Maria came boiling down the dustway, the first trucks following about fifty yards behind. She gave Crater a wave and kept going across the bridge. Crater wondered if her fastbug counted as one of the three trucks. He decided it didn't, fastbugs being so light, and, anyway, he thought she'd probably be across before the first truck arrived.

He waved the first truck on, then two more, then stepped

out onto the road and held his hand up to stop the next one, which, to his amazement, didn't even slow down. He had to dive out of its way as it rolled past, its driver hunched over its wheel. This meant there were now four, maybe five vehicles on the bridge. Crater hoped the captain wouldn't notice, which proved to be a forlorn hope.

"Crater! I told you no more than three trucks on that bridge!" Teller roared. "Get control of the situation. Now!"

After two more trucks whizzed past, Crater jumped in his fastbug and drove it onto the road to block the way. The next truck, dodging him, ran off the road, skidded, spun around, and finally stopped with its front bumper inches from the edge of the rille. The driver was a fellow Crater had seen around Moontown named Brian "Irish" Murphy, a hothead by reputation.

The captain yelled, "Doggone it, Crater. Get Irish back on the road and keep the convoy moving! What's wrong with you?"

Crater didn't know what was wrong except everything was happening too fast. He also thought the captain had given him contradictory orders. Which was he supposed to do first? Take care of Irish or move the convoy that was blasting onto the bridge, one truck zooming after the other. There were at least six on it now.

Choosing to save the bridge, he drove onto the road, completely blocking the trucks. The next driver skidded to a stop just inches away from Crater's fastbug and began to curse. Crater ignored him and ran over to Irish and jumped up on the running board of his truck. "Get back in line," he demanded.

Irish, who'd been staring into the deep rille, turned and looked at Crater. "I would've died if I'd gone over the edge."

"It was your own fault. Now, get back in line."

Crater hopped off Irish's truck and ran to his fastbug, moved it out of the way, and waved three trucks through, then stood in the road to stop any more. If they were coming, they'd have to run over him. He was not going to move. After a minute had passed, he waved on another three. The third one was driven by Petro, who yelled, "Here I go!"

Crater waved him on, then bodily blocked the road again. The next three trucks included Irish's. He provided Crater an insulting hand gesture, which changed to a salute as he passed. There was a rhythm now. Crater kept waving trucks on, three at a time. Finally, it was just Captain Teller and his chuckwagon.

"A poor job, Crater," Teller admonished. "And don't just stand there with your mouth open. Your day's just starting. Catch up with Maria. *Go!*"

Crater went. Driving on the bridge was breathtaking. The rille, probably a collapsed lava tube, was so deep, it looked like the Big Miner had reached down from the stars and dragged the prong of a gigantic pick through the dust.

Before long, Crater caught up with Maria. "All the trucks are across the bridge."

"I heard you had a little trouble," she said in a snarky tone.

"Well, they got across."

Maria looked dubious, then said, "Why don't you scout ahead?"

"Because Captain Teller didn't tell me to."

Maria's expression turned as cold as a shadow on the

moon. "Crater, let me explain something. I own this company and I employ Captain Teller. I give him the authority he has. I also employ you. Any questions?"

"I guess not."

"Then get going."

Crater mashed the accelerator and his fastbug's modified fuel cell kicked in, throwing up rooster tails of dust that covered Maria. Grinning while she sputtered in outrage, Crater sped away. Ahead lay the open dustway, the endless plains and craters, and the wild territories of the wayback. All of a sudden, Crater couldn't wait to see them.

::: ELEVEN

The convoy plowed on for twelve more hours with Crater and Maria alternating at the point. Then Teller ordered a halt for the drivers to rest. The blazing sun bore down as they raised their solar panels and pulled down their sun shields, most of them crawling into curtained bunks behind the bench seats for a nap. Crater joined Maria and Teller in the chuckwagon. "A good first day, absent Crater's failure at the bridge," the captain said. "Get yourselves something to eat and drink, then some sleep."

Maria went to the cupboard. "Peanut butter sandwich?" she asked Crater while Teller busied himself at his puter.

Crater was smarting from Teller's criticism, but he was also hungry and glad to have the sandwich. He poured faux powdered orange juice in plaston cups while Maria made her peanut butter and bread creations, adding strawberry jam—all of it artificial from the biovats, of course. She brought the sandwiches and sat down at the compact table. Crater joined her and they ate and drank in silence.

"What's wrong with you?" Maria asked after she'd finished the first half of her sandwich.

"What do you mean?"

"You're so quiet."

"It's hard to talk and eat a peanut butter sandwich at the same time," Crater pointed out.

"I think you're pouting because the captain said you did a poor job at the bridge. Well, you did, so what else was he going to say?"

"I don't want to talk about it," Crater said.

"You also don't like it when I tell you what to do."

"Now I really don't want to talk about it."

Maria took a bite out of the second half of her sandwich, chewed it thoughtfully, and then noticed the gillie move in its holster. "Would the gillie talk to me?"

"Gillies are only supposed to answer questions."

"Petro said yours does more than that."

The mention of Petro made his jealousy bloom again but Crater remained calm, at least on the outside. "What else did he say?"

"He said you loved that little blob of slime mold cells."

"I don't love it. I don't love anybody."

Maria apparently enjoyed needling Crater. "I would like to ask your gillie a question. Is that all right?"

"Sure, but it won't answer unless I tell it to."

"Then tell it. What's the harm?"

Crater thought it over. He supposed there was no harm, other than general stupidity for Maria to think she could stump the gillie. In fact, he thought it might be fun for the gillie to show off a bit so he said, "Gillie, this girl is going to ask you a question. I give you permission to answer it."

Maria blinked her big brown eyes. "Why did you call me 'this girl'? I have a name."

"I didn't think I should use the first name of my boss."

"Give me something of a break, Crater."

Crater shrugged. "Gillie, *Maria*"—he pronounced it with some disdain—"is going to ask you a question. Please answer it."

"Gillie," Maria said, "do you think Crater is nice?"

"It doesn't answer personal questions," Crater snapped.

Define nice, the gillie said, crawling out of its holster to Crater's shoulder.

Maria gave Crater a triumphant glance, then said, "Is he kind, brave, and clean? And does he like brunettes?"

The gillie turned a crystal blue and managed to look thoughtful, then said, *He is kind. He is brave, though he doubts himself. He generally bathes when he can, but he has at times worn underwear that is not clean. He likes girls, and the color of their hair does not matter.*

"How about me? Does he like me?"

"No more questions," Crater growled. For some reason, his face was feeling decidedly hot.

The gillie preened, changing its color to a golden yellow. *He alone can answer.*

Maria laughed softly. "Well said, Gillie. So, Crater, do you like me? Not many boys do. They think I'm too bossy."

"Well, I agree with them," Crater said.

"That was an honest answer," Maria said, though she didn't sound grateful. She didn't look grateful either. "I guess we've established at least one thing with your gillie. You don't like me and, guess what, I don't like you either." She raised her chin. "But we're professionals, are we not? We'll continue to work together, me telling you what to do and you doing it."

"Fine," Crater snapped.

"Fine," Maria snapped back. "Pick up our dishes, wash them, and tidy up the kitchen. I'm going to bed."

Crater did as he was told, his lower lip out in grumpy fashion, while Maria climbed into one of the bunks and snapped the curtain shut.

During the dustup between Crater and Maria, Captain Teller kept his eyes focused on his puter screen though he was listening. He was also smiling. "Kids," he said, then shook his head. He'd have to keep an eye on those two. They liked each other, though they hadn't figured it out yet. He also took a moment to think about something other than the convoy. He was wondering if maybe he'd done enough convoying. He had a fine wife and three marvelous kids in Armstrong City. He also had a nice savings account in Armstrong City stuffed with johncredits. Teresa wanted to invest it in a sundome that could hold a vineyard. She was from the Italian Amalfi Coast and her family had owned vineyards for centuries. Why not one on the moon? With enough water and fertilizer and sun, the grapes would grow, and during the long shadow, they could use sunlamps. She had it all figured out, and Teller was thinking perhaps it was time to follow her dream. After all, how many times could a man cross the moon and come through unscathed? Any man could run out of luck, and Teller figured he'd almost used up his allotment.

But that decision was for later. Now, he had a convoy to get across the moon, a convoy laden with the treasure of the Alpine Valley. He turned back to the puter, plotting his course, calculating the time line.

TWELVE

"Take the point, Crater," Teller said.

Crater was happy to do it, just to get away from Maria and the unhappy glances she kept sending his way. After an hour of driving, he approached a series of craters named after the old states of the original American union. He took them one after the other, Montana, West Virginia, and Texas, then drove down a long straightaway. He opened up the fastbug, just to see what it could do.

Sixty miles per hour, the gillie said.

Crater let off the accelerator. He could have gone even faster, but he didn't know the road ahead and feared hitting a hole or a bump. After an hour of steady driving, the captain called him. "Change out with Maria," he said.

Crater did a u-turn and sped back to the convoy, passing Maria who diverted her eyes from him. Crater turned around and began to pace alongside the leading trucks.

The gillie had been very quiet as if absorbing all the new things it was seeing but, Crater wondered, were they new? The gillie had crossed the moon, probably near this very track, when he was brought across as a baby by his foster parents. Could it remember that far back? It occurred to Crater he'd never asked the gillie what it recalled about that time.

But questioning the gillie would have to wait. He needed to focus on driving.

Number eleven truck out of line, the gillie said.

Crater checked his mirror and saw the gillie was correct. He called the driver. "Number eleven, please get back in line."

There was no response and the truck kept coming. The next time Crater looked back, number eleven had passed two trucks. Then Crater saw another truck move into the open lane to the left of number eleven.

Truck number twelve out of line, the gillie advised.

Crater couldn't figure out why the trucks had pulled into the other lanes. After all, Captain Teller had read the official rules of the convoy, and there was one that said there would be no passing. "Truck twelve, get in line," he called. There was no response.

Crater threw the wheel hard over, skidded around, and floored the accelerator to send the fastbug flying back. He zoomed between the errant trucks, then performed the maneuver again, coming up behind them. "Gillie, are they talking on another freq?"

Yes, the gillie said and made the connection.

"Move out, boys and girls!" he heard one of the drivers urge the others. "Race time!"

"Time to stretch it!" another driver called.

"You'll pay this time, Ching Hoo!"

Crater understood. The drivers were racing. "Get back in

line!" he demanded. The result was more trucks swerving into the open lanes.

"This ain't nothing to do with you, sonny boy!" came an anonymous reply.

"Yeah, watch yourself, youngster. This is a man's race!"

Captain Teller called, "Crater, why are those trucks out of the line?"

"They're racing, sir," Crater replied.

"Why are you letting them?"

"I'm not, sir. They just started on their own."

"Then stop them!"

Crater wanted to ask the captain how he was supposed to stop the trucks. They were ten times the size of his fastbug and could run right over him. He did the only thing he could think to do. He accelerated past the leaders, then swerved back and forth in front of them in an attempt to slow them down. The maneuver didn't faze the drivers, who bore relentlessly down.

Crater saw a curve ahead and knew he was going too fast. He slowed, then smoothly accelerated to get around the curve without skidding. As he came through it, he spotted a crack in one of the lanes. Although he'd covered the road on his scout, he'd not paid much attention to any of the outer lanes. Steering quickly, he avoided the crevice which was about eight feet long and looked to be about six inches deep.

"There's a crack in the road," he called to the trucks barreling along behind, but his warning came too late. Truck eleven hit the crack, its front wheels collapsed, and it smashed into the dustway and started coming apart. Right behind, truck twelve slammed into eleven and flipped, its heel-3 canisters tearing loose and raining down on top of it and scattering on the road. The rest of the convoy slid to an abrupt stop, some of the trucks forced into the dust off the road.

Crater turned about, going first to truck eleven where he found the driver's compartment separated from the rest of the truck. The driver within, a big fellow with a blond handlebar moustache, was lying very still, and Crater didn't know if he was dead or alive. "Condition of this driver," he said to the gillie.

Alive. Broken arm. Probable concussion.

Crater drove to truck twelve which had rolled off the dustway and was lying atop a crater rim. The driver's compartment was beneath a pile of heel-3 canisters. "Condition of number twelve driver," Crater asked.

The gillie took a moment, then said, *Dead. Driver compartment breach.*

Crater muttered an oath stronger than any he'd ever used, then got out and climbed through the debris. By the time Captain Teller and Maria arrived, he had the driver pulled free and lying in the dust. Her name, according to the name patch on her left breast, was Tilly. She was wearing an ECP suit, but she hadn't been wearing a helmet. When the truck flipped, the cab cracked and the big suck got her.

Captain Teller scowled at the sight, then said, "Maria, get the drivers out of their trucks. March every one of them over here to see this."

The driver of truck eleven limped up, holding his arm. "Think my arm's broke, Cap'n," he said.

"Klum, I'm sorry," Teller said, "because I wish it had been your neck."

Klum took on a sorrowful expression. "Aw, you don't mean that, do you, Cap'n?"

Teller pointed at the woman. "It was your stupidity that killed Tilly." He cut his eyes back to Crater. "Say a prayer for her, Crater."

Crater didn't know why the captain wanted him to say a prayer, but he gave it some thought and said, "Dear Lord, I didn't know Tilly, but I hope You'll take her into heaven. She messed up here at the last but that doesn't matter now, not to her and maybe not to You either."

"I said say a prayer, not write an editorial," Teller growled.

The gillie jumped in. *For dust thou art, and unto dust shalt thou return. Dust to dust, ashes to ashes, blessed be the Lord thy God who loves thee still. Amen and good-bye.*

Teller stared at the gillie, then said, "Well, at least that thing's got some sense."

Maria went from truck to truck, making sure the drivers were all in their ECP suits with their helmets on and properly latched. If they were going to act like children, she was going to treat them like children. She ordered them out of their cabs to gather at the wreckage of truck twelve.

Once all the drivers were standing in front of him, Teller raged at them for a while, calling them every name in the book of evil names, then said, "So now you've managed to kill one of yourselves. Don't give me those innocent looks. I saw most of you start to jockey for position as soon as those two numbskulls decided to race."

"We were just trying to have some fun," a driver said.

Though the man was twice his size, Teller picked him up and threw him, his arms and legs flailing into a small crater. "My suit coulda unraveled!" he protested, whereupon Teller went after him and tossed him into another crater, this one deeper.

Crater started to walk toward the driver to help him up but Teller said, "Crater, you take another step and you'll find yourself hiking back to Moontown."

Klum meanwhile was trying to lose himself among the other drivers, but Teller grabbed him by his broken arm and dragged him howling back. "This is the Colonel's convoy," he said. "When you signed on, you signed his articles. One of those articles says I have full control of every manjack or womanjill driver in it. The charge is murder, Klum, the evidence is in and weighed, and I sentence you to death."

Klum went pale and held up the hand attached to the arm that was unbroken. "Please don't do it, Captain." The supplicating hand sought out Crater and with it an accusing finger. "That child there shoulda seen the crack. He was down the road ahead of us and said it was all clear. It's his fault we wrecked. Otherwise, we'da just raced awhile, then we woulda backed off. You execute somebody, it ought to be him. Dereliction of duty."

The gillie, turning orange, said, in imitation of some long-dead king, *Balderdash, this man is clearly a fool and deserves to die.*

"Hush, Gillie," Crater said. "I can take up for myself."

Then Klum began to weep and sagged into the dust. Teller said, "Well, there you go, Klum. First, blame a mere boy and then start crying like a snot-nosed baby. You're not worth killing. If any of you pea brains care anything about this piece of trash, you'd best drag him out of my sight. Maria and Crater, get a detail together, gather up those loose heel-3 canisters, and spread them out amongst the trucks. We'll also need a couple of volunteers to bury Tilly."

"We can't take anymore canisters, Captain," Carlos said. "We're all overloaded as it is."

Teller was in no mood to be told anything by a driver, even one as respected as Carlos. "You'll do as I say."

Crater had an idea. "Captain?"

Teller cut his eyes toward his scout. "What do *you* want?"

"I could cut up those wrecked trucks and build some trailers out of them. All I need is a welding rig and a cutter."

Teller gave it some squinty-eyed thought, then said, "There's a welder in the chuckwagon. Cutters too. Get busy."

"I'll need some help. Petro's a fair welder."

Petro looked out from the crowd of drivers and said, "No thank you. I'll help bury Tilly."

Crater went to their private channel. "Why won't you help me?"

"Captain Teller's crazy and you're on his side."

"I'm just doing my job. So is the captain. The drivers were wrong to race."

"That's your opinion," Petro said.

"It's not an opinion. It's a fact."

Petro shrugged. "Good luck on finding someone to do your welding."

It took four hours to convert the truck beds into serviceable trailers, and Crater ended up doing most of the welding. The collected canisters were then strapped aboard. After seeing Tilly properly buried and the plot marked on his puter map—the plan was for her body to be picked up by a return convoy and carried back to Moontown later for proper cremation—Teller came over and inspected Crater's work, then took his scout aside. "You failed this convoy by not reporting that crack, Crater, but I suppose these trailers show you have at least some utility." When Crater made no reply, Teller said, "I'm surprised you didn't blame Maria."

Crater felt like the captain had slapped him in the face. "Do you really think so little of me?"

Teller's eyes went hard. "Why, yes, son, I do. I think you've got a good heart, which usually hides a host of other weaknesses. Maybe I'll think differently if you give me a reason, but so far you've been mostly a disappointment."

Teller walked away, yelling, "Pull those panels in and let's go, people! Maria, you have the point. And pay attention to the entire road, you hear?"

Maria mounted her fastbug and sped off. Crater, his face hot with embarrassment at the captain's opinion of him, didn't wait for Teller's orders. He climbed in his fastbug and took up station in one of the offside lanes. Teller waved the trucks forward and the convoy lurched ahead. Most of the drivers didn't look at Crater as they passed but Petro did. The look wasn't friendly.

::: THIRTEEN

The captain tried to call the Dustway Inn but there was no answer. "Likely their comm terminal is down," he said, then gave the situation some thought. The Dustway Inn was where they hoped to spend the night, but he knew well enough that the little inn wasn't the most efficient place in the wayback. He'd stopped there before without checking first, and he and his drivers had spent half their rest time waiting for beds to be made and food to be cooked. He needed a scout to go ahead and alert them. He started to ask Maria to do it, then decided to give Crater a chance to redeem himself. "Go ahead, Crater, and alert the proprietor of the Dustway Inn that we're coming. Tell him we'll need food, showers, and medical aid for Klum's broken arm."

"And don't get lost," Maria chimed.

Crater ignored her. "On my way, sir," he said and sped off.

Before long, he'd put some miles between himself and the convoy. The track led through craters and low hills, then wound through a series of tight turns and a run up a steep hill and down the other side. It was there he discovered a utility truck parked alongside the road. There were three people inside it, an older man and a woman with a young boy between them. The man waved him down. "Can I help you?" Crater called.

"S'pose you can, s'pose you can't," the man said. "Operate the Dustway Inn, we do, but we've run from it. There's a creature there scared me and the missus so we says to ourselves let's take the boy, run away, wait for Captain Teller and the convoy. You it?"

"A scout," Crater said. "What kind of creature?"

"Big one, like a giant. Black armor over its pressure suit. I'm a vet of the Sand War in old Persia. A trooper of the Legion Internationale is what the thing is, crowhoppers is what they're called because of that black armor and how they hops around in battle aboard spiderwalkers. Fights for money and blood and loves to choke their enemies to death. They're a genetic mush, grown in some awful laboratory. This one has itself a rifle that shoots lightning and a slug of some sort. It shot up the ceiling of my bar. Guess that was to get my attention. Then it asked when the convoy was set to come. When I told it I didn't know, the thing puts its boots up on a table, says it'll wait, and starts to drink my best earthshine. For the good of our boy, we evacuated out a hatch we got in a secret place. Saw where it had blew up our comm antenna, so glad we did."

Crater absorbed all that, then told the gillie to call the convoy. It did with no answer. "If you're thinking about going there," the innkeeper said, "you should think twice. Let Captain Teller deal with that thing."

Crater considered the innkeeper's advice, which he

supposed was good advice, indeed. On the other hand, if he was found huddled with the innkeeper and his family, Captain Teller would likely tell him he was soft again and a coward to boot. "I'll just take a look," he heard himself say and drove on, his nerves taut as banjo strings.

A few miles down the road, he reached a mound of yellowish dirt with a sign on it that read Dustway Inn. Below the sign was a hatch and below the hatch were six mooncrete steps leading up from the dust. On the other side of the road, he saw the communications tower that had been knocked down. Taking a closer look, he could see rough edges at the break in the legs and the discoloration of the lunasteel. An explosive had been used.

A spiderwalker was parked beside the steps. He'd seen such eight-legged contraptions on vidpix but the Colonel had outlawed them in Moontown. The reason, or so Crater had heard, was the Colonel had fought against the bioengineered troops who rode them and was unnerved just by the sight of the things. *Crowhoppers*, that's what the innkeeper had called the killers who rode spiderwalkers into battle. If a crowhopper lurked with mayhem on its mind, what chance would Crater have against it? On the other hand, Crater considered, maybe he could talk to it. Crowhoppers were still human, even though they'd been genetically altered, and surely they could be reasoned with. If so, maybe he could find out what it was after, then report it to Captain Teller. Maybe the captain would like that Crater had taken such initiative.

All of that thinking led Crater to the conclusion that he had to try.

Reining in his nerves as best he could, Crater climbed the

steps and entered the airlock, the gillie ordering the airlock puter to close the hatch behind him, pressurizing the chamber, and opening the first dustlock hatch. Crater hesitated. "Gillie, any advice?"

The inn is a lava tube. Gillie can hear through dustlock hatch. Acoustic readings indicate normal equipment noise. No sounds detected of biological creatures.

"Can you see inside?"

The rock is too thick for gillie's visual sensors. Gillie can see through the hatch. View is tube with more hatches inset along its wall.

Crater crept farther inside the dustlock. He found on a hanger rack two ECP suits with the Dustway Inn logo: a wavy line surrounded by small circles—the road going through craters—with the motto "The Dustway Inn, A Bed 4 Your Head" beneath it. Crater decided to keep his suit and helmet on. If he got yelled at by the innkeeper for bringing dust inside the inn, he'd just have to take the guff. In the next dustlock, he found showers, benches to sit on, and a cabinet with clean coveralls, all neatly folded. He also spotted on the deck an odd thin rod, pointed on one end and about four inches long. "Gillie, what is this?" he asked.

This object is a flechette. Sometimes called a dart. It is launched from a railgun.

The components of a railgun were simple: an electrical generator, a pulsed power supply, and an armature to launch a flechette, dart, or slug, the velocity of which could be dialed up or down by a rheostat. Crater was aware of their design but had never heard of one being made small enough to carry around. It seemed someone had managed to invent such a weapon.

"Gillie, what do you see through the dustlock hatch?" Crater asked.

Nothing moving.

Cautiously, Crater opened the inner dustlock hatch and stepped into the corridor. Its gray irregular walls were rough— not smooth like a Moontown tube—and it took a moment for Crater to recall why. It wasn't made out of mooncrete but was a natural formation, the interior surface of a small lava tube. The tube sloped downward toward a hatch that stood open. Crater eased toward it, then stepped through into what appeared to be the lobby of the inn. It had a desk cut into an alcove on one side that faced a restaurant and a small bar. The mirror behind the bar was broken, and tables and chairs were overturned.

Crater stepped back into the lava tube and peered down the natural corridor it formed where there were more hatches. Since the inn catered to convoy drivers, Crater supposed they led to rooms for overnight stays. Maybe the crowhopper was in one of the rooms, sleeping off the alcohol the innkeeper said it had drunk. Pleased with himself that he'd at least gone this far, and anticipating a grateful Captain Teller hearing his report, Crater retraced his steps back to the dustlock, planning to go through it into the airlock and outside. There, he'd try to raise the convoy again but, failing that, he'd drive back along the dustway to let the innkeeper know the situation and then wait for the captain.

In the airlock, he said, "Depressurize and open the hatch," and the gillie accomplished it. Crater stepped through.

Unknown biological organism, the gillie warned.

Crater ducked back inside, the gillie commanding the

hatch to close and the airlock to repressurize. The air hissed and Crater opened the hatch into the first dustlock, stepped inside, and locked it. That's when he saw the airlock hatch panel light up. Someone had entered the airlock from the outside. "Override the dustlock hatch," he commanded the gillie.

Override. Hatch superlocked.

Crater stood inside the dustlock hatch, his heart pounding even though he was safe for now. With the gillie overriding any commands from the outside, he could wait until the convoy arrived. Crater was thinking along those lines when the hatch blew. It flew off its hinges and ricocheted around the dustlock, followed by the crowhopper.

Crater, backed against the wall, stared helplessly at the terrifying creature. Its legs were like mooncrete pillars, and it was dressed in a black armored suit. Its helmet was also black with just a narrow slit for a view port. It was holding what appeared to be a rifle with a stiff wire butt, a flat, rectangular receiver, and a barrel about a yard long. A railgun. "Who are you?" it asked in a voice that was rough and guttural.

Crater, summoning his courage and doing his best to keep his voice from cracking, said, "I am a scout with a convoy of the Medaris Mining Company. The main body will be here any minute. The drivers are well armed. You'd better run."

"Well armed?" The creature laughed. "With what? Rocks? I think you're lying."

"They have guns. We heard there were robbers on the dustway."

"Then where's yours?"

"I have an elk sticker," Crater said. "And I know how to use it."

The crowhopper turned its headlamp on, playing it across Crater's face. "Well," it said, "this is a surprise. You are the one."

Crater didn't know what the crowhopper meant. He only knew he was looking down the barrel of its railgun. He therefore tried to change the subject. "Are you a crowhopper?"

"Talked to the innkeeper, did you? Crowhopper is what they call me and the fellows. I'm proud of it, boy, not that it's information you'll ever pass along. Now shut up and let me decide how to kill you. I could shoot you or I could amuse myself by watching you wave around your puny little elk sticker, and then I'd stab you to death and watch your blood drain out of your puny body. It's not a choice I thought I would get."

Then came an explosion of sound, but not from the rifle. It was a noise so loud that Crater was knocked to his knees. The crowhopper was also staggered. It dropped its railgun rifle and threw up its hands to its helmet as if trying to protect its ears. Crater's ears whistled, whined, crackled, and hurt. Still, somehow he heard voices. They sounded like Doom, or maybe it was Headsplitter. *Pick up the rifle, Crater. Pick it up!*

Crater's head swam, but he did as he was told and reached for the rifle. *Kill this fellow*, Doom said, except Crater knew it wasn't Doom at all. It was the gillie, somehow inside his head. There was another burst of sound, like a detpak going off, but Crater forced himself to focus on the rifle. The crowhopper leaned back against the lava tube, its head down, then suddenly straightened and ran through the opening of the destroyed dustlock hatch. Crater heard the hiss of air and knew the crowhopper had gone outside.

Crater picked up the rifle. To test it, he aimed at the wall and pulled the trigger, but nothing happened. He saw a handle on its side and pulled it back and felt the resistance of an internal spring. When he let it go, something seemed to snap home inside, a flechette ready to be fired. Then, the ringing in his ears subsiding, he cautiously entered the airlock. As he did, the gillie hopped back aboard his shoulder. *Can you hear?* it asked.

"Yes. What did you do?"

Acoustic burst. Directed toward crowhopper, not you.

"Where is he?" Crater demanded.

Spiderwalker.

Crater ducked through the ragged hole onto the mooncrete steps and saw the crowhopper on the spiderwalker heading across the dust. Crater waited until it had disappeared into a large crater, then walked unsteadily down the steps, keeping the rifle at the ready. He stopped to inspect the dust where the spiderwalker had been parked, hoping that he'd get lucky and find something the crowhopper had dropped. *Spiderwalker on collision course*, the gillie announced.

Crater looked up, saw the spiderwalker with the big crowhopper on its back running toward him, and raised the rifle. The crowhopper was a large target and Crater couldn't miss. Yet he found he couldn't pull the trigger. His finger stroked it, but he didn't pull, but then the rifle fired anyway. The flechette struck the crowhopper, disappearing into its thick armor. Still, the spiderwalker kept coming. Crater saw the gillie wriggling out of the trigger guard.

Crater dodged the spiderwalker, but one of its legs knocked him down. He rolled, jacking the rifle handle back to recharge it, but before he could get up, he saw the crowhopper slapping at something, then the spiderwalker running and then hopping away.

Crater watched the curious sight, then climbed up on the steps to make certain this time the crowhopper was really gone. He watched the spiderwalker until it disappeared, then sat down on the steps and tried to make sense of what had happened. After a while he realized the gillie was no longer on his shoulder or in its holster. He looked around and then remembered the crowhopper was slapping at something as he rode the spiderwalker off. Crater ran to his fastbug, jumped in, stirred up the fuel cells, and pressed the accelerator to the floor. Across the dustway, wheels spinning, dust flying, Crater steered the fastbug around the craters, large and small, following the spiderwalker's track. Finally, he came to a rille that the contraption had jumped. Crater kept going, soaring across the rille, but didn't make it. The fastbug struck the far side, pitched over, and began to fall. All Crater could do was hang on and pray he'd be alive when it finally hit bottom.

::: FOURTEEN

Brother!" Petro was in Crater's dream. "Brother, are you alive? Answer me!"

"What's wrong, Petro? What's wrong with you?" Crater cried.

"What's wrong with me?" Petro suddenly and inexplicably chuckled. "What's wrong with *you*, you moron! Come on. Wake up!"

"Is he awake?" The voice was Maria's. She was in Crater's dream too.

"You should kiss him," he heard Petro say.

"Kiss him? I'm dirty, I'm sweaty, and I stink from being in an ECP suit for days. Nobody would want to kiss me!"

"I would," Crater said because it didn't matter. He was dreaming, after all.

"Attaboy, Crater!" Petro said. "Go on, Maria. It's like a reverse Sleeping Beauty. You wake up the prince with a kiss."

Crater's eyes opened and he realized he wasn't in a dream at all because there stood Petro grinning down at him and Maria turning away, muttering, "You Moontown boys are crazy."

"Please tell me I didn't say I wanted to kiss her," Crater groaned.

"Oh, you said it, all right," Petro replied, "and she told you to stuff it, more or less."

Crater struggled to sit up but Petro held him down. "Take it easy. You're more than a little battered and bruised."

Crater agreed with Petro's assessment. It seemed he had a lot of bumps and bruises everywhere on his body, and he was beginning to recall things such as the armored giant in black. He recalled that the gillie had given him a chance to fight back, but he'd failed to shoot the crowhopper when the opportunity was there. And then the gillie had saved him but now the gillie was gone. And he'd rolled his fastbug while chasing the spiderwalker.

Crater pushed himself up on his elbows and saw he was in the bar area of the inn on one of the tables. Captain Teller shoved into Crater's view. "So you'll live, youngster," he said. "And I suppose you've got a story too. When you're ready, I'll hear it."

Crater, pleased to hear the very small note of concern from Captain Teller, swung his legs over the table, stood on wobbly legs for a moment, then sat heavily on the nearest chair. Looking around, he saw drivers at the other tables, all of them looking worn-out. There were bottles on the tables and Teller saw where he was looking. "We'll dry them out later. The innkeeper told us about the crowhopper."

Crater told his story, including his failure to shoot the crowhopper when he had the chance and how the gillie had done it for him. "Has the gillie turned up?"

"No sign of it," Teller said. "I wish you'd have killed that scrag of a bob. Now it's still out there."

"What I don't understand," Maria said, "is why the gillie doesn't use its acoustic weapon to get loose?"

"Sound waves don't carry in a vacuum," Crater said. "There was air pressure in the dustlock when it used it."

"Of course," she replied. "I guess I'm as tired as you are loopy."

"I was in a wreck," he pointed out.

"Tell me more about the crowhopper," the captain said.

Crater tried to remember. He thought he'd already said everything there was to say but as he thought back, he remembered the armor covered more than its chest. It had armor strapped to its legs, like the greaves the ancient Athenians wore in battle, and the helmet had a crest on it, not of feathers or horsehair like the ancients, but a metallic arc, like an ax blade.

"Maybe what we've got here is not a crowhopper but a lunatic dressed like one," the captain said.

Crater had heard of such men—they were indeed called lunatics—who'd somehow managed to set up a living tube for themselves in the wayback, usually in a collapsed lava tube, eking out a life with maybe nothing more than a biovat, a couple of beat-up solar panels, and a crusty old microbial oxygen generator. Given enough junk and technical savvy, some people, if they were desperate enough, could live anywhere, even in the wayback of the moon.

"How's my fastbug?" Crater asked.

"I towed it back," Petro said. "It's bent a little and the paint's scratched, but otherwise it's fine. Don't let anybody ever say you don't know how to bolt a vehicle together. But now my truck's sick. Wheel bearing, I think."

Crater rubbed the back of his neck and looked at Captain Teller. "We'll need to fix Petro's truck before we can go anywhere."

"Seems to me you ought to rest," Teller said.

"I'm fine, Captain," Crater replied.

Teller gave Crater a thoughtful look, then said, "All right. Go get what you need from the inn's store and I'll use the Colonel's chit to pay for it. You can use tools from the chuckwagon, just put them back where you found them."

Teller addressed the drivers. "Gentlemen, the bar is hereby closed. We leave in four hours. I suggest you get some rest."

Irish spoke up. "We ain't going nowhere, Captain. We didn't sign up to get murdered out here."

"There's no vote on a convoy. You'll do what I say or you'll end up like Klum."

"And who's gonna look after Klum now?" Irish demanded. "Poor man there with a broken arm."

"The innkeeper's wife set it," Teller said, "and injected some bone bugs in him. His arm will knit in a few days."

"It don't keep it from hurting like scrag, Captain," Klum complained. "I'm going to sit right here and wait for the next convoy heading back to Moontown."

"That's fine, Klum," Teller said. "But what if that crowhopper comes back?"

Klum had no reply. He just looked sour. "You're gonna get yours someday, Captain," Irish growled.

"Anytime you're ready, Irish."

Irish stared hard at Teller but there was no fight in him. The other drivers hastily drank what was already in their glasses. Teller was going to get his way.

Crater went off with Petro to see about the wheel bearing while Teller had another talk with the innkeeper. He didn't like it when the man confirmed Crater's description of the invader. He wasn't likely a lunatic but probably a real crow-hopper. God help them all, but what was such a creature doing in the wayback of the moon?

Teller wearily climbed back into his ECP suit. When he went outside through the inn's auxiliary hatch—the main one welded shut until it could be repaired—he saw that Crater already had Petro's truck jacked up. Teller went over and stood beside the ruined antenna. It wouldn't help him make the call, but at least he knew there was a clear view of the comm sats. He tapped in the necessary request, linked up with two comm sats, and chose the one that cost the least. The main operator at Moontown answered the call, then switched him over to the Colonel. Teller explained what had happened in as few words as he could manage. "Understood, Jake," Colonel Medaris said. "What are you going to do now?"

"I'm going to follow that crowhopper, have a look around."

"I need you to get your convoy to Armstrong City on time."

"I will, sir. Don't worry."

"How's Maria?"

"She's fine. A remarkable young lady."

"And the boy?"

"He's raw but he's doing his job well enough."

"I need him to get to Armstrong City on time too."

"If the rest of us get there, I guess he'll also get there, sir."

"Then get there. And on time, do you hear?"

Teller heard and signed off, then walked over to where Crater and Petro were working. "I'm going on scout with your fastbug," he told Crater.

Crater, his hands holding the new bearing, looked over his shoulder. "That crowhopper could still be out there," he said.

"That's why I'm going."

Petro stood up. "I'll go with you."

"No. Crater needs you more than I do." He nodded to the electric rifle Crater had leaned up against the truck. "But keep that thing handy. And next time, shoot to kill. Its neck is its most vulnerable spot."

Before Crater could answer, if he had an answer, Teller walked to the fastbug and stirred up its fuel cells. Before he began his scout, he allowed himself a brief moment to savor once more the idea of this being his last convoy, that perhaps at the end of it, he would join his wife and children in a little cottage tube within a vineyard dome. There, they would live a long, happy, productive life.

But then Teller shook off such pleasant thoughts. In the holster on his belt, he had a moontype nine-millimeter pistol, designed to work on the moon utilizing low-powder vacuum-sealed cartridges to decrease its recoil. The crowhopper was a threat to his convoy and was out there somewhere. He intended to find the creature and kill it.

::: FIFTEEN

It was a simple matter to follow the tracks of Crater's fastbug and Petro's truck. After Teller reached the rille where Crater had wrecked, he could also follow the splayed footprints of the spiderwalker that led southward. He'd seen a few of the war machines before and they gave him the creeps. With their eight legs, they moved almost like the real thing, and when they hopped and came down on an enemy with their hideous pincers snapping, they were terrifying.

Teller followed the tracks across a crater field and then across a plain of exposed basalt toward some rounded hills. After a few miles, he saw where the spiderwalker had stopped and another spiderwalker had joined it. A chill went up his spine. Two spiderwalkers meant certainly this was no lunatic he was following but some kind of military operation. He could tell by the boot prints that the two drivers had gotten off their machines, then remounted because the dual tracks of the two spiderwalkers continued on, still southward. Teller studied the horizon and then drove to the top of a small hill, got out, and switched on the binoculars in his helmet view port.

A few miles away, more or less—distance being difficult to judge on the moon even for an old hand in the wayback like Teller—he observed a black dot that didn't appear to be a regular feature. He got back in the fastbug and drove until he found a crowhopper lying sprawled on its back beside a spiderwalker. The tracks showed that the other spiderwalker had continued on. Teller inspected the crowhopper, which appeared to be dead, then stripped it of its armor and saw it was wearing a standard ECP suit. Teller pulled off the crowhopper's helmet. Its eyeballs were just blots of blood and its ears had bled out. When he turned the helmet over, Teller saw there was a small hole in the back. It looked as if a laser had bored through it.

Teller searched the thing for any identification, but there was nothing. He took a few pix with his helmetcam. The thing—Teller couldn't bring himself to think of it as a man—was normal-size, not the giant Crater had described. After stripping off its ECP suit, Teller saw it had a myriad of tattoos on its body. One of them said "Kill them all." Another said "Death is my trade." There were more such phrases, all praising death, doom, and destruction. The artwork included terrible and fantastic beasts, blood dripping from their fangs and lips.

There was little else to see. Teller took more pix of the creature, then tossed the armor and the bloody helmet in the fastbug and drove back along his path. Along the way, he felt as if he were being watched, but though he stopped twice to look over his shoulder, he saw no one, just the moon . . . the beautiful, deadly moon.

::: SIXTEEN

At the inn, Teller showed Crater and Maria the pix he'd taken, the armor, and the pierced helmet of the dead crowhopper.

"It's not the one who attacked me," Crater said. "The armor's too small."

"What could punch through a helmet like that?" Maria wondered, picking it up and pushing her finger through the irregular hole. It just barely fit.

"Nothing that I know of," Teller answered. "A battle-laser makes a much bigger hole. Maybe some kind of new weapon."

Crater was anxious to hear if there was any sign of the gillie but Teller told him there wasn't, though he'd looked around the spiderwalker. Crater kept reminding himself the gillie was just a biological machine that couldn't really think or feel. Still he said with a mournful tone, "I hoped it would get away."

Teller's reply was disdainful. "Even if it did, it's full sunlight, Crater. It would die out there."

"A gillie can take full sunlight," Crater replied. "It's always exposed when I'm on the scrapes."

Teller seemed hesitant to suggest another possibility. "Maybe that crowhopper killed it. From what you told me, it'd be plenty mad at it. You can kill a gillie, can't you?"

"I suppose so," Crater admitted. "I never thought much about it."

Petro strolled over. "Before we drive another mile, Captain," he said, "the other drivers and I want to know where we stand. You need to tell us what's out there."

Teller glared at Petro, then said, "Tell the drivers to meet me in the lobby."

When Teller joined the drivers, he noted there were more than a few of them with expressions of contempt. Still other faces were blank, impossible to read. Teller preferred the ones he could read to the ones he couldn't. A man with a blank face was a dangerous man. The others could be watched and handled.

"I've talked to the Colonel so he knows our situation," Teller said. "I followed a spiderwalker track and after a while, two of them. Not too much farther along, I found a dead crowhopper. There was a hole burned in the back of its helmet. That's all I know."

Klum, his broken arm in a sling, stood up. "Look, Captain, we need to get on back to Moontown, get ourselves armed guards, then try this again. It's crazy to go on."

"Your opinion is noted, Klum, and it will be given the

weight it deserves," Teller said. "How's that broken arm, by the way?"

"It aches and those little critters the innkeeper's wife put inside me give me the heebie-jeebies."

"You'll be healed and able to drive in a week," Teller said. "For now, you're riding with Mutt. He needs his rest, being the delicate creature that he is, so he may pay you something when you're able to drive for him."

The drivers chuckled at Teller's lame attempt at humor, then Irish spoke up. "Captain, it's clear you've decided we're going ahead. I'm going to wear my suit with my helmet on from here on, and I recommend that's what we all do so we can get out of our trucks in a hurry."

"That's fine, Irish," Teller said. "Any driver wants to follow your suggestion, I've got no objection. Just keep in mind most suits need refurbishment every one thousand hours. Keep an eye on them. All right, gentlemen and ladies. Mount up. We need to get across the moon."

Crater had asked for permission to drive Petro's truck for a while, just to be certain the new wheel bearing was turning properly. Maria took the lead in Crater's fastbug, since it was faster than hers, and Teller brought up the rear with Maria's fastbug in tow behind the chuckwagon. "I'll need to go a little slow at first," Crater told Teller.

"Don't fall behind," Teller said. "And if you break down, call me."

"Oh, you can be sure I'll have him do that, Captain," Petro said from the driver's compartment. Both he and Crater were in their ECP suits. Although they weren't wearing their helmets, their skull buckets were within arm's reach.

⁂

The convoy moved out, with Crater falling in behind the chuckwagon. Before long, the line of trucks was rolling along at a good clip, following the dustway through several crater fields and around a few small hills. The sun and the Earth were both visible, the dust below turning a shimmering luster of silver. The shadows within the pale-lipped craters were a tawny black. In direct sun, the temperature according to the truck gauge was a steady 260 degrees Fahrenheit although in the shadows, it was minus 290 degrees, about the same as every day on the scrapes when it wasn't in the long shadow.

Petro was looking at the Earth and its swirling clouds. "I wonder what weather is like," he said. "Here, all we have is night and day."

"You've seen vidpix of tornadoes and hurricanes and such," Crater said.

"I don't mean that kind of weather. Here it's boiling when it's light, it's the deep freeze when it's dark. What would it be like if it was just average? And what would it be like to have rain? Can you imagine such a thing, Crater? I recall Asteroid Al saying it made a sound on the roof that was like music being played. It could even lull you to sleep."

"I was in the maintenance shed one time," Crater remarked, "when a loader accidentally dumped dust on top of it. The mechanic in there said it sounded like a heavy rain."

"I bet it didn't sound like rain at all," Petro said. "Water would have a soft sound, not like a bunch of rocks."

"Well," Crater said, "I'll take the moon over Earth any day, rain or no rain."

"The ignorant speaks of that which he has no knowledge," Petro accused.

Crater decided to stop talking to Petro and pay attention to the fuel cell that was producing erratic power. Reluctantly, he called Teller, told him his problem, and said he was going to stop to see about it. "Okay, but don't tarry," Teller replied.

Crater wasn't about to tarry. Being alone on the dustway was obviously not a good idea but he felt like he had no choice. "The microbes need a boost to make their energy transfer," he said, "so we'll put up the solar panels and let them soak a bit. Let's put our helmets on, just in case."

Petro pulled on his helmet and pushed his seat back. "Fine, whatever. I'm going to take a nap."

Crater wouldn't have minded a nap himself. He thought briefly that he should tell the gillie to keep watch and to wake him when the solars had done their job—but then he remembered the gillie was gone. He couldn't help but miss the little thing, although it was nothing more than a blob of slime mold. He also wished he'd told it just once that he liked having it around, although a machine—even one made of organic cells—didn't need to hear such things.

After a soak of thirty minutes, Crater started the truck and was pleased to see the fuel cell gauges turn green. Petro awoke and yawned. "Want me to drive?" he asked.

"I'm good," Crater said. "We should catch up with the convoy in no time with all this power." He pressed the accelerator and watched the speedometer tick up.

As predicted, in about fifteen minutes, Crater drove the truck up a rise and was pleased to see the convoy just ahead—although he was surprised to see it was stopped. Some of the trucks were parked at odd angles too, and two of them were off the dustway entirely. "Something's wrong," Petro said. "Maybe we ought to take a look before we go down there."

Crater stopped and turned on the binoculars in his helmet. He could see some of the drivers out of their trucks nonchalantly leaning on the fenders. He scanned up to the head of the convoy and saw Maria's fastbug tilted at an odd angle. She was standing nearby with Captain Teller and what he thought were a few of the drivers. Crater looked again and saw that they weren't drivers at all.

Petro figured it out at the same time. "Umlaps! Look there, Crater," he said. "See how filthy and patched their old-fashioned pressure suits are? Only Umlaps would have those."

"Let's see if we can help," Crater said, then drove down the hill and past the trucks until he reached Teller, Maria, and the Umlaps. Captain Teller was talking and waving his arms. The Umlaps were just standing there, their faces inscrutable. The convoy frequency was quiet so Crater put his helmet comm set on automatic and, after a few seconds, found the frequency Teller was using to talk, if yelling was considered talking.

Teller snapped a glance at Crater as he came walking up. "About time you got here," he said.

"Sorry, Captain," Crater said, then looked at Maria. "Are you all right?"

"Why do you care? I'm just a bossy girl."

Crater didn't know how to reply to that but at least it told him she was okay. "What happened to my fastbug?" he asked.

"These idiots stepped out in front of me and I swerved and hit a boulder."

"You broke its axle."

Maria rolled her eyes. "Really? I hadn't noticed."

The Umlaps had been watching and listening to Crater and Maria with some interest, but the one who seemed to be in charge suddenly got restless and spoke up. "Give us your money," he said, in the Umlap tongue which was a combination of Russian, Chinese, and tribal Siberian.

"He wants money," Crater advised Teller.

"You can speak this gibberish?"

"A little."

"Then tell them to get out of our way."

Crater did as he was told and the Umlap leader smiled. "Is your commander an idiot? Pay us or we are not going to let your trucks pass."

"What's he smiling about?" Teller asked.

"They smile when they're unhappy," Crater answered. "They're kind of backward about showing their emotions."

"Do they cry when they hear a joke?"

"I don't know," Crater confessed. "Do you want to tell them one?"

"Just tell them to move," Teller snapped.

"I already did."

"Then tell them again!"

Crater passed along Teller's request again, which caused the Umlap leader to be so unhappy that he grinned, showing off big yellow teeth. "My name is Hit Your Face. I am astonished you speak Umlap. Tell this stupid man if he does not give us money, we will stick you all with our spears."

"My name is Crater Trueblood," Crater said. "It is good to meet you."

"What is good about it? Did you not hear me? I want money. Give it to me or . . ." He pointed at Maria. "She will be the first to die."

"Why her?"

"I saw the way you looked at her."

"What's he saying?" Teller demanded. "Why did he point at Maria?"

When Crater didn't answer immediately, Teller pulled his pistol. "If these fellows don't move in about three seconds, I'm going to start shooting. Tell ugly there he's first."

Without appearing to hurry, lest he cause spears to be hurled and bullets to be shot, Crater walked over to stand in front of Maria. "Get out of my way," she said. She took a step to the side but, glancing over his shoulder, he moved to stay between her and the spears. "Crater, what are you doing?"

Ignoring Maria's complaints and trying to calm things down, Crater asked the Umlaps, "Why are you reduced to common thievery? Why don't you sell your heel-3?"

"We can't."

"Why not?"

Hit Your Face smiled. "Our scraper doesn't work."

"What's wrong with it?"

"If we knew that, we would fix it."

"Do you have a machine shop?"

"A very nice one. The Russians built it for us."

Crater thought he saw an opening to end the confrontation. "How about I have a look at your scraper? I know a little about machinery. Maybe I can fix it."

Hit Your Face pondered Crater's offer, then said, "I will discuss it."

When Crater explained what he'd told Hit Your Face, Teller replied, "Let's just shoot them and be done with it."

"You don't have to protect me," Maria griped. "I can take care of myself."

"But the Colonel asked me—" he said, but caught himself in time. She didn't need to know her grandfather thought she needed him to watch out for her. If she did, she'd probably make the job twice as hard, just for spite.

Hit Your Face came sauntering back. "We agree," he said.

Crater translated and said to Teller, "I think I can get down there, fix their scraper, and get back on the dustway in eight hours or less. I should be able to catch you well before you get to Aristillus."

Teller internally debated Crater's idea and supposed it wasn't an entirely bad one. "All right," he said, then nodded toward the damaged fastbug. "Can you repair it too?"

"No problem. I'll fix it, then catch up."

"The railgun's in the fastbug stowage locker," Teller said. "You might need it. Anyway, catch up with us as fast as you can."

Crater turned to Hit Your Face. "I will need the damaged fastbug if you'll be so kind as to carry it for me."

Hit Your Face gestured to his group. The Umlaps lowered their spears and picked the fastbug up on their shoulders and marched off, Crater following. He passed Maria, who said nothing, but before he got out of range, she called him on a private channel. "Crater? I don't think this is a good idea. We need two scouts and now we have one. What sense does that make?"

"I'll catch up with the convoy in no time," Crater replied. "Don't worry."

"Is that another way of saying don't be bossy?"

Crater couldn't help himself. "Yes, it is."

The immediate click in his comm unit told him Maria had signed off.

::: SEVENTEEN

rater had never seen a more dismal sight than Baikal, the Umlap settlement. Strewn everywhere were ruined mining equipment and piles of garbage that glittered with the shards of shredded plaston bottles. Beyond the airlock entrance was a low hill and beyond it was disturbed regolith, indicating a scrape. There sat an idle loader and a scraper, a conveyor belt that was conveying nothing, and a solar tower with all its panels pointing in the wrong direction. Nothing about the scrape was encouraging, and Crater fretted he only had a few hours to fix it, else the convoy would get too far ahead of him.

The Umlaps set the fastbug down and wound their way through the litter to the airlock hatch, which had been left open—a safety violation that would not have been tolerated in Moontown. Crater climbed inside behind the Umlaps. Hit Your Face closed the hatch and pushed a button on a panel, causing air to be pumped in to whatever the Baikal standard was. When Hit Your Face opened his suit and didn't keel over,

Crater unzipped his, climbed out of it, then hung it beside the others on a line of hooks. His nose involuntarily wrinkled at the reek of grease, sweat, and dust. When Crater saw Hit Your Face take a filter mask off a peg, he grabbed one too.

An Umlap, apparently the airlock dustie, appeared and began to hook the backpacks to a compressed-air station. Crater asked him to take care of his ECP suit too. In response, the technician made a dismissive gesture. Hit Your Face walked over and struck the Umlap dustie in the face with his helmet, staggering him. Blood oozed from the wound on his skull. He gave Crater a dirty look, then took his gear and slunk off.

"Why did you do that?" Crater asked.

Hit Your Face frowned, which, Crater had to keep reminding himself, meant he was happy. "It was my way of reminding him to be courteous to a guest even though, technically, you are not a guest. You are a captive."

This was news to Crater. "I volunteered to come here," he reminded the Umlap.

"No, you came because your captain was happy to be rid of you."

"That's not true," Crater said. "It was my idea."

"But he didn't try to convince you otherwise, did he?"

Crater thought it wise to change the subject. "Is that scraper out there the one that's broken down?"

"Since it is our only scraper, yes. Can you fix it?"

"I'll have to look at it first."

"First you must see the king. His name is Wise Beyond Belief."

"I have to catch up with the convoy," Crater said.

"I don't care," Hit Your Face replied, and Crater realized he was in big trouble. He had to catch up with the convoy to get to Armstrong City and aboard the Cycler on time to collect the Colonel's artifact, whatever it was. And even though his primary reason for coming to Baikal was to keep Maria from being stuck on an Umlap spear, he'd allowed her to go off on her own. How could he protect her if he wasn't around? His idea to go with the Umlaps, he confessed to himself, was a bonehead move, and he needed to figure out how to get away from them as soon as he could. He was tempted to just take off running, but even if he escaped outside, the fastbug required repair. Crater accepted there was nothing to do but chalk this one up as another example of his bad judgment and do what he could to get out of it. And fast.

Crater stripped down to his underwear and passed through the next hatch to a dustlock where there were three showers. The Umlaps skipped them and kept going. From the pungent odor wafting from them, Crater thought they should have taken advantage of the showers. But that wasn't his problem, so he followed them into the next dustlock where their town clothes, black pantaloons and red vests, were in piles on the floor. There was an argument between two Umlaps claiming the same pair of pantaloons, and punches were thrown and kicks were kicked. Hit Your Face battered them both down with a flurry of fists, then took a pair of pantaloons and a vest from a cupboard and handed them to Crater. They seemed clean so he put them on.

Outside the dustlock was a tube made of raw mooncrete. Hit Your Face swung open a hatch, its unoiled hinges protesting, and led the way into another tube as dismal as the first.

Some Umlap men sat on the deck playing some sort of board games. They were arguing and, as Crater watched, started wrestling. Hit Your Face went over, kicked them both, and turned their game board over, scattering the little figurines on it. The two crawled off, rubbing where they'd been kicked.

"What is the population of Baikal?" Crater asked.

"Twelve," Hit Your Face replied. "There were thirty before the women left and took the children with them."

"Where did they go?"

"Who knows and who cares?"

They kept going through two more dingy tubes. The exit hatch of the last tube opened into a small tube where a man sat cross-legged on a gray blanket. On his head was a peaked red and black cap. "King Wise Beyond Belief," Hit Your Face said, "I have brought you a captive."

The chief had two teeth, one on the top and one on the bottom. He also had eyes like hard, black beads and a livid forehead scar. He grinned at Hit Your Face, clearly very unhappy. "What nonsense is this?" he demanded. "Where is the money?"

Smiling broadly, Hit Your Face said, "They would not give us any, so instead we took this boy."

"Ah, for ransom," Wise Beyond Belief replied, nodding.

"No, I came to fix your scraper," Crater said.

"He appears petulant. Why have you not beaten him?"

Hit Your Face grimaced, obviously pleased by the question. "It slipped my mind!"

"There is no reason to beat me," Crater said. "Let me fix your scraper and I'll be on my way."

"There is nothing wrong with our scraper," the king replied, then said, "Sit down. Hit Your Face will bring us refreshments."

Hit Your Face laughed in outrage. "Do I look like a serving wench?"

"Do not test me," Wise Beyond Belief said with a chuckle that was clearly a warning.

Hit Your Face grinned, then left. Crater sat. "What did you mean there is nothing wrong with your scraper?"

"Just because a thing doesn't work doesn't mean there's anything wrong with it."

Crater pondered the king's philosophy, if that's what it was, then said, "Since it is designed to work and it doesn't, by definition, there is something wrong with it."

"Do not argue with me. You are just a boy. Perhaps I should kill you."

"If you do, I won't be able to fix your scraper."

"I already told you there's nothing wrong with it."

"But you also said it didn't work."

"And if you cannot make it work?"

"I will have tried."

"Try and not do could get a boy killed."

Crater was trying to decide if Wise Beyond Belief was serious about killing him when Hit Your Face reappeared carrying a tray. On it was a bottle and three dirty glasses. He poured the liquid from the bottle into the glasses and handed one to the king and one to Crater.

"Cheers," Wise Beyond Belief said and drained his glass.

Crater sniffed the liquid, which smelled nearly as foul as the Moontown grease traps. "It is made from turnips," Hit Your Face said. "The turnip biovat is the only one we have that works."

Hit Your Face drank, then looked at Crater. He took a brave

swallow. "Good," Crater croaked, though he came close to throwing it up.

The king said, "I require a nap. Take this boy away. Bring him back after he's fixed our scraper."

"I can't stay, your majesty," Crater said. "I must catch up with my convoy."

"That is not possible," the king replied. "If you are able to make our scraper work, what would we do if it stopped again? No, you will stay." He fluttered his bony hands. "Go."

Hit Your Face led Crater back to the dustlock. "Your suit is in there. You saw the scraper."

"Is there a maintenance shed?"

"Bad Haircut will guide you."

"Who is Bad Haircut?"

"The creature who insulted you whereupon I hit him."

Crater pulled on his ECP suit, then went outside and looked in the fastbug stowage locker. Inside was the railgun rifle and a bag of tools. The rifle did him no immediate good. He still needed a working fastbug.

He left the tools but took the rifle, lest it be stolen, and trudged down to the scrape and took a walk around the scraper. It was a standard design and, other than being filthy and probably poorly maintained, Crater could see nothing obviously wrong with it. He sat in its seat and gave a go at starting it. When nothing happened, he swung open the engine hatch to have a look at the fuel cell. The reason the scraper didn't work became instantly clear. It had no fuel cell, just a vacant cavity where one was supposed to be.

"The scraper can't be fixed. The fuel cell is ruined. I have told everyone this. Are you going to shoot me with that rifle?"

It was the Umlap who'd been hit by Hit Your Face. "You would be Bad Haircut," Crater said. "No, I'm not going to shoot you. Could I see the fuel cell?"

"The maintenance shed is just over there."

"I need the fastbug to be brought there too."

"I will see to it."

The interior of the shed had piles of trash, but it held shop machinery that looked useful. Bad Haircut pointed to a fuel cell that Crater recognized as a Stewart Y21A5 design. No tests were needed to identify the problem since there was an obvious crack in it. "Have you tried to weld it?" Crater asked.

"Yes, but after a few hours, it cracked again."

"Do you have a spectroscope?"

Bad Haircut said he did, and before long, Crater had the fuel cell in a fixture studying it. The lunasteel around the crack was a fractured mess. "There's no fixing this," Crater said, then noticed a shuttle parked on the other side of the shed. "What's wrong with that shuttle?"

"Its braces are broken."

"Does it have a fuel cell?"

"It is too small to power a scraper."

"How about two shuttle fuel cells? If we had two, we could link them together and that would be enough power to run your scraper."

"I have a spare shuttle fuel cell," Bad Haircut said. "But your idea will not work."

"Well, let's give it a try, eh?" Crater said, then started to remind him about the fastbug when four Umlaps carried it inside, set it down, made many rude gestures to Bad Haircut and Crater, then departed. "Nobody seems happy here," Crater observed.

"Why would they? This place is a scrag dump."

"But you have everything you need to make it into a nice place."

"We are an unlucky people."

"Asteroid Al says people make their own luck by hard work and being decent to one another."

"He is obviously a fool as are you. Here we are much smarter."

"Then why are we happy and you're miserable?"

Bad Haircut smiled. "You make my brain hurt with your illogical logic. Let us try your dumb idea."

Crater could see he would get nowhere with Bad Haircut when it came to bucking him up, so he got to work. Over the next few hours, he and Bad Haircut connected the two shuttle fuel cells, then installed them in the scraper. When tried, the combo instantly came to life, and Crater tested the combo by running a straight scrape and piling up a tent. Bad Haircut picked the dust up with a shuttle, carried it back to the conveyor belt that didn't work, and ran up to the vibrators and solar tower that also didn't work.

Crater picked rocks out of the belt, fixing it, then walked to the vibrators, adjusted them, ran them for a little while, then walked on to the solar tower, fiddled with its controls, redirected its collectors, and burned off a little heel-3 from the dust. Then Bad Haircut and Crater exchanged the Baikal version of a handshake, slapping each other on their respective helmets and frowning deeply. "I'm sure the king will be grateful," Bad Haircut said. "Now, we can work ourselves to death while he sits on his backside and does nothing."

Crater turned to the fastbug, which proved an easy fix. All he had to do was weld a broken strut on the axle joint, which he accomplished quickly. He put on his ECP suit and climbed in its seat. "I'll take it for a test drive," he said to Bad Haircut, although he actually meant to keep on driving. He could be on the dustway within minutes and gone before the Umlaps could react.

Unfortunately, Hit Your Face showed up at that moment, along with three of his fellows, all holding spears and looking menacing. "I saw the scraper working," he said. "Now we will make money and get our wives back, although they are all ugly." He pointed at Crater. "You will be the chief foreman. Establish the shifts immediately!"

"I can't be your chief foreman," Crater replied. "I have to catch my convoy."

Hit Your Face smiled. "Bad Haircut will be your assistant. He was our foreman but a poor one. You will be much better." Then, without further ceremony, Hit Your Face and his troops marched out through the airlock.

Bad Haircut stared after them, his eyes burning with hatred. When he saw Crater watching him, he pointed at a hatch. "There's a tube through there where you can sleep. There is turnip paste and water in the refrigerator."

Crater said, "Now, see here, Bad Haircut, I have to go. You and I are friends, aren't we? How about looking the other way and I'll just drive out of here and be on my way."

Bad Haircut seemed to be considering Crater's proposal, but it didn't last. "Hit Your Face will kill me if I let you go," he said. "He has killed before. He and Wise Beyond Belief murdered the previous king and their court. By the way, while you were working on the scraper, I went through the stowage locker in your fastbug in case it contained something good to eat. I found a bag with something in it that must be yours. It's disgusting and I am afraid of it."

Curious, Crater opened the stowage locker of the fastbug and retrieved the tool bag. Inside was a wrench, three screwdrivers, and a jack. It also contained a shapeless clump of slime mold cells. "Gillie!" Crater cried. When the gillie did not respond, Crater said, "Turn yourself on." But there was still no response. "Poor thing," Crater said, wondering how it had gotten inside the fastbug locker.

Crater carried the gillie to the tube that Bad Haircut said he could use. It was as dismal as everything else in Baikal: bare walls, bare floor, a mooncrete table, a plaston chair, a bunk with dirty blankets, a small refrigerator that, when opened, proved to contain several containers of what Crater presumed was turnip paste, some bottles of water, and the turnip drink. There was also a flash oven where Crater supposed he could heat up the paste. A cupboard revealed some cracked plaston cups and dirty dishes. That was it.

Crater sat on the bed and contemplated his plight and the gillie. "What's wrong with you?" he asked. If it was dead, Crater hoped at least it wouldn't stink. Suddenly very tired, he curled up on the bed and slept, waking to the sound of himself singing "Moon Dust Girls." Except it wasn't him. The gillie stood on the table, though it had no legs, and sang, though it had no mouth, and looked at Crater, though it had no eyes. "Status?" Crater asked.

Normal, it replied.

"What happened after the crowhopper took you?"

Show you, it said.

The gillie projected a view of something blurry, then

Crater saw a spiderwalker ridden by a crowhopper. Then he heard the voice of the giant who'd attacked him. "Take this thing back to the jumpcar," it said, handing the gillie over. "And give me your rifle. I'm going to follow the convoy."

"I'll take that ugly thing but I'm keeping my rifle," the other crowhopper said.

"I've had a bad day," the giant growled. "And if you don't do what I say, you'll have a bad one too, and it will be your last."

The smaller crowhopper took the gillie from the giant and put it in the stowage locker on the spiderwalker. The picture went dark until Crater saw the back of the crowhopper. Then the point of view changed and Crater saw the gillie crawl up the rider's back, then onto its helmet where it began to change color until it was perfectly clear. The gillie grew a tripod of legs, holding what appeared to be a convex lens. A hot spot developed on the back of the helmet, and the crowhopper suddenly jerked, then fell off the walker. The gillie returned to its own view, which was all red. It seemed to swim in a red liquid for a while, then it was in the dust.

"You used the sun to burn a hole in its helmet," Crater said in awe. "I didn't know you could make shapes like that."

Hard to do. Made gillie tired. Big sound also required much energy. Needed to recover so gillie did not move for long time. Fastbug arrived, I crawled inside. Do not like Captain Teller so did not communicate.

"I'm glad you're back," Crater said, which caused the gillie to somehow look pleased. "And thank you for saving me with the big noise."

The gillie did not answer and appeared to be asleep if, in fact, it could sleep. Crater picked it up and gently placed it on the pillow of the bed, then heard someone rap on the hatch.

Bad Haircut, without waiting to be invited, came inside. "I have found enough miners. We will begin in the morning. Do not try to escape. There are guards." He crawled back through the hatch and slammed it shut.

Sighing fretfully, the convoy getting farther away by the minute, Crater found he couldn't sleep. He got up and took the rifle to the machine shop. He had an idea how to improve it. He disassembled the receiver and considered its design. It was ingenious in every way except how the flechette was inserted into the chamber. This required a handle and a spring mechanism to push it into place. Crater found a slab of lunasteel and used a milling machine to produce another receiver, this one with a dual spring design that made it semiautomatic, eliminating the need to pull back the handle. Every time he pulled the trigger, a flechette was launched and another one sprung into its place. All a rifleman had to do was keep pulling the trigger until the magazine was empty. Crater also made the magazine bigger, plus turned out a hundred new flechettes made from an iron alloy he found in the bar stock. Satisfied with his work, Crater could finally allow himself to sleep, and he did, managing a couple of hours.

::: EIGHTEEN

When Crater woke, he made a breakfast of turnip paste, which tasted so putrid he had to choke it down. He then went out into the maintenance shed, disappointed that Bad Haircut and seven other Umlaps were already there. He intended to escape, one way or the other. Based on their smiles, they were not happy to be there either.

On the scrape, Crater gathered the Umlap miners and assigned Bad Haircut as the scraper driver. Consulting a reader that held their names, Crater assigned the other positions, which brought more unhappy smiles.

"We'll say a prayer now," Crater said, using English for the term. "Who's the oldest man?"

"What is prayer?" Bad Haircut asked while the other miners looked puzzled.

"It is talking to God," Crater answered. "Asking the Big Miner to keep us safe and that kind of thing."

"We don't think there is a Big Miner. We think there are

many gods that are everywhere, in the dust, in the turnips, and so forth, and every one of them is angry and mean."

"Well, I'll say a prayer, anyway." Crater did so, silently asking that everything would go smoothly and safely on the scrape and that he would then be able to escape. Afterward, he said, "Let's go to work."

Crater showed Bad Haircut how to build up a good tent with the scraper, then showed the shuttle drivers how to properly scoop and load the dust. He showed the scragline pickers how to use a shovel and a hook pick, then walked up to the solar tower and showed the operator how to find the sun and burn out the heel-3. Soon, he was exhausted from all the showing he'd done.

Bad Haircut drove up and announced a problem with the scraper blade. Sure enough, there was a big rock lodged in between the frame and the blade. Crater was a bit surprised. He'd looked over the scrape that morning and had not seen a rock that big. Still, Bad Haircut had managed to find one. "Take it out," Crater told one of the scragline pickers who had wandered over.

"I don't know how," he said.

Crater grabbed a pry bar and climbed onto the scraper to dislodge the big rock. Bad Haircut chose that moment to make an announcement. "I have asked our leaders to come visit us, and here they come. It will be good for them to see us work."

Crater popped the rock loose, then picked it up and heaved it off the scraper. "Well, if you want them to see you work, you'd best actually do some."

Bad Haircut got back on his scraper as Hit Your Face and King Wise Beyond Belief came walking up. "What idiocy is this, boy?" the king growled at Crater. "Why did you insist we come outside to look at the scrape? It is just dust and rocks. Why should I waste my time out here when I could be thinking?"

"I didn't insist on anything," Crater answered.

"But we received an urgent message from you," Hit Your Face said. He stopped talking when he noticed the scraper, driven by Bad Haircut, had turned in his and the king's direction and was coming fast with its blade raised. The pair started to run but they didn't run far. Bad Haircut smashed them with the scraper blade, then ran over them. Three times.

Crater was shocked and sickened. He was also wondering if he was going to be next. "Are you the new king?" he asked Bad Haircut after the scraper came trundling back. He figured it wouldn't hurt to ingratiate himself with the murderer, especially since he doubted he could outrun the scraper.

Bad Haircut grimaced from his driver's perch. "I suppose I am. But what shall I do with you?"

"Let me go, of course," Crater said. "You don't need me anymore."

"But you are a witness," Bad Haircut said.

Crater pointed at the other Umlap men who were staring in their direction. "There are many witnesses."

"One is my partner. Eats Many Turnips, the shuttle driver. He and I will kill the others later."

"Why would you do that?"

"Because we can then sell Baikal to General Nero, who has been trying to buy it and the scrape. That's what King Wise Beyond Belief was going to do. The difference is we won't have to share the money with anybody. Perhaps I will also kill Eats Many Turnips. I shall think on it."

"Those are evil ideas, Bad Haircut."

"It is but life, Crater Trueblood, although I fear your living is at an end."

Bad Haircut pulled the lever to raise the scraper blade so as to kill Crater, but as he did, the fuel cells within suddenly exploded in a gush of fire and smoke. Bad Haircut was knocked off his seat and thrown into the dust, whereupon the scraper blade fell on top of him. Crater knelt beside Bad Haircut and discovered he was still breathing, though it didn't look like for long. "What happened?" Crater asked.

The new king laughed, his helmet fogging as the suit's ventilation system failed. "I bet your gillie did it." Then, after a few gurgles, which may have been chuckles, he died, and the fog in his helmet faded away.

Crater stood up and looked at the other Umlaps who stared back at him, then walked toward the Baikal entry hatch. Crater trudged to the maintenance shed, opened the airlock door, and climbed into the fastbug's seat. The gillie was there waiting for him and crawled up on his shoulder. Crater drove into the dust and kept going, leaving Baikal and the Umlaps behind. As he neared the dustway, Crater said to the gillie, "Did you make the fuel cells explode?"

Yes. I stopped the stirrers through the scraper puter. Heat buildup. Only a matter of time.

"How did you know Bad Haircut's plan?"

Tapped into vidcams, do4us, and puter systems. Could see, hear, and read everything.

"You're not supposed to do anything unless I tell you to do it."

Gillie helps you.

"But only when I ask for help."

Gillie helps Colonel too. You must catch Cycler on time.

The gillie's response caught Crater by surprise. "How do you know about that?"

Gillie pays attention to all Moontown systems.

Crater said, "You are a bad gillie."

The gillie looked sad, although it could look no way at all.

"Let's catch the convoy," Crater said, then turned onto the dustway and pressed the hammer down.

::: NINETEEN

The convoy would stop for a rest at Aristillus Crater, and that was where Crater hoped to catch it. If not there, the next place might be at the Bessell way station in the great empty *Mare Serenitatis*—the Sea of Serenity—which was mostly Russian territory. Crater couldn't imagine driving that far alone. He was more than a little afraid the giant crowhopper might catch him out there too.

He worried over the fuel cell status, then asked the gillie, "Can we make Aristillus?"

Yes, if the fuel cell retains its charge.

"Well, I knew that," Crater replied.

Tired, the gillie replied.

Crater supposed this was an apology. "I didn't know you were so fragile," he admonished.

Gillie only flesh and blood.

"I didn't know you had any blood."

It's a metaphor. My tissue must be occasionally restored.

Crater drove on until he felt fatigue seeping into his bones.

His tissue had to be occasionally restored too. He pulled over, put up the solar panel, and leaned back for a nap. "Keep track of my suit pressure," he told the gillie, which responded with a simple chirp. Crater supposed it really was tired if that's all it could do.

When Crater awoke, he climbed out of the fastbug to stretch his legs. He slung the rifle on his shoulder, chose a direction, and walked for a while, then picked a small crater and sat on its lip and contemplated the view, which was a handsome brown plain with some nearby rolling hills.

In the distance he saw some mountains that he presumed were the Caucuses, named after a mountain range on Earth. He looked around for the Earth and found it high overhead and thought it would be ironic if he could see the Earthly Caucuses that were in western Russia. But all he could see were the Americas, and they were mostly hidden beneath clouds. Crater tried to imagine what it would be like to live beneath a white shroud. He tried but it was beyond his imagination.

Then he spotted something glittering in the sun. He walked toward it and found an ancient robotic lander. Long ago, people on Earth had sent robots to the moon, and this was one of them. Fascinated, Crater walked around it. It had crashed, that much was clear, as it was a crumpled mess. Its spherical fuel tanks were split, its dish antenna was bent, and everything else was twisted aluminum and steel. Its solar panels were also shattered, their shards glittering in the sun.

Crater spotted a metal plate lying in the dust. There was a symbol engraved on it that he recognized, the hammer and sickle of ancient Russia when it was part of something called the Union of Soviet Socialist Republics. The letters

CCCP were also on the plate, the Cyrillic letters that stood for USSR.

Crater again looked up at the Earth. All the countries there had changed since the smashed robot had flown, but the physics of spaceflight had not changed at all. It still took a lot of energy to move things from the Earth to the moon.

Crater found himself admiring the people in those extinct countries who'd sent such machines to the moon, but he also felt sorry for the ones who'd sent along this particular robot. From his reading of the old USSR, those scientists and engineers might have been shipped off to Siberia which, in those days, was a terrible place. It was still no place to take a vacation, or so Crater had heard.

Crater began to think about time. Time was a peculiar thing and no one had a real grasp on it. Crater had a fair understanding of quantum physics. Albert Einstein, the physicist who had first explained the relationship between time and space, said the only reason time existed was so everything didn't happen at once. During a sermon, the Moontown preacher had once quoted a little piece of Scripture from Ecclesiastes: *He has made everything beautiful in its time. He has also set eternity in the human heart; yet no one can fathom what God has done from beginning to end.*

Crater sat companionably with the old robot, thinking about time, until he decided it was time for him to go. He was confident he could catch up with the convoy, but not if he kept taking detours.

As he walked back, retracing his path, he came across a set of tracks he hadn't noticed before that crossed his own. He studied them and concluded he'd never seen such strange tracks. Each was the shape of a U and made deep, gouging marks in the dust. "Gillie, what made those tracks?" he asked.

Unknown, the gillie said.

Crater was astonished that he'd stumped the gillie. Maybe, he thought, he'd asked the question wrong. He considered a better question, but never got the chance to ask it because that was when the creature that had made the tracks appeared. It was the strangest thing Crater had ever seen: a monster with the head of a dragon, wild eyes and flaring nostrils, and four stout legs that had heavy, thick feet if such strangely shaped things could be called feet at all. The awful creature advanced on Crater, shaking its terrible head, each heavy step producing an angry spurt of dust and leaving behind the strange U-shaped tracks.

::: TWENTY

ooking back on it, Crater would wonder why he hadn't used the rifle on the monster. Maybe it was for the same reason he hadn't been able to shoot the crowhopper. He was soft, that's what Captain Teller had said, and Crater supposed he was right.

When the monster came for him, Crater took off. He ran through a field of craters, leaping over the smaller ones, stumbling across the bigger ones, weaving back and forth where he could. But the thing was too powerful and too fast. It came up behind him, then alongside, bumping its thick shoulder into his, a shoulder that seemed dense as mooncrete and crackling with energy. Crater fell hard into the dust. He scrambled to his feet, started to run again, but then stopped because the creature was standing in his path.

It appeared to be studying him as if to decide what part of Crater to eat first. Crater took a step to the right and the monster matched him with a sidestep in that direction. Crater took a step to the left and it matched his movement again. Since it appeared to be content for the moment, not quite ready to race up and crush the life out of him with its pile-driver feet, Crater was about to ask the gillie what the monster was when the gillie answered on its own.

Gillie believes it is the Earthian animal known as a horse.

Crater, being well educated by Q-Bess and the denizens of the Dust Palace, knew very well what a horse was and what one looked like, and this wasn't it. Jockey Jill, a diminutive but intense woman, had even taught him about horses in some detail. Looking closer, however, he saw that the creature could indeed be a horse except it was wearing some sort of suit and a helmet. But what was a horse doing on the moon in such a rig? Crater simply could not accept it, even though the evidence was standing in front of him.

The gillie said, *Let it approach you.*

"How do you know about horses?"

Gillie listens to Jockey Jill.

Crater waited and, sure enough, the horse took a step toward him, stopped, then took another. It kept raising its head, as if to sniff the air, but of course there was no air except what was in its helmet.

Finally, the great head pushed within arm's reach of Crater.

Touch its nose.

Crater touched the front of the horse's helmet. He didn't know if the horse was male or female but he said, "Good boy. That's a good boy."

The gillie had apparently searched for the horse's comm channel and found it as the horse made a peculiar nickering sound that Crater had never heard or imagined that any animal could make. "Is that sound normal?" he asked, worrying now that the horse might be sick.

Normal for this species.

Crater noticed something protruding from the thick, armored material on the horse's neck and was startled to see it was a flechette. It had struck at an angle so had been captured by the armor. There was another flechette, Crater could see now, on its flank, similarly captured by the armor. Crater plucked the one from the neck cover, then pulled out the one from the flank. The one from the flank had blood on it, and the horse shuddered when he pulled it free. The flechette had penetrated into the horse, but its suit still hadn't leaked.

"You have a biolastic suit, don't you?" Crater asked. Crater inspected the flank wound and saw no blood leaking out. To repair the sheath that quickly, Crater supposed the biolastic material on the horse was of a superior type.

Then Crater saw a vidpin attached to the armor. He pushed it and read its message.

PEGASUS

Born Stallion Aug. 14, 2116

STEEL PRIZE STABLES

Madison, Alabama

Warhorse: Alabama Irregulars

Silver Moon Medal with four Red Bud Clusters

Eight Campaign Medals including

Battle of Nashville

Battle of Western Kentucky

Battle of Atlanta

Corporate owner: Deep Space Suits, Inc.

Manager: Major Ellis Justice, late of the Ala. Irregs.

"Pegasus." Crater tried the name on and concluded it was a good one for this big horse, even though it had no wings.

The horse looked back along its track. Nickering softly, it started walking away, and, curious, Crater followed it. The horse walked along the path it had made and kept walking with Crater behind, his rifle at the ready. The crowhoppers that had shot the horse might be nearby. The horse's owner had to be nearby too, and Crater wondered if it might be a lunatic who was so much a *real* lunatic that he had brought a horse from Earth, built it a suit, and kept it. In that case, he would have to be a very wealthy lunatic.

The horse was walking faster than Crater could keep up. It looked back once, then stopped. Crater walked up next to it and inspected the suit it was wearing. Built into it, unless Crater was mistaking its purpose, was what he thought was called a saddle. Horses had been used by humans for centuries for transportation. He'd seen the old vidpix of American cowboys riding them. With these images in mind, and knowing he could not keep up with the horse, Crater climbed upon the lip of a small crater and stuck his leg over the horse's back, then slipped into its saddle while tucking his rifle beneath elastic straps sewn to the fabric, apparently for such utility.

The fabric over the armor automatically curled around Crater's boots. The horse took a few steps forward, then looked over its shoulder again and waited patiently until Crater saw a button on the saddle. He pushed it, and two straps were unreeled from the nose of the horse's helmet. Crater reached over the horse's neck and took the straps in his hands. There was a snap buckle to join them together, which Crater did, creating what he recalled were called reins. "So I can steer you, right?" he asked the horse, which pondered him with one of its big brown eyes, then turned and began, without warning, to run.

And how it ran!

Crater hung on and it was glorious. Pegasus ran through the crater field and then began to stretch its legs, soaring with every step in great bounds. Ten yards, twenty, fifty, and more! Crater reckoned Pegasus was going faster than even his fast-bug could go. The dust below became a blur but Crater was not afraid. He loved the sensation of being aboard a beast that ran with such fluid grace. The gillie whooped and yodeled as if it were a cowboy from an old western movie. This made Crater laugh, and he whooped and yodeled himself.

The horse ran on, leaping over great craters, up a small hill, launching itself and soaring so high, it was almost as if it were flying. Pegasus, the flying horse in Greek mythology, brought thunder and lightning from Olympus, and every-where Pegasus's hoof struck the earth, water was supposed to have sprung forth. Crater wished that might also be true on the moon, and maybe it was true because this was truly a miraculous creature. "Fly on, Pegasus!" Crater cried with joy and abandon. He had never, in the entire history of his life, felt such freedom as on the back of the great horse as it galloped and flew.

Crater saw the dustway and a big truck parked on it. He pulled gently back on the reins, and Pegasus slowed and stopped. Crater got off and led the horse into some rocks for cover. He wanted to study the truck before going any closer.

The truck was a van of some type, designed perhaps to carry Pegasus. Crater activated the zoom setting on his helmet binoculars. His heart sinking, he saw two crowhoppers and their spiderwalkers. He also saw a man lying in the dust, apparently the driver of the truck. He was spread-eagled, his hands and feet tied to stakes driven into the regolith. Crater saw the man's bearded face was twisted in pain. Crater also saw a line of tracks leading off the dustway and realized they were hoof marks. A ramp from the big truck in the back was where Pegasus had come down and apparently gotten away from the crowhoppers.

Crater yelped involuntarily when the crowhopper shot the man tied down.

"Check his suit, gillie," Crater ordered.

It was a tough order. They were miles away, and the gillie did not know the freq the bearded man's suit was transmitting on, or if it was transmitting at all. A long minute passed before the gillie said, *Five flechettes in the suit, none leaking.*

"A biolastic suit, for certain," Crater muttered. "But a better one than I've ever heard of. Five flechettes penetrated a suit and none leaking? Amazing." It was also amazing that a man with five flechettes in him was still alive. Apparently, the crowhoppers were shooting the man with their rifles set to their weakest setting. Crater supposed it was a type of torture.

The gillie transmitted the signal from the man on the ground. "Is that the worst ye can do, ye ugly creatures? Why, that ain't nothin' to me. I'm a moon mountain man, by Joe! I can shoot straighter, jump higher, cuss worser, fight longer, smell badder, and spit farther than any man on the moon! My maw were a collapsed lava tube and my pap were a volcano! My brother's the dust and my sis is a roller! My wife's a crater, my kids are Helium-3!"

"Shut up, old man," one of the crowhoppers croaked. "Nothing you say is going to help you. You will die today."

"Death ain't nothin'," the tied-up man retorted. "It's how you die. Watch me, boys, and learn somethin'!"

Pegasus walked around the rocks and looked at Crater. "What?" Crater demanded. "We can't do anything about this."

The horse kept looking at him until Crater felt ashamed. He checked his rifle, clicked it to its lowest setting, rethought that, clicked it to its middle setting, then climbed aboard Pegasus.

Crater didn't know why, but the horse made him feel not only brave but almost foolhardy. He faced two crowhoppers, bioengineered Earthian killers. What would the outcome be? Surely disaster.

Yet he was not afraid.

Crater clamped his legs tight against the sides of the great horse, the material flowing around his legs, steadying him. "What kind of horse are you?" he asked. Then he knew the answer. It was on the vidpin, after all. Pegasus was a warhorse.

"All right, boy," Crater whispered. "Let's ride."

The horse made a shrill sound—an angry whinny. Then Pegasus flew down the hill in great leaps, reaching the crowhoppers in what seemed to Crater no more than a few bounds. Crater rose up in the saddle and pulled the trigger of his rifle, and one of the crowhoppers fell. The other crowhopper raised his rifle to fire, but Pegasus soared over him, circled behind the truck, then turned and, though Crater scarcely believed it was possible, leapt completely over it. Caught by surprise, the crowhopper fell beneath Pegasus's hooves, never to rise again.

Crater jumped off the horse and ran over to the bearded

man. He knelt beside him. "Sir, are you all right?" Crater asked, though five flechettes sticking in him told their own story.

When Pegasus nickered, the man's eyes fluttered and then opened. "Ah, Pegasus," he said. "You came back to save me, eh? Good horse." The man smiled at Crater. "And who are you, boy?"

Crater untied the man and told him who he was and why he was there. The man sat up unsteadily while Crater held his shoulders, giving him support. The flechettes had no doubt bled him. "I'm Ellis Justice," he said. "And this is my horse, Pegasus. I work for the Deep Space Suit Company. My job is to visit heel-3 towns and demonstrate our wares, which are suits of all kinds, space suits, dust suits, fabric ECP suits, and the latest BCP suits. Pegasus is along to demonstrate the amazing capabilities of our new biolastic material. He also gives rides to the children of these places. Or at least that's what we did until these ruffians killed me. Who are they?"

"Crowhoppers, Mr. Justice, Earthian mercenaries. But what did you mean they killed you? Your suit has sealed."

"One of the flechettes entered my right lung. It was the first shot. It was before they slowed their rifles down." As if on cue, a pink froth escaped Justice's lips and his eyelids fluttered. "Take good care of Pegasus, will you? He is a dear friend, though he was once a warhorse with the Alabama Irregulars. His previous owner told me he was feared by every man and horse who ever faced him, but since he's been with me, he's been gentle as a lamb and patient with children."

"Gillie," Crater said, "is it true what Mr. Justice says about his lung, and is there something to be done?"

The gillie crawled off Crater and onto Justice's neck, then

disappeared into the helmet seal, reappearing inside. Justice, though apparently dying, was delighted. "A gillie, by golly! But it's illegal!"

"It knows," Crater said, and then to the gillie, "How did you do that?"

Gillie cousin to biolastic microbes. Gillie fool them into thinking gillie all the same. But these are different from Moontown biolastic microbial sheath. Much stronger. Much meaner.

"These *are* different," Justice confirmed, then hacked and coughed some before speaking again. "State-of-the-art, just put on the market for long endurance. Put it on, you can leave it on up to six months. Pegasus has one, and except for the plaston girdle along his hindquarters that needs cleaning every week or so, and the need for food and water, he could run along on the moon for months."

The gillie climbed next to Justice's lips. "I think it wants to go into your mouth," Crater said.

Justice didn't look pleased at that prospect, but he still opened his mouth and the gillie wriggled inside. Justice gagged, then relaxed. A few minutes later, the gillie reappeared out of Justice's mouth carrying, though it had no hands, a flechette that was dripping blood. *Repaired tear in his lung*, it said, then put the flechette down and worked its way through the neck seal, reappearing on the other side.

"That thing's a wonder," Justice said and drew a clear breath.

"Status report," Crater said, as if what the gillie had done was normal. The truth was he was in awe.

The gillie said, *Lung function good, biolastic sheath holding.*

Nickering softly, Pegasus walked up and allowed Justice

to stroke his nose. "Thank you for coming back with help, old friend," Justice said.

"Maybe we ought to get you out of the dust, Mr. Justice," Crater suggested. "And pluck out these other flechettes."

"Just help me up."

Crater helped Justice to his feet, noticing as he did that one of the crowhoppers was moving. It was the one he'd shot. When Justice noticed the crowhopper too, Crater said, "I had the rifle on midpower so it wouldn't kill."

The gillie said, *Crowhopper suit leaking. Death in twenty minutes.*

"Can we take it inside your trailer?" Crater asked, but Justice threw off Crater's arm, staggered over to the crowhopper, picked up the creature's rifle, and aimed it at its heart.

"Mr. Justice, don't!" Crater cried.

Justice glanced over his shoulder. "Stay out of this, Crater." He turned back to the crowhopper. "Answer me quick and I might let you live. Why did you attack me?"

The crowhopper's eyes were filled with hate. "Questions we had to ask you," he grunted.

"You shot me, old son, and you tortured me, but you didn't ask me any questions. Better come up with a better answer."

"First we decided to have our fun."

"Torture is fun?" Crater asked.

The crowhopper turned his head toward Crater. His eyes almost had weight, like two slimy worms crawling on Crater's face. "You want to hear about that heel-3 camp we were in the other day? Killed 'em all, we did. Oh, that was fun, boy. You should join us. We'd show you how much fun it can be when nothing means nothing."

"What was the name of the town?" Crater asked, fearing the answer.

"Something Japanese. Nekko? Yes, that was it."

Nekko was a small Japanese heel-3 camp south of the lunar equator near a lava flow that was the shape of a cat, thus the name. "Did you say you killed everyone?" Crater asked, his voice turning to a near whisper.

"Not all at once. We played around first."

The shock on Crater's face seemed to surprise the crowhopper. "What's with you, boy?"

"He's not a veteran," Justice said. "He don't know war, what it's like, what creatures like you are bred to do."

"Well, old man, I'm not the worst of the lot, I can tell you that."

"Where's your base?" Crater asked.

"We don't have a base. We travel on our spiderwalkers, take sustenance where we find it."

"But you have to come from somewhere," Crater said.

"I'm getting tired of answering your questions," the crowhopper replied. "Name, rank, and serial number, that's the ticket. My name is Henri Vallemarte, my rank is private, serial number is echo seventeen eighty-one—or used to be when I was in the Legion. You're not going to get another word out of me."

Justice shot him, the rifle reset to full power, and the crowhopper died, quivering in the dust.

Crater was aghast. "What did you do that for?"

"When he said he wasn't going to talk anymore, I believed him."

Using the rifle as a cane, Justice stumped toward the trailer. "Let's go inside. We can talk there."

Crater looked at the dead crowhoppers and sensed that everything was changing from what he'd always believed to be true, and it was not for the better. The horse came over and pushed him in the back with his nose, then crowded in, demanding attention. "What about Pegasus?" Crater asked.

"He comes inside too. I know he's itching to smell you. Come on. I promise you'll like what's going to happen next."

::: TWENTY-ONE

Crater couldn't imagine that he'd like anything much for a while. He was far behind the convoy, and if he didn't catch up, he was going to miss the Cycler and fail the Colonel. He'd also promised to look after Maria and, though he'd had the best of intentions, he supposed he could be accused of abandoning her. There was also a dead trucker buried miles behind, a woman who'd just wanted to race, a race Captain Teller had blamed on him. There was also a dead crowhopper out in the wayback not too far from the Dustway Inn, three dead Umlaps—the king, Hit Your Face, and Bad Haircut—and now there were two more dead crowhoppers plus a report of a destroyed heel-3 town down south.

All the death and destruction was a great drag on Crater's morale. He was also in the company of a man who didn't mind killing other men, not to mention a giant warhorse who could pretty much fly. Well, that last one wasn't so bad. Meeting Pegasus was marvelous, but everything else about the convoy was a scrag shambles.

He told the gillie to keep watch, though he doubted it had the strength to do much, and left it outside on the truck, then helped Justice inside. Pegasus followed up the ramp. When he saw the interior of the trailer, Crater almost forgot the misery of his situation. It was amazing. Once through the big airlock, there were three sections, a set of complete but compact biolastic dustlocks made of the finest lunasteel, Justice's sumptuous quarters, and Pegasus's stall. Justice was suddenly feeling faint, so after opening the hatch for Pegasus and seeing him inside his domicile, Crater helped Justice remove the flechettes and take off his coveralls.

After sitting down in the biolastic removal dustlock, Justice waved Crater away from the shower handle. "Not for me, Crater. I'll keep my biolastic sheath on. It's good for another four months and I can scarcely feel it. Just remove my helmet by pushing that button at my neck. Ah, there you go. See how the helmet comes right off? The microbes at the neck are programmed to dissolve when a small current at a precise phase passes through them. They come back together when the helmet goes on. Pegasus's helmet works the same way. Go unburden him, if you will. He won't mind getting loose from his gear."

"This truck is amazing," Crater said.

"My own design, bucko."

Crater climbed out of his ECP suit, put on some coveralls he found in a cupboard, and went inside Pegasus's quarters. Taking off the horse's helmet was as easy as removing Justice's, and Pegasus gave him a thank-you nicker.

After Crater removed Pegasus's armor, the horse pushed a large dome-shaped button on the wall with his nose and was rewarded with a bucket of green pellets. He quickly had his huge head deep in the pail.

Going back to see how Justice was doing, Crater found him sitting in an easy chair in his quarters, having limped there from the dustlock. He looked ill, his face as gray as the dust outside. "Blood poisoning from the flechette, maybe," Justice said, coughing. "Your gillie can't fix that by crawling into my lungs." He pointed to a white cabinet. "Some antibiotics in the medicine chest with injectors. You ever injected anybody?"

Crater admitted he hadn't, but promised to give it a try. The injector had a place to press, and when he did, a reader on the wall played a vidpix of how to use it. Crater watched intently, then, as instructed, wiped down Justice's shoulder with an alcohol swab, also thoughtfully provided by the medicine chest, and pressed the injector on Justice's shoulder. It emptied itself and Crater tossed the spent injector into a waste bucket.

"Most likely got pneumonia, too, from the blood in my lungs," Justice said. "But I guess I can make it for a few days."

"I was heading for Aristillus," Crater said. "You can travel along."

"West to east? I was going east to west."

"I guess things have changed for you, Mr. Justice," Crater said.

Justice thought that over. "I suppose they have. With crowhoppers on the moon, they've changed for all of us, I suspect. Looks like we might have to dig up the tomahawk, do battle with those old creatures. But all right. If you don't mind our company, Pegasus and I will tag along."

"Tell me about the crowhoppers," Crater said.

Justice leaned back in the chair. "I first saw them in my

rearview mirror whilst they were trying to sneak up on me on their spiderwalkers. Fought 'em when I was with the Irregulars so I knew what they were. I didn't have anything to fight them with so I had no choice but to stop. They didn't want to come inside—maybe they were afraid I'd ambush them—so they ordered me and the Peg out.

"They knocked me around a bit, then got interested in Pegasus. One of them said he'd race the other, him on Pegasus, his buddy on his spiderwalker. They were just having a good time. But Pegasus fooled them when he ran off into the dust. They shot at him and may have nicked him. Not sure."

"They shot him twice," Crater said, "but his suit held."

Justice lit up in a grin. "He wears a suit of the latest design by my company. Of course it held. It's designed to hold."

Getting back on track, Crater asked, "What did the crow-hoppers want?"

"They never said, except I heard them talking to each other and gained they were looking for someone on a truck convoy. I guess I was a diversion. Maybe they thought I'd seen the convoy. I don't know. The only thing I know for sure is if you hadn't come along, I'd likely be dead and so would poor Pegasus, who clearly has taken a shine to you. Children he'll let ride on his back with no complaint, but most men, he's pretty particular. Now, tell me what you're doing out here and let's see if we have common cause."

Crater told Justice most of it, in a shorthand way, and Justice smiled at the end of the tale. "I know Captain Teller. A tough fellow, not too bright or imaginative, but honest, and honest goes a long way out here in the wayback. You'll learn a few things from him if you pay attention. One thing for certain, he'll like to hear what a brave scout he has, charging those two crowhoppers like you did."

"All I did was hang on to Pegasus," Crater said.

"You did more than that. You shot one of 'em. That was some great shooting. But why did you have the rifle on half-power?"

"I didn't want to kill anybody."

Justice closed his eyes for long enough that Crater thought he'd perhaps fainted, but then he opened them and said, "Crater, these crowhoppers are on the dustway to kill. That's what the people who made them designed them to do. They got no heart or souls neither. You get mixed up with one, you got to kill it. In war, it's okay to kill a man as long as that man's going to kill you if you don't. But anyway, crowhoppers don't qualify as men. Do you understand?"

"I think so, sir. I'll try to keep that in mind."

Justice nodded as if he believed he'd convinced the boy, but he knew better. He'd seen lots of boys like Crater on Earth, unable to kill a man even though there was a war going on all around them. Those boys never lived long. He worried about Crater, then sensed there might be more to the boy than he showed. At bottom, the boy probably had a lot of sand. He was all by himself in the wayback of the moon, after all.

"Say," Justice said, "how'd you like to try one of our new suits?"

Crater thought that was a splendid idea, and an hour later—after some measuring—he was wearing a Deep Space special biolastic suit. When he touched his arm, it felt as if he had nothing on at all. "This is amazing," Crater said.

Jumpcar in sight.

Crater had nearly forgotten about the gillie left outside

on watch. He snatched up the helmet Justice provided, pulled on his coveralls and boots, and went through the airlock. He saw it immediately. A jumpcar was hovering on its jet about a mile away, its triangular fins a hundred feet above the ground. Then, it began to rise until the flame from its engine had turned into a sparkling star, then disappeared altogether.

"I saw it on the monitor," Justice said when Crater came back inside. "Crowhoppers, I suppose, looking for their fellows. They saw them, probably, and went off to make their reports to whoever brought them to the moon. We'd best get on to Aristillus before they come back."

"I'll hitch my fastbug to the motorbarn," Crater said, then got busy. Within an hour he had accomplished the task, made sure Justice was comfortable, that Pegasus was fed and watered and his stall cleaned—Crater's work in the grease traps was good training for that—and began to drive the motorbarn.

He drove for the next ten hours straight, the gillie on the dashboard, prepared to sound the alarm if it sensed the crowhoppers or any other kind of problem. The gillie looked off-color to Crater so he asked it for a status.

Gillie sick, it said.

Crater felt bad. He should have asked it earlier. "What's wrong?"

The gillie's voice was weak. *Biolastic cells tried to absorb gillie. Gillie fight. Big drain.*

"What can I do to help you?"

The gillie didn't answer, which was an answer itself. "I'm sorry," Crater said and still the gillie did not respond.

When he needed sleep, Crater pulled the motorbarn off the dustway and sought out a hill and its shade. This became his plan, to drive as long as he could, then seek out the shade, either of a hill or a crater. The motorbarn had a low-powered radar that could pick up anything moving nearby. Crater set the alarm on the radar during the rest period so he could sleep, but sleep was difficult. He worried for the gillie, which was still very quiet and maybe about to die, and he worried about Justice, who was running a fever, and he worried about Pegasus, who was dependent on Crater to recognize the colic or all the other problems horses might have. Of course, he also worried about catching the convoy and getting to the Cycler on time, and whether Maria was okay. He even managed to worry a little for himself, but not much. There wasn't time.

After a day of driving, Justice rallied enough to stand watch when Crater slept. Over breakfast, he told Crater more about himself and Pegasus, how in fact his son had been the soldier of the Alabama Irregulars who'd owned the warhorse. "He died in the battle of Nashville," Justice said, his voice trembling with pride and pain. "Pegasus is all I have left of him." It reminded Crater that the gillie was all that he had left of his parents and, if it kept getting sicker and stopped working, he would not even have that.

Justice spun a few stories of battles in the North American war in which his son and Pegasus had fought and other stories of his own experiences in the various Earthian wars that had absorbed his life.

"I don't understand your pride in being a soldier," Crater said after Justice had told of an impossible charge his son and his horse had made with his cavalry unit—one where so many had been killed, the battle lost, but glory found.

"Wars are not noble, nor are battles, for they are bloody,

nasty, and awful," Justice replied, "but have you heard of King Arthur, his Round Table, and his knights?"

Crater had heard of them, of course, being thoroughly educated in American and English literature by a former professor from Oxford University turned scragline picker. Yet he'd never read any book about the old English king and his famous knights. "It's just a legend, isn't it?" Crater asked. "Not real history."

"Sometimes," Justice said, "the legend is more real than the history. It's not what happened but what we choose to believe happened that matters the most."

Justice revealed himself to be a scholar of the Arthurian legends and had texts on his reader that went as far back as Geoffrey of Monmouth's Latin work, including the *Le Morte d'Arthur* by Thomas Malory, and on to the *King Arthur vs. the Aliens* movies of the 2040s, just before the great wars erupted. No matter when the tales were told and in what method, they still were about the old king, his battles, his knights, and his enemies. Justice told Crater about each of the knights, of Elyan the White who was beloved by Arthur but betrayed him in the end, and Lancelot who was a virtuous warrior yet would steal Arthur's wife, the beautiful Guinevere. He told Crater about Sir Galahad, the purest knight of all, who quested, along with Sir Percival, for the Holy Grail. Then there was Sir Gawain, the brash, talkative, womanizing knight who made Crater think of Petro even if he was supposed to be a king. And there was Sir Kay, who was the unrelenting warrior, fighting the king's battles without caring why they were fought, and Mordred, Arthur's son, who detested his father and would eventually fight him to the death. Crater was particularly intrigued by

Orgeluse, the haughty maiden of Logres, who tempted and taunted Gawain, nearly causing his death before they were united in love and marriage. He saw parallels with Orgeluse and Maria and mentioned it to Justice.

"This is why the Arthurian legends are still told," Justice replied. "The characters are so rich and so defined that we begin to see them in ourselves and the people we know. This Maria is a worry to you, yes?"

"I wouldn't say a worry," Crater said, but then he confessed that she was a worry, indeed. "I see Petro as Gawain," he allowed.

"Ah, sibling rivalry for the same girl," Justice said. "I understand. But, Crater, which of the knights are you?"

"Galahad," Crater said, instantly.

"And what is your Holy Grail? What is the perfect thing you seek?"

Crater had surprised himself by picking Galahad, but he supposed he had done it for a reason even if he didn't know what the reason was. He therefore gave Justice's question serious thought. "I seek the perfect thing in myself," he concluded. "I want to be perfect in everyone's eyes. If I mess up, I feel embarrassed and ashamed."

"Yet you realize no one is perfect and no one can avoid failure. It is the human condition."

"I know it but I can't stop how I feel."

"Oh, but you can, Crater," Justice replied. "You have to keep telling yourself that you are doing your best—just make certain you are, of course—and leave the rest to the big Fellow who looks after us all. And remember that Galahad ended up being isolated from everyone he loved because he became obsessed with finding the Holy Grail. The irony was when he found it, it was no longer perfect just because it was found."

Crater mused on that for a long second, then told Justice of another quest, this one not within himself, but the one the Colonel had sent him off to accomplish aboard the Cycler. It felt good to let someone else know.

"Is it a worthy quest?" Justice asked.

"I don't know. It seemed important to the Colonel."

"Do you see the Colonel as King Arthur?"

"Not really," Crater concluded after thinking it over. "King Arthur always had the best of intentions. When I stop to think about it, I'm not sure what intentions the Colonel has or why he's sent me after this package."

"But you clearly intend to do it whether you understand his motivations or not."

Crater nodded, saying, "I will do it. I told him I would, and I will."

"Still, it's something to think about," Justice said, and that's what Crater did as the motorbarn crawled across the face of the moon, and the gillie died a little each day, and the crowhoppers, for all he knew, circled above, ready to pounce.

::: TWENTY-TWO

The high and irregular rim of Aristillus formed a circle surrounded by ejecta-rays that speared out hundreds of miles. In the center were three peaks, the tallest at least a half-mile high, the result of the impact of the meteorite that had formed the crater. Aristillus was an example of a complex impact crater with an uplift in the central region. As the energy from the impact of the meteor had dissipated, the center of the crater had swollen upward, creating the tall mountains.

Along the northern rampart, Crater could just make out the remains of an unnamed and even more ancient impact crater nearly submerged in brown and gray lava flows. To the south he could see Autolycus, a smaller, simpler crater, and to the southwest was the vast Archimedes crater with its complicated geometry. To the southeast, he could see the opening between the Caucasus and Apenninus mountains called the Serenity Gap that ultimately led to the vast ocean of dust and lava that was the Sea of Serenity—or, as it was called by the dustway truckers, the Serene Killer. It was all magnificent, and Crater sat there in the driver's seat of the motorbarn admiring it. When he looked a little closer at the settlement, he beheld, with relief, a line of trucks he recognized. He had caught up with the Moontown convoy.

Crater walked back into the motorbarn to ask Justice permission for something he wanted to do. Justice thought the idea jolly and pulled himself into the driver's seat while Crater got Pegasus ready for the outside. The horse, perhaps sensing a nice run, shook eagerly as Crater led him down the ramp, then climbed aboard. "There it is, Pegasus. Aristillus. Ready?"

Pegasus raised and lowered his head and stamped his hooves in anticipation. "Let's go," Crater said.

Pegasus leaped, landed on the downslope, and began to run, every step covering fifty feet or more. Crater yodeled with excitement as he and the great horse closed in on the convoy, then galloped through the huge parking area, snaking through the trucks. As he passed them, he saw other trucks, some from Neroburg, New St. Petersburg, the Luna Water Company, and various freight haulers from Armstrong City. The drivers waved and whooped as he passed, Pegasus's great hooves tossing up plumes of dust.

Then he spotted the chuckwagon. Captain Teller, Petro, and Maria were standing beside it, perusing a checklist. Since he'd left the gillie in the motorbarn, Crater ran up and down the freq list the convoy was likely using, catching Petro saying, "... if my brother ever catches up with us, then—"

Teller interrupted. "I think we have to assume he will not catch up anytime soon."

"But I have caught up!" Crater cried as he and Pegasus rounded one of the trucks, a driver standing there—Irish, as it turned out—falling backward in astonishment.

"What the—!" Teller yelled as Pegasus leapt over the chuckwagon.

"Yeehaw!" Crater cried in joyful abandon as Pegasus landed and kept running in astounding strides. Crater looked over his shoulder and was surprised to see Maria coming after him in a fastbug. He pulled back on the reins, and Pegasus slowed to a canter until Maria drove up alongside. She grinned and pushed the accelerator down hard. The fastbug spun its wheels, then soared up the lip of a collapsed crater and flew through the vacuum.

"Come on, boy, catch her!" Crater cried, leaning forward.

Through the craters and plains Pegasus ran after Maria. She slowed, letting them catch up. "To the Autolycus Crater," she proposed and jammed the accelerator pedal again to the floor.

"We can do this, Peg old boy," Crater said, and the great horse, its breath coming in joyful, swelling puffs, surged forward, and they caught Maria at the crater. Crater gave the horse a gentle tug on the reins and Pegasus got the idea, wheeled around the crater, and took off back toward the convoy. On a straightaway, Maria caught up again, then waved them down. "Stop, Crater," she said. "Please!"

Crater brought Pegasus to a canter, then a walk. The horse quivered beneath him and then stopped beside Maria. Crater hopped off Pegasus and was astonished when Maria ran to him. He was so unprepared, she knocked him down. Pegasus looked at him with concern, then at Maria, and stamped his hooves. "It's all right, boy," Crater said from the dust. "She's a friend. I think."

Maria helped Crater up, then, to his further astonishment, gave him a hug. "I'm so glad you're back!" she cried.

"Who are you and what have you done with Maria?" Crater asked.

Maria laughed. "It's me, silly. Even though you have a low opinion of me and my bossy nature, I can be nice."

"I have never had a low opinion of you," Crater swore, even though he supposed he had, sort of.

"Then let's start over. Deal?" Not waiting for him to answer, she put her hand on the nose of Pegasus's helmet. "And who's this?"

Crater told her about Pegasus and about Ellis Justice and the crowhoppers that had attacked them. Then he told her about the Umlaps and how the gillie had returned. Maria listened to it all in solemn silence, then said, "I worried about you while you were gone."

"You did?" Crater fought to hold back a grin but he just couldn't.

"Of course I did!"

"Why?"

"Because you're my friend, Crater."

"Only your friend?"

"Oh, I see. You want more than that. You know, even when you were calling me bossy, I kind of suspected that. All right. I will give it due consideration, but don't rush me. Don't rush anything. We're living through a special time. Don't you see that? We need to just be in the moment, not look beyond even if that beyond includes, well . . . us."

"Of course you're right. We're much too young to get serious," Crater responded with a cheerful shrug, even though he didn't mean a word of it.

"You know what we should do?" Maria asked, coyly pressing her helmet faceplate to his, her lips puckered.

He concluded he must be in a dream but, if so, it was a wonderful one. "What?" he asked, dreamily, his lips prepared to kiss hers, at least through the plaston helmet.

"Finish our race!" she cried, pushing him away and laughing. She jumped back into the fastbug and, wheels throwing dust, zipped across the short plain before plunging into another field of craters.

Crater threw himself aboard Pegasus. "Get after her, boy!" he shouted. Pegasus took off, though he had cooled down and couldn't catch up with Maria this time.

When Crater and Pegasus trotted back into the convoy parking area, Captain Teller walked out from the chuckwagon. "Ellis Justice arrived, told me all, Crater. You apparently did fair work out there."

"As good as I could manage, sir," Crater said, climbing down from the great horse.

"These crowhoppers are worrisome," the captain said. "Why are they stalking the dustway?"

"I don't know," Crater said. "Is the convoy ready to roll? If not, I'd like to see Mr. Justice to a doctor, Pegasus to an inside domicile, and the gillie is sick too."

Teller's face was drawn. "Not to worry. I've dispatched

Justice to the clinic and the horse, per his instructions, will go to the maintenance shed where he will be looked after. As for the gillie, you'll have to take care of it. Unfortunately, there should be plenty of time. The mayor here has declared a week-long holiday for all government workers to celebrate their team winning the Lunar League Shovelball championship. That means we can get the trucks serviced—which we have done—but we can't pay the town taxes because the tax office is closed and the local police won't let us leave until we do. See there? They've posted guards."

"That doesn't make sense," Crater said.

"Mayor Trakk is eccentric. He hates the Colonel and every-thing that has anything to do with Moontown. His father was in the Colonel's original party and was dropped off here to build a way station. Something happened—something to do with money, I'm sure—and there was a falling out. Because of that long ago history plus the result of an unfortunate shovel-ball game, we're stuck. All this and we have crowhoppers afoot. Crater, this convoy is well and truly scragged."

And so am I, Crater thought. If the convoy was stuck, he wasn't going to make it to Armstrong City in time to catch the Cycler. He was also doubtful the Colonel would take into account it wasn't his fault. Somehow, Crater knew he had to get the convoy moving, but how? He was just a scout. There had to be a way but, try as he might to come up with an idea, he couldn't come up with a single one.

::: **TWENTY-THREE**

In the dustlock, the Aristillus dustie told Crater, "You leave your suit here and I'll clean it for you. Tube clothes are in a locker in the shower room if you need some. Just tap your convoy code in the puter to rent them."

"I don't have a suit," Crater said. "Just these coveralls." He applied a battery-operated current to the helmet base and removed it. "I'll need a place for this."

The techie took the helmet. "Wearing a biolastic, eh? There's showers in the second dustlock that'll take the sheath off. There's no biolastic server to put one back on, though. You'll have to find an ECP suit."

"No, I won't," Crater said, taking off the shoulder holster holding the gillie and carefully placing it on a bench, then taking off his coveralls and folding them before handing them over. "This sheath stays on. It's good for six months. There's no bio-girdle required either. The sheath opens and closes, um, down there, and knits itself back together after relief."

The techie nodded. "One of the new Deep Space suits. They work well."

Since the dustie was friendly, Crater said, "I'm curious about this holiday for your shovelball team. Who did your team beat?"

"Armstrong City, of course. The Lunar League only has two teams."

"Your team beat the only other team in your league and your mayor declared a weeklong holiday?"

"What's wrong with that?"

"We need to get our heel-3 to market."

The dustie chuckled. "Perhaps you haven't heard. Our mayor is eccentric. Is that a gillie? They're illegal, you know."

"It's also dying," Crater said.

"Don't let the constabulary catch you with it. They'll run you in, sure. They're a rough bunch."

Crater thanked the dustie and carried the gillie into the next dustlock to go through the process of dedusting. After he was scrubbed clean in the water shower, he marveled at how the biolastic sheath was almost a second skin, so thin and supple it was as if he didn't have it on at all. He rented tube clothes, strapped the gillie to his arm, then stepped out into a long corridor that was filled with people wandering this way and that, and poking into the shops that lined the hallway. By the lost and sullen looks of most of the people, Crater was sure a lot of them were stranded drivers.

Crater headed for the clinic, finding Justice in a ward staffed by nurses and doctors in starched whites who were efficiently moving about carrying instruments, bedpans, and medicines. Justice was in a bed with starched white sheets, his head resting on a starched white pillow. Everything inside the clinic tube was so white it hurt Crater's eyes, but he appreciated the obvious attempt to make everything look as antiseptic as he supposed it actually was. Certainly, the air had an antiseptic perfume.

Justice had tubes running in and out of him and was asleep when Crater sat down alongside him. Justice opened his eyes and said, "The lookouts on the south perimeter are ready, Major."

He blinked a few times, then turned his head and smiled in recognition. "Crater. Good to see you, though I just saw you several hours ago. Since then, I've been pinched and prodded and shot full of medicinal bacteria the doctors tell me will soon absorb my pneumonia. Getting some other microbes— perhaps through that yellow tube, I'm not certain—that will soon have me feeling like a sixteen-year-old again. For that I can scarcely wait, as there are several pretty nurses I'd like to chase around the clinic."

"It's good to see you're being cared for so well, sir," Crater said. "I'll go see Pegasus to make certain he is as well."

"You may do that, but I've stayed at Aristillus many a day and the boys in the maintenance shed love that old horse as much as I do. He'll be fine. I'm more concerned about the motorbarn."

"Captain Teller is seeing to its care, sir," Crater said.

"So all is well, all is well."

"Not quite," Crater said and explained that they were all stuck for a while.

Crater was anxious to see to the gillie. Justice sensed Crater's anxiety and waved him along. "Well, get on and let me sleep. If things open up, don't leave without me and the

Peg, promise? We'd like to get on down to Armstrong City and stay there until this crowhopper business gets settled."

"How will that be done?" Crater asked.

"I guarantee you Colonel Medaris will see to it," Justice said. "If this is war, he'll be in his element. He'll pull the other heel-3 towns together, get them organized. They won't like it, but they'll have no choice if these assassins have a larger purpose more than raiding way stations and convoys. Maybe that package you're going after has something to do with it. The Colonel was always a good one for anticipating what the enemy might do."

After talking to the head nurse and making sure she understood that Justice was to be given every medical aid possible, and then having his head handed to him by the nurse who let him know, in no uncertain terms, that *every* patient she and her nurses looked after got the same, *superb* care, he left the clinic and walked through the tubes until he reached the shopping tubes. He wandered around until he found a shop that sold puters and readers, called Clara's Puters & Stuff. The woman at the counter noticed the gillie as soon as Crater walked inside. "My goodness, haven't seen one of those for a very long while! It's illegal, you know."

"It knows that but it's sick," Crater said. "Can you help it?" Then he told her about its encounter with biolastic cellular structure.

"Oh, that Deep Space biolastic bacteria can be a nasty bunch," she clucked. She delicately withdrew the gillie from its holster and laid it down on a cloth on a workbench, then probed it with her finger. Crater watched it squirm and it made him anxious. "Maybe you shouldn't do that," he said.

The woman smiled. "I worked with gillies on Earth. Don't worry. I just wanted to see how much energy it has left. Precious little, I fear. It's very sick but here's what I can do. I can put it in the detox bath I use for polluted bio-diodes. It will either work or kill it."

Crater felt he had no choice. "Go ahead," he said.

She wrapped the gillie in the cloth, then gave Crater a receipt for it. "I'm Clara, by the way. Come back in an hour. We'll know if the bath is going to work by then or not."

Crater went looking for Petro, finding him in a side tube that housed a cafeteria unlike any he'd ever seen. The sign over the entrance announced Olde USA Coffee House. It had big shiny metal cylinders that dispensed something hot into plaston cups. There was a pictogram of some drinks that Crater gradually deduced were types of coffee. Until that very moment in the entire history of his life, Crater had never imagined there was more than one type of coffee or, for that matter, why there needed to be more than one. It didn't make sense. Coffee was to help wake you up and get you going on a scrape and that was about all, as far as he knew. But here were people lined up to get coffee in all kinds of flavors and retreating to small round tables where they sat, sipping the hot drink, and generally doing nothing except staring at their readers. It was all very odd. Petro, sitting with Irish over a deck of cards, waved Crater over.

"Captain Teller briefed us about your adventures," Petro said. "Very well done, but you look kind of glum. What's up?"

Crater told him about the gillie being sick. "How did you get it back?" Petro asked.

Crater gave Petro a condensed version of everything that

had happened since he'd gone off with the Umlaps. Petro looked at Crater with astonishment, then whistled. "Well, Crater, I'd say you've done a few crazy things. I admire that."

"What kind of cafeteria is this?" Crater asked, wanting to get the topic off himself.

"It's not a cafeteria at all. It's a coffee shop like they used to have in the old USA. See the sign and all those kinds of coffee? Pick one out. You can use your convoy number to pay for anything but electronic doodads, clothes, shoes, that kind of thing. Food's covered. Lodging, too, if you can't sleep in your truck."

"We're gonna be stuck here forever," Irish said. "And when the long shadow arrives with us still sleeping in our trucks, if a heater fails, we wake up a big, pink slab of ice."

"You see?" Petro said. "This whole convoy could fall apart any minute."

Crater waited out an hour with gloomy Petro and Irish, feeling more than a little gloomy himself, then looked at the time and said, "Got to go check on the gillie." He ran to the shop, and Clara waved him inside. "The bath did some good, I think," she said and unwrapped the gillie. It immediately got up and crawled into its holster. It still looked limp. "Let me keep it overnight," Clara said. "I'll give it a fresh bath every few hours. No extra charge. I've gotten attached to the little thing."

Crater thanked Clara, used the convoy number to pay her, and walked back to the main corridor. He tossed up a prayer to the Big Miner on behalf of the gillie, even though it was just a biological machine.

Crater next decided to seek out Maria. He wanted to talk to her, to see if this surprising turn-around on how she felt about him was real or a dream. Along the way, he encountered a group of women and children who were wearing red and black robes that draped their bodies from their necks to their ankles. After a second look, Crater realized they were Umlaps. The facial features of the women and children were softer than the men's harsh angularities and they seemed a bit taller than their men, but Umlaps they were for certain. The children appeared to all be girls, none more than eight years old by Crater's estimate, huddled within the knot of women and looking out with wide, frightened eyes.

The Umlap women had big hands, short legs, no ears, and long arms, physical characteristics expected of Umlaps, but Crater was struck by how normal the children looked, if normal was the right word to use. Their limbs were the proper ratios, and their ears, the ones he could see, seemed to be just like any other attached to a human child.

The Umlaps were peering into various shops, then consulting with each other before wandering on to the next shop, buying nothing. Finally, the women sat down on some mooncrete benches in the center of the tube, the children sitting in their laps or hanging on to their shoulders, and just stared at people as they went past. Crater wondered what they were doing at Aristillus, then supposed that was as far as they had gotten after running away from Baikal.

Petro came strolling along and stopped beside Crater. "What pathetic creatures," he said. "I meant to tell you they were here, seeing as how you did away with their king. As a potential king myself, I think perhaps you went a bit too far."

"I didn't do away with their king. Bad Haircut did that. Why are they here?"

"The truck they drove from Baikal broke down about a mile away. They abandoned it and walked here."

"They look scared."

"They should be," a woman shopkeeper said, stepping outside her store. "From what I've heard, they've had a lifetime of being beaten and generally abused by their men. Now they're getting another fresh dose of abuse. Mayor Trakk has slapped a fine on them for every day they're here. He expects their men to pay for their return."

Petro said to the shopkeeper, "My brother killed the Umlap king, so I imagine they won't be paying anything."

"I did no such thing," Crater said. "I tried to help the king."

"And where is he now?"

"Dead."

"I rest my case."

The shopkeeper clucked her tongue, shook her head at the strange outlanders who'd washed up in her hometown, and went back inside her shop.

Crater watched the Umlap women and children and wished there was something he could do to ease their burden. After a while, he realized some of the women were begging from passersby, all of whom were hurrying past without even glancing their way. "They're hungry," Crater said, alarmed.

Petro shrugged. "Just ignore them, Crater. They're not your problem."

The way Crater saw it, they were as much his problem as anyone else's. He walked down the corridor until he reached a shop with a sign that said Meal In A Box. He checked with its manager, then went back to where the Umlaps were sitting.

He didn't quite know what to say, but one of the women gave him a hard look. "Look, girls," she said in Umlap, "this one likes to stare at our misery."

"We should grab him for ransom," another of the women said. "Perhaps someone would feed us if we let him go."

"My name is Crater," Crater said in Umlap to the first woman who had spoken.

She was taller than the rest, her robe slightly cleaner, and she wore a cap on her head that was black with red piping like Wise Beyond Belief's cap. "How do you know Umlap?" she demanded.

"There are Umlap miners in Moontown, my home. They taught me and I am a quick study. Also, I was recently in Baikal."

"Were you?" Her eyes narrowed. "We escaped from those evil men there who chained us to our beds at night and whipped us when it suited them, which was most of the time."

"I'm very sorry to hear that," Crater said. He hesitated, then said, "King Wise Beyond Belief and his assistant, Hit Your Face, are dead. So is Bad Haircut."

This news caused nearly all the women to frown, which meant, of course, they were happy. But then, perhaps upon reflection, they began to smile, and tears leaked slowly down their faces, for even the backward Umlap expressions couldn't change that physical reaction. The children, sensing something terrible had happened, started to wail.

"Why did you tell them that?" the woman with the black and red cap scolded. "Those men, as awful as they were, were Umlaps."

"It was the truth," Crater said.

"Do you think it so virtuous to tell someone the truth even though it will ruin what little happiness they have?"

Crater thought that over, then said, "But you would have found out eventually."

"But not so soon. Therefore, you are responsible for their present unhappiness." She eyed him until her anger seemed to subside. "My name is Queen No Nonsense Talker. My husband, Thinking Great Thoughts, was the king before Wise Beyond Belief killed him and took over. Thinking Great Thoughts was not a good king either. He allowed many evil things to happen."

Crater pointed at the shop. "If you and the others are hungry, go there and get what you need. I gave them my convoy number."

The queen pondered Crater. "And what do you get out of this sudden charity?"

"Nothing. Do you want the food?"

"Yes, of course. We've been eating out of garbage cans."

"Then please be my guest."

The Umlap queen grimaced and stood up, saying, "Ladies, this kind stranger, for reasons I'm not certain, is offering us and our daughters food. If we go over to that shop and get what we want, he says he's willing to pay for it."

Actually, it was the Colonel paying through his convoy number, but Crater couldn't imagine he would mind, considering his generous spirit. The women and children headed for the shop. Crater followed them, reminded the proprietor of the convoy number, and watched while the Umlaps were handed meals in little paper boxes whereupon they retreated to the benches to eat.

Petro, who'd been watching, came over. "The Colonel is going to love paying for this," he said, chuckling.

"Leave me alone," Crater said.

Petro shrugged. "I've got a card game in the casino anyway." He walked away.

Crater sat with the women and their daughters and enjoyed watching them eat. All the while, he considered their situation, and being a sequential thinker, he gradually resolved in his mind what they should do. When they were finished eating, the women tidied up the area, threw all the boxes in the trash receptacles, and the queen came over and sat in front of him, her hands on her knees, and regarded him carefully and deeply.

"Are you looking for a bride?" she asked. "I'm thirty-eight but still healthy. I have had my one girl child so would not burden you with raising another since she is already grown."

"What do you mean you've had your one girl child?"

"Umlap women can have but one child, always daughters. After that, we become sterile."

"Why is that?"

"I don't know. Something in the way we were engineered. But look there. See that young woman?"

Crater looked and saw a young Umlap woman looking back at him with hopeful eyes.

"That is my daughter. She is a normal human being, and it may be she can have more than one daughter. She might be more suitable to you for a wife than me."

"I don't need a wife," Crater said, then processed the other thing the Umlap queen had said. "What do you mean your daughter's a normal human being?"

The queen glanced lovingly at her daughter, then said, "The men who made us did so by modifying our DNA while we were still in egg form. It changed us to be as we are but did not change our progeny. Perhaps you are familiar with the dinochicken that these doctors invented before us, the dinosaur made from a chicken egg? Two of the dinochickens mated, an egg was laid, but out did not come a dinochicken but a normal chicken. We are the same except, of course, we aren't dinochickens. We are humans."

"Yet you can only have one daughter."

"Yes," the queen mused. "That part we do not understand. I don't think the men who made us understood it either. There is so much more to us than DNA, or protein, or nerve endings, or anything else. There is something that is beyond matter."

"You mean your spirit," Crater said. "Or maybe your soul."

"Yes," she said and, though her expression didn't change, Crater could tell she was crying inside. Perhaps all the Umlaps were crying inside, including their poor men who were self-destructive, because they could not find their souls within the bodies and minds constructed for them by other men. All Crater could conclude was he was glad the laboratory that had made the Umlaps had been burned down.

"You seem lost in thought," the queen said.

Crater focused on the situation at hand. "I've been thinking over your problem. Why don't you travel to Moontown? The Colonel has always been happy to hire Umlaps."

"It is where we actually meant to go," the queen admitted, "but we weren't sure of the way and ended up here."

"You should have turned left at the dustway, not right," Crater said.

"The men never allowed us to study a map," the queen answered, brushing her hair out of her eyes. She, like the other Umlap women, had thick, black, lustrous hair.

Crater looked around at the truck drivers listlessly wandering the shopping corridor or picking around the shops. "Heel-3 trucks have an extra seat. You could ride on them to Moontown or whatever heel-3 town suits you."

"And what payment would these drivers take?"

She had him there. The drivers were, after all, independent contractors. "They would want to get paid," he conceded.

That was when Captain Teller showed up. He pulled Crater away from the women. "Please tell me you didn't feed them with our convoy number."

"I fed them with our convoy number," Crater said.

Teller's face, already pinched, pinched some more. "You are insubordinate, Crater, the worst scout I've ever had. If it wasn't for your mechanical ability, I would have fired you long ago. The Colonel will have both our hides for this expenditure."

"I'm sorry, sir," Crater said, though he knew he didn't sound very convincing.

"Come to think of it," Teller said, "the solution is simple. It will come out of your pay."

Pay was something Crater had never asked about, was uncertain would occur, and had no clue to the amount. "That's fine, Captain," he said.

"Why did you do it?" Teller demanded. "I am a bit of a student of human folly and think I could get a college degree just by studying you."

"I felt sorry for these poor women. Besides, I told them the Colonel would hire them."

Captain Teller coughed, then choked on his cough. "You did *what?*"

Crater couldn't figure out why the captain was so upset. "There's a labor shortage at Moontown."

The captain struggled to regain some semblance of control. "Perhaps so, Crater. But you can't just go around promising jobs from the Colonel. You have to get permission first. Why don't you understand these things?"

"The Moontown preachers always said I should do the right thing."

"Promising that the Colonel will hire these women is not the right thing!"

Maria arrived at that moment, got the gist of the conversation, pondered the women and their daughters, went over to have a closer look, then came back. "They are somewhat smelly," she announced. "That is a problem that needs to be addressed."

"I've been thinking about that too," Crater said. "Suppose we got some rooms and allowed them to wash and launder their clothes. Then maybe our drivers won't charge much to take them with us to Armstrong City and then back to Moontown."

"*With us?*" The captain choked again.

"Those robes can't be laundered," Maria said. "They should be burned. We'll need to buy them some new clothes."

Crater smiled at Maria, pleased that she had joined his project. Captain Teller, however, was still a long way from joining anything, especially anything that Crater had thought up. "Look, Maria," Teller said, "if you want this to come out of your grandfather's hide, then I can't stop you. It's your family that would be hurt. But I urge you to think this over."

Before Maria could reply, there came the piercing shriek of a whistle, and Crater, Maria, and Teller turned toward it in time to see the Umlap women pluck up their robes, gather their daughters about them, and start to run, though there was nowhere to go except into the shops. The shop owners quickly shooed them out and pulled down metal screens. Then three men in uniforms—Aristillus police, obviously—came charging out of an adjoining tube, one of them blowing a whistle as if his very life depended on how loud and irritating he could blow it. The women and children ran over to Crater and crouched behind him as the constables thundered up. One of them pointed his baton at Crater. "Boy, remove yourself so we might arrest these women."

Crater looked over his shoulder at the crouched Umlaps, then said, "Why would you arrest them?"

"Because they are a public nuisance," the officer said.

"They don't seem to be bothering anyone," Crater replied.

The officer lowered his baton, squinted at Crater, then assumed a relaxed posture. "Ah, so you want to debate. All right, I always enjoy a good one. Here is my postulate. It is quite possible to be a nuisance whether one is bothering anyone or not. Also, the mayor has proclaimed these women and their progeny officially as a public nuisance. He has also decided that they must pay what they owe the city or depart. As the police force, we therefore must arrest them or we break our oath. Over to you."

Crater searched around in his mind for a good answer but Maria beat him to it, although with a question. "How can they leave or pay a fine?" she asked. "They have neither money nor transportation."

"Then they should acquire both," the officer said.

This was too much for even Captain Teller. "That's a sentence of death," he said before adding, "and I know who you are . . . Mayor Trakk!"

Behind Crater, in a small, terrified voice, the queen said in Umlap, "Please help us. We will do whatever you say."

It broke Crater's heart to see the queen so reduced as to beg a mere boy, even if it was him, for help. He sorted through the possibilities, then said, after glancing at Maria and Captain Teller, "We have discussed renting them rooms so they would not have to wander your tubes. They wouldn't be nuisances then, would they?"

The mayor gave that some thought, then said, "No hotelier would be willing to rent to Umlaps."

"I'll bet I can find one that will," Maria said.

"More money spent," Captain Teller moaned.

The mayor and sometimes policeman eyed Maria, then the Umlap women, before his eyes lit on the queen. "Since clearly none of you here know the rules of debate, I am therefore bored and see no reason to continue this discussion. All right, men, move forward and escort these women and their kids outside. Alert the dustlocks to have their ECP suits ready."

Crater improvised. "Mayor, is it true your shovelball team is amateurish and bush-league?"

The mayor and the two officers froze, their mouths unhinged at the affront. "We are the champions of the Lunar League!" the mayor cried.

Crater shrugged. "A league with but two teams. You're bound to come in first or second. How would you like to have a match with the drivers of our convoy? I'm certain even a pickup team would clean your Aristillus clocks."

This provoked a round of laughter from the mayor and the officers. "Play shovelball with a bunch of dustway drivers? It would be no contest!"

"Oh, well, if you're scared of losing, I understand . . ."

"Give me one good reason why we should play," the mayor said.

"A wager," Maria said.

Still improvising, Crater added, "If we win, we pay our taxes and leave. Right away, no waiting for a week, but within the hour. And we take the Umlap women with us. And they'll owe no fines."

The mayor narrowed his eyes. "And what would we receive should we win, which, of course, we will?"

"One percent of the value of our heel-3 load," Crater said.

"Are you crazy?" Captain Teller screamed.

"Ten," the mayor said.

"It's not going to happen, Crater!" Teller exclaimed. "You have no right. *We* have no right."

"Three," Crater said.

"No, no, no!" the captain yelled.

"Five and it's agreed," the mayor said.

When Teller started to protest again, Maria said, "It's all right, Captain. I'll explain it to Grandfather if our team loses. Anyway, we first have to lose—which hasn't happened yet and I don't think it will."

"But I'm responsible for this convoy!" Teller sputtered.

"A convoy that's stuck and going nowhere," Maria pointed out.

"We play rough in Aristillus, Missy," Mayor Trakk growled.

"My drivers will beat you and the other fat men on your pathetic team like a drum," Maria replied.

Maria's words were like vinegar in a wound to the mayor and his officers, who reacted with flushed faces. "We'll meet at nineteen hundred hours at the arena," the mayor said before he and his men stalked off.

"What is to happen to us?" Queen No Nonsense Talker asked.

Crater explained the situation as best he could and the queen considered the plan, before asking, "Can you beat them?"

Crater didn't have a certain answer. First, he had a shovel-ball team to recruit, train, and field, all in little more than eight hours.

::: TWENTY-FOUR

etro looked up from his cards. He had several stacks of chips in front of him, more than anyone else at the table. "Play a shovelball game with a bunch of pickup players and expect to win against a championship team? Are you nuts?"

"I need you. You're a great player."

"True, but I've gotten old and stiff."

"You're only nineteen."

"I'm mature for my age. It's a genetic thing for we royals."

"I'm going to take that as a yes," Crater said. "So it's you, me, and Maria. Who else can we get?"

Petro looked Crater up and down to see if he was serious and concluded that, unfortunately, he was. He raised the other poker players, they all dropped out, and he raked in his winnings. "Gentlemen, I'm cashing in."

"Good thing," one of the other players said. "Give the rest of us a chance."

Petro clapped Crater on the back as they walked out of

the bar. "Typical Crater, a lunar Don Quixote out to save some Umlap women nobody gives a fig about. Well, all right, brother, I'll be your Sancho Panza. How about Captain Teller? He's been known to play a round or two of shovelball. Tell you what. I'll recruit a couple of players for you. You go after Captain Teller."

Crater went after Teller, finding him coming back into town after checking the trucks. "Maybe we should make a run for it," he said. "All we need is a distraction of some kind."

"If we win the shovelball game," Crater reminded him, "the mayor has promised to let us pay the tax and go."

"We can't win."

"How can you be so sure? I mean, we're playing not just for ourselves but for the Umlap women and children too. I recall the preacher saying when you do the right thing, there's always a reward."

"I recall that sermon," Teller said. "I was in Moontown picking up a convoy. The good reverend also said that we wouldn't always recognize the reward and sometimes it wouldn't come until we're in heaven. It was a perplexing sermon. I reflected on it and came up short."

"It's still the right thing to do," Crater said.

Teller took on an expression of disappointment. "Crater, I'll say it again. You're too soft. I've tried my best to toughen you up but I've gotten nowhere."

"Does that mean you'll play?"

Teller sighed. "I suppose I have no choice. I have a couple of helmets and shovels in the chuckwagon. You can buy the rest of the gear with our convoy number."

Crater grinned. "Thanks, Captain!"

"Don't mention it," he said. "And I mean that. Don't mention it!"

Crater went looking for Maria to tell her the news. A convoy driver said he'd seen her with the Umlaps, shepherding them into the Starland Hotel. Crater ran through the tubes until he found the hotel marked by a sign over a hatch. He entered it, finding himself in the shabby lobby of Aristillus's finest lodgings. Marching up to the counter, he was about to ask after Maria and the Umlap ladies just as an inner hatch opened and out came a basket of faded, dirty, multicolored robes carried by a bellman who wrinkled his nose. "Take those rags outside and bury them!" the counter clerk ordered, then turned to Crater. "What might I do for you, young sir?"

Crater pointed at the bellman. "Where are the women who were wearing those?"

"Room 107," the clerk said with a sniff. "Surely you're not with those filthy creatures."

"I'm just helping out."

"Then tell the witch who brought them into my hotel that she will be responsible for any damages. That includes cleaning out my grease trap."

Crater grabbed the clerk's tie and drew him across the counter. The clerk made choking sounds, mostly because he *was* choking. "That witch, as you call her," Crater said, "is Miss Maria Medaris, the granddaughter of Colonel John High Eagle Medaris himself."

The clerk tried to say something but nothing came out except gasps and gulps until Crater released him. "My apologies to her and to you, young sir," he rasped. "Room 107, sir. Thank you for choosing the Starland Hotel!"

Crater hadn't chosen the Starland Hotel, but he recognized that he and the hotel clerk had completed their business. He went through the hatch and down the corridor until he found the room. Along the way, he reflected how he had, without really thinking about it, grabbed the prissy hotel clerk's tie. He felt bad about that. On the other hand, maybe he was finally learning to be strong like everybody kept telling him he was supposed to be. On the other-other hand, he supposed he could overdo it. He would have thought more about it but he didn't have time. He knocked on the door marked 107, got no answer, and knocked a little harder. The door opened and one of the Umlap women peeked around the door and said, "You can't come in. We are bathing."

Crater looked past her and briefly saw several Umlap women—nothing but towels wrapped around them—scurrying past before the door was slammed in his face. Blushing furiously, Crater stood there astonished.

::: TWENTY-FIVE

The shovelball rules were simple enough, derived as they were from the ancient Irish game known— perhaps unfortunately, considering the term had a double meaning—as hurling. Since Irishmen and Irishwomen were among the first heel-3 miners, they brought the game with them, modified for the moon's light gravity and the equipment that was available. At first, the playing fields were maintenance sheds. Later, most of the towns built shovelball fieldhouses with rubberized floors and ceilings for increased traction.

The object of the game was for players to use shovels to hit a ball, four inches in diameter, into the opponents' goal. Goals were round nets six feet in diameter and set halfway up the wall at each end of the field. Full pipe ramps were at midfield. By running through the pipe, players could travel to the roof of the court where they could advance the ball until they lost momentum and fell to the floor.

There were several ways to advance the ball. One was to

hit the ball with the front or the back of the shovel. Four steps were allowed before it had to be batted away. The ball could also be batted by an open hand, usually for short-range passing. A player could run with the ball, but during the run, the ball had to be bounced on the player's shovel, something exceedingly difficult to do in the light gravity. Serious players, however, practiced hard until they mastered the maneuver.

The fieldhouse arena began to fill with spectators. The game was the only entertainment in town, and the Aristillus team was obviously very popular. On the scoreboard, the legend read Aristillus Aces versus Moontown Truckers.

Petro showed up with two players. One of them was Irish, and another fellow Irishman named Claddy. Irish and Claddy immediately sat down on the sidelines. Crater thought they looked sick or drunk or both. "Do they even know how to play?" Crater asked.

"Irish and Claddy were on the Irish national hurling team until they got kicked off for cheating."

"Cheating?"

"They took a bribe."

"You mean they threw a game?"

"Pretty much."

"Leave it to you to recruit untrustworthy felons for my team."

"What do you care? They play like gods."

"Up the Irish, down the English," Claddy grunted.

"You see?" Petro grinned. "Full of spirit, these lads."

Crater was dubious. Irish and Claddy had stopped sitting and were lying down, their arms across their eyes. "Right now, it looks like they'd have trouble standing up. In fact, they look like they're about to hurl."

Petro looked around. "You're short a man. Where's Maria?"

"I don't know. She said she'd be here."

Carlos, his arthritis affecting his knees, limped up. "Message from Maria. She's still cleaning up the Umlap women."

"Great," Crater grumped, then pondered Carlos. "All right, Carlos, you're in the game."

"Me? I can't play."

"You're all I got."

Carlos shook his head. "Then you don't have much, son."

The Aces had cheerleaders, a dozen or so young women in tight outfits. Their cheers were so loud it was hard to hear when the teams met in the center of the field. Since the referees were naturally from Aristillus, Crater knew the Moontown Truckers weren't going to get a fair shake, but it didn't worry him too much. Since just about anything went in lunar shovelball, except deliberately beating the opposing players with shovels, the referees had little to do other than hand the ball over and get out of the way.

"Give up now," Mayor Trakk said to Crater, "and you won't be humiliated."

"Get ready to take a whipping," Crater snorted, though he had his doubts. Compared to the Truckers, the Aces were huge and looked fast.

The referee reminded the teams of the few rules, then flipped a coin. Crater called it and lost, a harbinger he feared of what was to come. The teams lined up. Crater swatted the ball downfield with his shovel and the game was on.

An Ace caught the ball on his shovel and started running,

then swatted it with amazing strength, bouncing it off the roof. Another Ace emerged from the pipe onto the roof and swatted it farther up the field. The mayor, who was also the team captain, leapt high, caught the ball with one hand, and tapped it to another of his players who slapped it back. Teller leapt after it and missed, Petro leapt at it and missed, and the mayor powered it into the goal. Six points.

Crater noticed that neither Irish nor Claddy had moved much from where they'd started. He trotted over to them where they were lethargically looking at the cheerleaders. "Have you forgotten how to play this game?"

Petro came to their defense. "They just need to get warmed up."

"What about you?"

"I told you I was old and stiff."

Scoring teams had the option of going one-on-one for three points or using three players against one opposing player for one point. The Aces easily took the single point against Crater.

The Aces swatted the ball to the Truckers who fumbled it away, and the Aces quickly scored, again taking the extra point. Then the same thing happened again. Only minutes into the game, the Truckers were behind by twenty-one points.

Captain Teller walked over to Crater. "What are you going to do?"

"I'm going to suggest we play harder," Crater said.

Teller looked around at the other Truckers. They were all, including Petro, admiring the cheerleaders. "Maybe you ought to tell them your superb plan."

Crater gathered his team. "Look, fellows," he said. "We've got to set up a pattern. Irish and Claddy, I'm looking to you to get us downfield. Captain Teller, you run along the sidelines, get ready to receive. I'm the center man. Petro, guard the goal. Carlos, try not to have a heart attack."

"These guys are good," Irish said, and Claddy nodded agreement.

"You're supposed to be good too," Crater replied.

About then, Crater heard a weak cheer and looked over his shoulder and saw the Umlap women and children were the source. The women were dressed in new skirts and blouses, the daughters in coveralls. Their hair was washed and combed and glistened in the lights of the stadium. "Listen to them," Crater said. "They haven't given up."

"Who are they?" Irish asked while Claddy also studied the women.

Crater told the two Irishmen who they were. "I didn't know we were playing this game for them," Claddy said.

"Does that mean you might play harder?" Crater asked.

"Of course," Irish said. "An Irishman always helps the ladies. That's the way we roll."

Crater had renewed hope, especially since Maria trotted on the field, replacing Carlos. "Let's do this," she said.

The Aces shoveled off to the Truckers. Irish received it and Claddy ran up the ramp, whipped through the pipe, and emerged on the roof. Irish tossed Claddy the ball who shoveled it in, slung it across to Captain Teller who hit it downfield. Crater caught it on his shovel, bounced it for a fast run, then shot it to Petro who leapt to catch it, and shoveled it to Maria who slammed it past Ace's goalie. *Score!*

Two more times the Truckers scored, picking up the extra points. By the third and final period, the score was tied, 21–21.

Crater was sure the Truckers had the momentum, but the Aces came roaring back, keeping the ball on the roof as they ran up the ramp, bursting out and slamming the ball into the goal. They got the extra point and were ahead by seven points.

The clock was ticking down. The Truckers tried a desperate maneuver, all of them racing to the roof and shoveling the ball between them as they fell to the floor. As soon as his feet touched the field, Claddy ran up the tube, caught the ball while performing a flip, and drove it into the goal. If they went after the single point, the game would be tied up again.

Crater chose to go for the win, one-on-one. Mayor Trakk was the goalie, Irish the attacker. Irish came running at the ball, scooped it up, leapt with it, and swung halfway. The mayor threw himself to where the ball would have gone except Irish deliberately missed it, spun all the way around, switching his shovel to his left hand to bat the ball in the opposite direction. At one hundred and fifty miles per hour, Mayor Trakk had no chance to recover. The Truckers were ahead 30–28.

The clock ran down, the buzzer sounded, and the Truckers ran off the field, holding their shovels aloft in triumph. At the sidelines, Crater was hugged by the Umlap women, all of whom smelled sweet and looked marvelous—the power of soap and water.

Crater and Captain Teller walked over to have a word with the mayor to see if he was going to keep his end of the bargain. Mayor Trakk reluctantly shook their hands. "I think you had some ringers in those two Irish lads. And the girl. The Colonel's granddaughter? She's a terror."

"Yes, she is," Teller said. "Now, can we pay our taxes and leave? And take the Umlap women with us?"

"You may not think much of how we run things here," the mayor said, "but we don't renege on a bet."

Captain Teller grinned and went off to get things organized. The queen came over, and the mayor couldn't take his eyes off her. "Would you mind introducing us, Crater?" He added, "I'm a bachelor, you know."

Crater saw no harm in it, so he introduced the mayor to the queen who shyly batted her eyes.

"May I offer you dinner, madam?" Mayor Trakk asked.

Queen Talks No Nonsense frowned deeply, then said, "You may, indeed. I think we have much to discuss."

And off they went, arm in arm, across the field while Crater watched incredulously. Petro sidled up next to him and Crater said, "Just when I think I've got them figured out, I discover I don't know a thing about women."

"Who does?" Petro replied. "They are the strangest creatures there are. Give me a deck of cards anytime. You might lose your money but at least you keep your mind."

Captain Teller was gathering his drivers from the stands, herding them toward the dustlock to get their trucks ready to go. "Two hours!" he yelled. "Two hours and we're on the road!"

Petro joined the others while Crater headed for the dispensary to say good-bye to Mr. Justice.

::: TWENTY-SIX

The convoy moved out in the desired two hours, including the motorbarn with a revived Ellis Justice at the wheel and a rested Pegasus in his domicile. When Crater went to the clinic, he found Justice's bed empty and the head nurse flustered. She even had a tendril of hair hanging from beneath her perfectly starched cap, although it was slightly askew. "Mister Justice said he had a convoy to catch," she said. "I told him he was still too ill to go anywhere. Then he took my hand and kissed it and told me I was the most beautiful woman he'd ever seen and that he intended to return and marry me." She put her hand to her cheek. "Then he kissed me on my cheek and was off. When do you think he might return?"

Crater didn't know when and said so, then went off to Clara's to see how the gillie was faring. "It's still sick," Clara said, handing it over wrapped in a blue kerchief. "But I think I perceive a little more life in it."

"Has it said anything?"

"It said your name and Armstrong City before lapsing back into its little coma. What you should do is keep it warm and hope for the best. It's a sweet gillie for a gillie. Otherwise, I'm sure it's untrustworthy as they all are."

"That's why they're illegal," Crater said in unison with Clara, then headed for the convoy in time to see Justice walking Pegasus up the ramp into the motorbarn.

"The head nurse said you were too sick to leave, Mister Justice," Crater said while he helped get Pegasus comfortable.

"Ah, isn't she a pretty thing?" Justice chuckled. "I was always a sap for a woman in uniform. Anyway, the Peg and I need to get on back to Armstrong City. We'll stay there until this crowhopper business is sorted out."

Crater removed the plaston girdle from Pegasus and placed it in the sanitizer. "I hope you're right about the Colonel taking care of those crowhoppers."

"Well, he's a capitalist of the old order, the kind that builds companies and, if need be, nations too," Justice replied. "You could do worse than hitching your star to him."

Crater thought about that, then said, "If you ever need somebody to work for you and the Peg, sir, please think of me."

Justice beamed and nodded his shaggy head. "Aye, I will, son. You'd make a fine addition, and I know Pegasus would love to have you around. Tell you what. When we get to Armstrong City, I'll have a talk with Deep Space Suits. But for now, are you going to be able to make the Cycler?"

"If all goes well from here, yes."

"Good. A man should honor a promise made."

Crater left the motorbarn, feeling a little dazed. He hadn't meant to ask Justice for a job but it had just popped out. And now that it had, he felt good about it. Maybe his life wasn't on the Moontown scrapes after all. But if that proved true, it didn't change his determination to get to the Cycler on time. And take care of Maria.

The convoy moved away from Aristillus, all the trucks in fine condition, the drivers in good moods, but Captain Teller was worried as always. Crater and Maria zipped ahead on the scout. The long shadow was coming inexorably at them but nothing could be done about that. Above might be crowhoppers but the convoy was moving, and that was all that counted. Ahead lay the Russians' Sea of Serenity and then the Ocean of Tranquility. Once there, the convoy would make the dash to Armstrong City.

The Umlap women and their daughters had all hitched rides in various trucks. The women proved to not only be excellent drivers but required little sleep. It didn't take long before the drivers were arguing over who got the women in their cabs. The deciding factor eventually was who paid the women the most.

The one exception was Queen No Nonsense Talker who had decided to stay in Aristillus, a guest of the mayor who had promised to put together a little army and march on Baikal to reclaim the town for the queen. Crater was confident she would do fine.

The dustway and the surrounding plain turned dark gray, then black as coal. The volcanic dust filtered into hubs, wheels, axles, and gears and poured over the trucks, scouring their paint, even seeping inside the cabs. Suits and helmets were required.

Teller pushed the convoy past Linné, an impact crater that

was nearly a perfect circle three miles in diameter. Its bowl was a quarter-mile deep and its ejecta was milk white. Well ahead of the convoy, Crater and Maria had time to climb its lip, marveling at the perfection of the impact.

Then they sat on the lip and scanned the dustway southward. That was when Crater spotted the glint of something metallic in the sky. With the long shadow approaching, the sun was low and the silvery flash was just for an instant. It could have been anything, but he couldn't shake his fear that it might be a jumpcar containing crowhoppers. Maria patted the rifle Crater had given her and said, "We'll fight them off if they come." Her smile was proud. "Whoever hired them must really hate my grandfather. I imagine those creatures don't come cheap, but we'll get our heel-3 through."

"I don't think they're after our heel-3," Crater said. "I think they're assassins."

"Really? Who are they trying to assassinate?"

"Maybe me."

Crater half expected Maria to laugh. Instead, she took on a thoughtful expression. When she didn't say anything, Crater became suspicious. "Do you know the real reason I'm on this convoy?"

"Of course. I'm a Medaris. We keep no secrets in our family. And I think you may be right. The crowhoppers could very well be trying to kill you."

"How would they know about me?"

"There are spies everywhere."

"And who hired them? Do you know that?"

Maria hesitated, then said, "There are a number of candidates. General Nero, for instance. He opposes the monorail, but he's not the only one. There are organizations on Earth who'd like to come up here and take over. The monorail would show that we're in charge of our own destiny. It would only be the first one too. Grandfather plans on eventually linking all the towns together with a network of monorails."

Crater had sudden insight. "That would put him in control of all transportation on the moon!"

Maria shrugged. "Who better?"

Crater thought it over and reached no conclusion except for one. "If the crowhoppers are after me, why doesn't the Colonel send a jumpcar to carry me to Armstrong City? I know his is broken but he could hire another one."

"You don't understand, Crater."

"Enlighten me."

Maria sighed. "Look, two men assigned by my grandfather to pick up the package have already been murdered in Armstrong City. It's impossible to keep you safe there. We think the convoy's still the best place for you to be, even with the crowhoppers around. At least we don't have to worry about an elk sticker in your back. Anyway, we don't know for sure they're onto you. It may be the crowhoppers were hired to keep Moontown's heel-3 off the market. Who knows? We've decided to just keep you where you are."

"Who's this 'we' you keep talking about?"

"My family, Crater. We need that package to be delivered."

Crater was beginning to feel like a pawn in a game he was just beginning to understand was being played. "Do you know what I'm to pick up?" he asked.

Maria bit her lip, then said, "Yes, but I don't think you should know. If you were captured . . ."

"If I was captured, they might torture the truth out of me. Is that it?"

"Yes. I'm sorry, Crater."

"But don't they already know?"

"We don't know what they know."

Crater didn't know what to say or do. He'd never been caught up in such a web of lies.

Maria provided a possibility of what to do. "I think it's time we shared a kiss."

"We're wearing space helmets," Crater pointed out.

"Remember what we almost did when we raced? Let's give it a try for real this time."

This they did, pushing their helmets together and kissing the plaston between their lips. "I really like you, Crater," she said.

"I really like you too," he replied, wanting to say much more.

"Come on," she said, laughing. She pushed off the rim, sliding on her backpack all the way down until she ended up beside her fastbug. Crater did the same, the ejecta powder slippery as wax. He spun around and around and slid into her. She laughed, got up, dusted herself off, and jumped into her fastbug, spinning wheels as she drove back onto the dustway.

Crater watched after Maria, his heart singing, then hurried to catch her. But then he stopped and gave everything some thought. He concluded he was in deep scrag. The Medaris family had decided he should be on the convoy, even though they knew he could be killed. Lies of omission had definitely been told, and Maria was probably in on every one of them. He'd have to think about that. Or maybe he'd get killed before he could think about much of anything.

It worried him, either way.

::: TWENTY-SEVEN

The dustway went past the crater named Bessel, where there was a small inn and way station. Captain Teller called for a brief halt to allow the solar panels to soak up the last rays of the sun before the long shadow claimed its victory for two weeks. To give Pegasus some exercise, Crater had ridden him all day, the warhorse easily keeping up with Maria in her fastbug. Crater even allowed her to ride and was astonished to see how she took to the saddle. "I'm not a moon rube like you, boy," she said as Pegasus leapt over the small craters that covered the ground at the approaches to Bessel. "I learned to ride when I was but a child and on horses not so polite as Pegasus, but mean little vicious horses anxious to throw their riders off and stomp them to death."

Crater wasn't certain if Maria was kidding or not although he suspected she was. In any case, she was a good rider and the Peg seemed to enjoy having her in the saddle. His leaps were almost like flying with Maria urging him on. Crater was pleased to be the link between them.

The convoy crossed into the long shadow when it entered

the Dorsa Lister hills, a corrugated terrain of low mounds and shallow valleys. Sensing trouble, Crater put Pegasus back into the motorbarn, and he and Maria went back to their fastbugs.

In the darkness, it was excruciating driving for the scouts as they strained their eyes for cracks or boulders in the road. Crater also tried to watch the sky. He saw occasional lights but they were unidentifiable. Possibly, they were merely the flash of sunlight off the solar panels of satellites or jumpcars traveling out to the heel-3 towns.

The dustway turned east, preparatory to rounding Plinius and going southerly to Plinius Village, the town that rested at its base. If it could safely be reached, the convoy would only have a short run to Armstrong City and the next phase of Crater's journey.

Captain Teller brought up the rear in the chuckwagon, shepherding the trucks and their precious cargo along. He was uncommonly happy. It had been a rough run, but with Plinius Village only a few hours away, he could almost taste the end of perhaps his last convoy. The glow on the horizon told its story, of the town ahead, of a day of rest, of a chance to talk to the Colonel and give him the good news that very soon his heel-3 and the boy would be delivered on time.

And then, there it was, Plinius Village in their sights. Maria led the way into the parking area with Crater dropping back to run along the length of the convoy, whooping the good news. The drivers whooped with him and the Umlap women trilled their tongues. "Settle down, people," Teller called on the common freq. "Let's act like we've done this before."

The trucks were parked, and the maintenance crews from Plinius Village swarmed over them. Crater stayed behind to talk to the mechanics about repairs that needed to be made. A few hours later, he entered the Plinius Village tubes, which were not tubes at all but big geodesic domes. Beneath the largest dome, there was a park with real trees and flowers and winding bricked paths. Crater had never smelled air so sweet and cool. He walked along the path with the gillie, still silent and still in the holster on his arm.

"So, this is where you're hiding out." It was Maria walking into the dome. She inhaled deeply. "Oh my! It smells like Earth in here!"

"Is this what Earth really smells like?" Crater asked.

"In those places where nature has its way, yes."

Maria linked her arm in his. "I have a surprise. I've decided to go aboard the Cycler with you. We'll pick up the package together."

Crater didn't like the sound of that. "I think it's too dangerous."

"I doubt seriously the Cycler will be more dangerous than this convoy. Anyway, I'll be your bodyguard."

Crater shook his head. "But—" which was all he got to say, mainly because Maria wrapped her arms around him and kissed him, this time with no plaston between them.

"We'll make it fun," she said and walked off, waving at him over her shoulder.

The kiss had been like an electric shock to Crater followed by paralysis. Then, to his delight, the gillie crawled out of its holster to lie on his shoulder. It still looked tired and sick, if it could look any way at all, but it stared without eyes at him and the plants and the flowers and the geodesic dome, then crawled back into its holster and went very still.

::: **TWENTY-EIGHT**

The convoy plunged on into the darkness, Plinius Village miles behind, trillions of stars crowding the sky, the dustway a pale white track through the gray dust of the Ocean of Tranquility. Crater, far ahead on the scout, trundled down the dustway with Arago Crater passing to his right. On its rim blinked the lights of a communications tower.

When the flechettes hit, Crater at first thought it was rocks being thrown up by the wheels of his fastbug. But then a shot burst through the dust shield, just missing him. He wheeled off the dustway, skirted a small crater, then came around again while unholstering his rifle.

He used his helmet starlight scope to look in the direction he thought the flechettes had come and caught sight of a crowhopper dodging through a boulder field. Crater pressed down on the accelerator and chased after him. The crowhopper ran down a small rille and then reappeared on a spiderwalker. Crater gave chase, but as he did, he saw the flare of two jumpcars landing north of his position. He feared they were attacking the convoy.

Still, he kept chasing the spiderwalker, hoping for a clear shot. When he saw the contraption run down a crack, he took a calculated risk that it would reappear at the other end. He jumped over another crater and cut off the spiderwalker as it came out of the crack, ramming it. The crowhopper was knocked off and Crater, though he tried to avoid it, ran over the creature.

A terrible accident, the gillie said.

"Gillie!" Crater cried with joy at the sudden communication from the little thing. "Status report!"

Sick.

"You sound good, anyway," Crater said, as he walked over and kicked the leg of the crowhopper. There was no response.

Sick, the gillie said again.

"Stay in your holster. We've got a bumpy ride ahead of us."

Crater drove back to the convoy, swerving through boulder and crater fields. When he reached a small rise, he saw the convoy had circled up. The muzzles of the crowhoppers' railguns were winking in the darkness, and Crater knew their flechettes had to be beating up the trucks. Winks of light showed that some of the drivers were fighting back with old-fashioned powder guns and a bright flash where Maria was probably shooting back at the attackers with her railgun rifle.

"Gillie!" Crater said, hoping it would wake up. "Can you tell me how many and where the crowhoppers are?"

The gillie crawled to his shoulder. *Gillie hears six crowhoppers.* Crater switched on the helmet infrared scanner, saw that it was overwhelmed by the flashes of the rifles, and switched to thermal imaging. He saw the signature of the two jump-cars, their engines still warm. Crater headed there.

He worked his way to a jumpcar, sitting upright on its fins. He climbed up its ladder, crawled inside, and sat down at its controls. He threw the necessary switches, heard the auxiliary power units rev up, then set it on autopilot to blast off in sixty seconds. He emerged and went to the next jumpcar. A crowhopper spotted him as he climbed aboard and came after him on the ladder, trying to grab his legs. Kicking the thing off, Crater climbed to the cockpit, fired up the engines, and twisted the throttle stick. The jumpcar roared aloft, the crowhopper clinging to the ladder. Somehow it managed to climb inside. Crater saw it and threw the bullet-shaped ship into a steep climb, then looped over into a twist, the crowhopper bouncing off the interior until it was thrown out of the hatch and then disappeared.

Switching to his helmet's infrared, Crater rolled the jumpcar on its back so he could get a view of the fighting and saw the flashes from the crowhopper railguns had stopped. Another scan showed five of them running toward the other jumpcar. They clambered inside just as the timer Crater had set reached zero. The jumpcar blasted off, streaked straight up, then flipped over and plummeted down to crash and burn.

Not trusting his piloting skills enough to land, Crater flipped the jumpcar over and put it on autopilot. The landing still proved to be a hard one since a fin clipped a boulder. The jumpcar teetered, then fell over. Crater jumped through the hatch and ran, the jumpcar exploding behind him.

He walked back to the line of trucks and came up beside

Captain Teller. "I'm back, sir," Crater said, then briefly described what he'd done.

Teller's expression said as much as his words. "You're a brave, courageous lad. I take back everything I ever said about you."

"You set the example, sir," Crater said and meant it.

"I thought perhaps they had ambushed you," Teller said.

"One did. I got him."

Maria came over and hugged Crater's neck. "That was amazing. *You're* amazing."

Petro came running up and pumped Crater's hand. "Well done, brother!"

"Be careful," Captain Teller said. "There could still be one out there. Oh gosh."

Crater didn't understand why Captain Teller had said "Oh, gosh," but then he understood. A spreading stain of crimson covered Teller's chest as he began to fall. Maria turned and fired her rifle into the darkness as Crater caught Captain Teller and gently lowered him to the dust.

Part Three

THE CYCLER

rater walked out of the dustlock into the most amazing place he'd ever seen, the main corridor of the bustling marketplace of the moon's largest town. Maria was still dealing with the Armstrong City clerks and inspectors who'd emerged from the airlock to register the convoy, tax the heel-3 canisters aboard, and assist in their further transport. She also had to attend to the handling of Captain Teller's body, including seeing his family. Crater wanted to see Teller's family too, but there was an urgent message for him to go to the Medaris Mining company offices and meet a representative sent from the Colonel. In the dustlock, the Armstrong City dusties insisted that he remove his Deep Space BCP suit with the explanation that the biotechnology had not been approved by the city health department. Crater didn't mind removing it—the sheath was pretty dusty, after all—and the hot water showers afterward felt very good.

He headed for the company office, but before he got there, the sheriff of Moontown appeared out of the crowd, took him by the arm, and turned him around. "We have to be careful, Crater! There may be assassins."

Crater was surprised to see the sheriff. "How did you get here?"

"Jumpcar," he said. "The Colonel had a visitor and I hitched a ride."

That sounded awfully convenient to Crater, but the sheriff seemed sincere. So he let himself be led to a ticket counter that had a sign that said See the Site of Humankind's First Landing on the Moon. There were photos of the American astronauts Armstrong, Collins, and Aldrin for sale along with other souvenirs, including models of the Apollo capsule and the *Eagle* lander. The sheriff handed over an adequate number of johncredits and the clerk handed back two paper tickets. "Let's hurry. We don't want to miss the tram," the sheriff said.

The sheriff pointed at a dustlock that said Tours to Tranquility Base Landing Site. They went through it, emerging into a pressurized tram filled with tourists. "Welcome," the tour guide said. "I hope you enjoy your excursion to Tranquility Base."

The sheriff pointed at two empty seats and he and Crater sat down. The tram pulled out, following a well-used track, while the tour guide announced that only one mile away was the landing site of Apollo 11, the place where humans first walked on an "astronomical body." Calling the moon an "astronomical body" was something of an insult to Crater, but he didn't say anything, just looked out the window at the boring view that was mostly devoid of craters or anything else other than a mildly sloping plain of pebbly dust. Before long, the bus arrived at the famous landing site, which was lit up by big spotlights. The tourists immediately started to take pictures.

Crater gazed with some wonder at the truncated base of the landing craft called *Eagle*. Beside it was the American flag on a staff stuck into the dust. The flag was a recreation, of course, since the original flag had been knocked down when the upper half of the *Eagle* had taken off.

The tour guide had already exhausted his spiel on how close Armstrong had come to aborting the mission because of an overworked guidance computer, and how the brave American had landed anyway, completing the promise of the long-dead and little known President Kennedy who had ordered the landing to occur before the Russians could get to it.

The guide was Russian, so he proceeded to tell the tourists that, of course, the Russians had launched the world's first Earth satellite called *Sputnik*, and also launched the first person into space, whose name was Yuri Gagarin. He also went on to say that during the civil war, poor Gagarin's body had gone missing from the Kremlin during an attack by Siberian revolutionaries, but that was neither here nor there.

The tour guide next turned to what had happened to the Apollo 11 site in the years following the landing. He mentioned the outrage in the provinces comprising the old United States of America that had occurred when a Chinese robot on tracks had barged into the site and destroyed many of the footprints while also knocking over some of the experiments left behind. A mission by the Independent States of America, which claimed the Apollo sites since it included among its member states Texas, Florida, and Alabama—where much of the Apollo hardware had been designed and built— studied the site to see if it could be reconstructed. One of its interesting findings was that it wasn't the Chinese who had destroyed Armstrong's famous "first step for man, giant leap for mankind" boot print but Astronaut Buzz Aldrin, who had inadvertently stepped on it as he climbed off the ladder of the landing craft.

While the tourists clicked their photos, the sheriff said, "I have your ticket for the elevator and the Cycler."

"I hope whatever is in that package is worth Captain Teller's life," Crater said.

The sheriff took a moment, then said, "I guess nothing's worth that."

"The crowhoppers were after me. That's why they attacked our convoy."

The sheriff looked incredulous. "You shouldn't take these things so personally. The Colonel has many enemies. There might be any number of reasons why his convoy was attacked."

"Then why did you mention assassins?"

The sheriff shrugged. "I'm a cautious man."

"I think maybe you're also capable of lying when it suits you. What I don't understand is why the Colonel didn't send me here by jumpcar in the first place."

"His is broken and I hitched a ride," the sheriff reminded him. "Anyway, if you go around questioning why the Colonel does what he does, it won't be too long before you're thoroughly confused. I can tell you this much. He's got Plans A, B, and C. You were Plan B."

"If I'm Plan B, what were Plan A and Plan C?"

"Plan A was a couple of fellows who've already got themselves killed. I guess they were sort of 1A and 2A."

"I know about them," Crater said. "How about Plan C?"

"Ah, well, that would actually be Plan 1C and 2C. Plan 1C is me and 2C is another employee in the Armstrong City office. You see, Crater, the Colonel isn't one to put all his eggs in a single basket, not that you'd know what a real egg looks like. Anyway, you will be happy to learn that the Colonel has decided you are to be the chosen one to ride the Cycler. He is pleased with the reports he's received about you from poor Captain Teller."

"Captain Teller said something good about me to the Colonel?"

"He extolled your capabilities every time he called Moontown. He said you had true grit."

Crater reflected that it was only at the very end that Teller had praised him to his face. Crater didn't know whether to be happy or sad. He chose sad.

The sheriff noticed. "You see? Now you're upset. That's why it's not good to know too much when it comes to the schemes of the Medaris family."

Crater lapsed into a kind of melancholy until he was galvanized by the tour guide. "If you'll look out the right side," the man said, "you'll see the remains of a lander that lost power and crashed about sixteen years ago. It was one of the main reasons the elevator was built."

"Sheriff," Crater said, "I think that was the lander my parents were on." Then he felt the gillie wriggle out of its holster. It was looking better, although Crater didn't know why he thought that since it always looked the same, other than an occasional color change.

It is the lander where your father died, it said.

"How do you know?" Crater demanded.

Gillie there.

This shouldn't have been a surprise, although it was. After all, the gillie was owned by his parents. Crater had never thought about it before. He supposed there was a lot he hadn't thought about.

The gillie said, *Hospital.*

"What about the hospital?"

Go. You. Me.

"Oh no you don't, Crater," the sheriff said. "The hospital is on the other side of the city. You don't have time to go over there and, besides that, some assassin might put an elk sticker in your back."

When the bus returned to the dustlock, Crater got up and joined the tourists clambering back to Armstrong City. Maria was waiting for him and the sheriff came up behind. "Ready to go to the elevator?" she asked.

"I'm going to the hospital," Crater said.

"Why? You look fine."

"Something that crazy gillie said," the sheriff said. He handed Maria the tickets. "Don't be late."

Maria looked at Crater, who was determinedly studying a map of the city posted on the wall. She grabbed him by the arm and pushed him into a taxi. "Hospital," she said, and off they went.

See Nurse Soichi, the gillie said on the way.

When they arrived, Maria paid the taxi driver, and she

and Crater descended into the labyrinth of tubes that made up the hospital which, as it turned out, was officially called the Colonel John High Eagle Medaris Hospital and Medical Research Facility. "Grandfather funded this place," Maria explained.

At the desk, Crater asked for Nurse Soichi. "Third tube, Obstetrics," the receptionist said and pointed toward a pink stripe that they should follow.

The doctors and nurses in Obstetrics wore crisp, starched whites, and the place looked modern and well organized. At the nurses' station, Crater asked for Nurse Soichi and was told to wait. "We have an elevator ascension to make," Maria said.

"Believe me," the nurse said, "Nurse Soichi will be along shortly. She is the most efficient and punctual person on the ward."

Sure enough, in a few minutes, a small woman in white arrived with a reader in her hand and a stethoscope draped around her neck. "These two young people asked for you," the nurse at the station said. Nurse Soichi, identified by the name tag on her uniform, glanced at Crater and Maria, and asked, "How can I help you?"

"I was born here sixteen, almost seventeen years ago," Crater said.

She smiled. "My dear, many babies are born here and I have attended most of them."

"Yes, ma'am, but my parents were in a lander crash. My father was killed. My mother was brought here for me to be born. I was adopted by another couple after she died."

Hello Nurse Soichi, the gillie said.

The little nurse's mouth fell open. She placed the reader

on the nurses' station, then took Crater into her arms and held him. "What a beautiful young man you've turned into!" she exclaimed. She felt his arms. "Strong too. Your mother would be so proud. What happened to you? Where did you go?"

"Moontown. I became a heel-3 miner. My name is Crater. Crater Trueblood."

"Who's this?" she asked of Maria.

"A friend," Maria answered.

Nurse Soichi led them into a small room that had some plaston chairs and they sat. After primly smoothing out her skirt, the nurse said, "Your mother was so brave. The doctors wanted to abort you. It was her only chance to live, they said, but she said you were more important. So you were born. She held you in her arms until she slipped away."

Nurse Soichi leaned over and touched Crater's knee. "Your mother said I was to tell you when you grew up how much she and your father loved you, that you were the most important thing to them, and that was why they'd come to the moon. They wanted you to live in a place where there were no wars and where people had a chance to live free."

Gillie was there, said the gillie.

Nurse Soichi smiled tenderly at the gillie. "Yes, Gillie, I will tell them. Before she died, your mother told the gillie to always stay with you and to protect you."

Crater was grateful for the news about his mother and about the gillie. It made the little thing's attachment to him more understandable.

"Nurse Soichi, who were Crater's parents?" Maria asked.

"Ah," she said, "who were they, indeed? Well, your mother didn't say much, Crater, but there was enough paperwork for me to figure things out. Paul and Juliet Trueblood were inventors, rather famous ones. They invented many things, their most famous being an electro-biological filtering system that converted seawater into fresh, which revolutionized life in some desert countries on Earth."

"Why wasn't Crater sent back to Earth to stay with relatives?" Maria asked.

"At that time, dear, there was no elevator and there were no Cyclers. Getting here was a risky thing and very expensive. Orphans were routinely taken into local families, usually without paperwork. The couple who took Crater seemed very nice. Did you stay with them, Crater?"

"Yes, ma'am, but they got killed on the scrapes. I was taken in by Q-Bess who manages the Dust Palace, such being what we call the bachelor's tube. I've had a good life."

"I am heartily glad to hear it," Nurse Soichi said, rising from her chair. She gave Crater a hug. "I have to continue my rounds," she said, then patted the gillie, which actually seemed to like her touch. It turned a restful blue before lapsing back to gray. "Good old thing. You were brave too." And off she went, a nurse on her rounds.

Maria studied Crater. "So you're the child of famous inventors. That explains why you like to tinker with things."

Crater supposed Maria was right, and he resolved to think about it later. For the time being, he was satisfied. "Let's go," he said. "We have a package to pick up. The way I see it, Captain Teller died for it and we should see it through. Are you coming?"

"Are you kidding?" Maria demanded. "Go up the elevator, then aboard the Cycler, then meet a renegade scramferry with a secret payload? Wouldn't miss it for the world or the moon. Anyway, you need a bodyguard."

"True is," Crater acknowledged with a tinge of regret, then led the way.

::: THIRTY

etro found Crater and Maria just before they climbed on the tram that carried passengers to the elevator terminal. He took Crater aside. "I wish I could go with you," Petro said. "I think you could use me."

"I think you're right," Crater said. "But there're only two tickets. Listen, will you check on Pegasus for me while I'm gone?"

"Every day," Petro swore.

"And stay out of trouble. No gambling. There's a rough crowd here. And don't be talking about how you're the Prince of Wales. Likely, somebody would stab you just for that."

"I can take care of myself," Petro replied with a crafty smile. "Just worry about yourself."

Crater stuck out his hand to Petro. "Well, farewell, brother."

Petro ignored his hand and gave Crater a big bear hug. "Farewell and Godspeed, Crater Trueblood."

"Come on, Crater," Maria called from the tram, which had started to move.

Crater climbed aboard and turned to wave to Petro. To his disappointment, the boy had already disappeared in the Armstrong City crowd.

The paperwork process at the elevator terminal was designed to be simple and easy. Maria and Crater showed their tickets and that was it. Once upon a time, according to the history Crater been taught by a Yale University president turned heel-3 miner at the Dust Palace, transportation terminals on Earth, especially airports, were a nightmare of presenting papers and getting luggage inspected and even personal body searches of the most intimate type. With the collapse of most of the world's governments in the mid-twenty-first century, the harassment at airports collapsed with them, mainly because most people were forbidden to travel for a time. In any case, the people prone to highjack airplanes or blow them up were among the first to be eliminated by the harsh new governments that took the place of the old ones. After those governments were in turn overthrown, the terrorists still didn't come back, so travel was just a matter of buying a ticket, at least for those who lived in tough, young republics such as the Independent States of America.

Maria and Crater got on the tram going out to the elevator and watched the dull gray plain slide by. When they got closer, Crater saw two wide ribbons rising from a huge mooncrete terminal. The fibrous material of the ribbons was turned to shimmering rainbow hues by spotlights directed from the ground. "Wow," Crater heard himself say in awe.

Space elevators worked by putting a counterweight into geosynchronous orbit, meaning they stayed over the same spot on the ground and brought up a ribbon from a fixed

base at that spot. To balance gravity against the centrifugal force of the moon's rotation, the counterweight of the
lunar elevator was required to be many thousands of miles
high. The elevator wasn't designed to take passengers to the
counterweight, only to a terminal located sixty miles off the
surface. That was plenty high for the Cycler ferries to manage a rendezvous.

Maria's delight at seeing the ribbons was obvious. She
couldn't stop grinning. She put her arm around Crater's waist
and said, "The first time I saw the elevator I was coming in on
the Cycler *Wernher von Braun*. There was only one ribbon then
and it looked to me like it went all the way to heaven." She
mused over her own words, then said, "Of course, I was just a
little girl back then."

The tram stopped and its driver announced that everyone
should exit and be sure to take their hand luggage, packages,
and souvenirs and proceed directly to the elevator. Most of the
other passengers were Earthian tourists who were chatter-
ing excitedly and comparing the treasures they'd bought on
their exotic journey to the moon. There were also a few moon
residents going back to Earth for a visit. And then there were
Crater and Maria, doing their best to look like a happy, young
couple heading off to college.

The elevator car was designed like a lounge, with plush
chairs and couches. An attendant walked in and sealed the
door. "Ladies and gentlemen," she said, "the Lunar Elevator
Company truly wishes you a very pleasant lift up to the Apex
terminal. Please be aware that once we start our ascent, we will
not stop until we have arrived in approximately six hours. As
we rise, the effects of lunar gravity will gradually diminish

until you will be essentially weightless. You will notice that we have a number of freshly laundered pillows and cushions in bins along the wall on which we invite you to lounge, or you may take advantage of the various chairs and sofas. There are seat belts to use if you wish. If you are prone to motion sickness, I recommend using them. There are plastic bags located conveniently in several stations in the event sickness should occur. Most of you won't have any problems in that regard, so we have a small lunch counter and bar available. Please let me know if you require food, drink, or other refreshment, all of which are priced quite reasonably and are served in disposable containers designed for microgravity. As we ascend, please feel free to enjoy the view. If you prefer to converse, play games on your readers, or anything else, please be careful not to disturb your fellow passengers. We have a brig for such offenders." She smiled prettily. "Are there any questions?"

There being none, the attendant said, "Then, welcome aboard! The management of the Lunar Elevator Company, the crew of this ascension, and I hope you enjoy your journey. We will be ascending soon." She took up position behind the bar and began to prepare complimentary drinks.

After a few minutes, the car began to creep slowly up the ribbon. It was so slow, it was some minutes before Crater realized it was climbing at all. He chose a couch that had been evacuated by a family who went after pillows to spread out on the floor. The couch faced one of the window view ports.

Maria came over and sat beside him, and together they enjoyed watching more and more of Armstrong City come into view as the car got higher. The dome on its eastern edge was the town's signature feature. Constructed of lead-infiltrated plaston, lunasteel, and mooncrete, it dominated the skyline. Observation towers here and there indicated the locations of many of the buried tubes that housed offices, stores, warehouses, maintenance facilities, heel-3 shipment docks, and homes. Some suburbs had been established with minidomes covering parks.

As they were lifted ever higher, Crater and Maria began to look farther out. When they spotted the serpentine trail of the dustway emerging out of the great shadow, they fell silent, thinking of all that had occurred there. When they climbed even higher, they saw the Alpine Valley.

Maria borrowed binoculars from the attendant, and she and Crater took turns trying to see Moontown. The town itself and its towers were too small, but the Copperhead Bridge was big enough to be seen. It was enough to make Crater terribly homesick for Q-Bess, his friends, and the Dust Palace.

Eventually, Crater noticed he was no longer sitting on the bench but floating slightly above it. About then, he also started to get sleepy and, excusing himself from Maria, found an empty cushion, strapped himself to it, and promptly fell asleep. He woke only when the car bumped into the latch at the Apex terminal. "We are so glad you ascended with us today," the attendant said. "Please use the rails to pull yourself to the lounge. Your ferry will arrive in thirty-two minutes."

In precisely thirty-two minutes, with sparkling jets, the rocket ferry arrived and docked. Its hatch swung open and there was a mild rush of air as the pressures between the terminal and the ferry were equalized. Maria grasped the railing that led to the hatch. "Here we go," she said, with what sounded to Crater like merry abandon.

Crater pulled himself hand over hand through the hatch into the ferry. He felt his excitement rising. The next step was to catch the Cycler as it swept grandly past the moon.

There were five Cyclers constantly orbiting around the moon and the Earth, the *Burt Rutan*, the *Konrad Dannenberg*, the *Elon Musk*, the *Jack Medaris* (named after the Colonel's great-grandfather), and the *Wernher von Braun*. All of them had essentially the same design. There were five main tubes, four situated like spokes around the interior core tube. The core was twice the diameter of the spokes. The bridge was at one end and a set of rocket engines at the other. The core also provided attachments for the spokes, observation decks, holds for storage and cargo, and two airlocks. Attached to the spokes was a tubular ring forming an outer rim. Since the Cyclers slowly rotated, centrifugal force provided gravity of varying degrees to the spokes and the rim, where all of the passenger and crew cabins were located.

Once aboard the *Elon Musk*, Crater retreated to his cabin. After getting a good six hours sleep, curiosity brought him out and he started to explore. The core turned out to be his favorite place. Weightless flying was fun and he practiced a variety of acrobatics. Then, fatigue again washed over him and he headed back to his cabin. Maria apparently was also feeling tired, no doubt the result of the grueling convoy, and was nowhere to be seen.

The next day, while exploring anew, Crater came to the attention of the chief purser, a graying man named Strickland. "Here now, youngster," the old spacefarer called as Crater zipped through the spokes. "Where are you off to in such a hurry?"

Crater's natural curiosity amused the purser, who sent him along with various crew members to inspect the parts of the Cycler ordinarily off-limits to passengers. Crater loved most of all the engine room with its pumps and fans and fuel cells and fuel tanks that fed the rockets.

Crater also met the ship's cat, although it came as a surprise. He became aware of something black and white and furry lounging on top of the couch in the crew's lounge. After he stared in amazement at the creature, the gillie, which seemed to be much healthier, stirred on his shoulder and said, with something akin to reproach before scurrying into its holster, *It's a cat.*

Crater had heard of cats but never imagined he would get so close to one. According to his readings of Earthian species, cats had teeth and claws and were carnivorous. The bigger ones were known to eat humans, and Crater wasn't certain about the little ones, although he supposed the crew wouldn't keep one in their lounge if it was a man-eater. Crater crept closer to the cat and studied it. After the cat made a languorous stretch, it opened its eyes, saw Crater, and began to mutter and shake which caused Crater to jerk back.

CP Strickland came inside the lounge. "I see you've met Paco. Go on. You can touch him. He won't hurt you. He's the ship's cat and belongs to everyone."

"But there's something wrong with it! It's making a terrible sound."

"A sound? Oh, I see what you're getting at. He's purring. See? When I pet him, he does it even louder. It's his way of saying he's happy."

Very carefully, Crater reached out and touched the cat, which erupted with more rumblings. He pulled his hand back, which made CP Strickland laugh. "Go on. Keep petting. He likes you!"

Crater tentatively put his hand back on the cat, then began to pet it while CP Strickland gave him a little history lesson about the first cat in space. It was a cat in an experiment called FLEA, for Feline Epistemology Attitude experiment, its purpose lost in the mists of time. FLEA was carried aboard a space shuttle that was supposed to go into low earth orbit but ended up going to the moon. The cat was a black and white long-haired cat named Paco. In fact, CP Strickland said, the errant shuttle was piloted by none other than Colonel Medaris's great-grandfather, Jack Medaris, in the world's first spacejack. Medaris had become famous after that mission along with the other crew members which included Paco. Ever since, a lot of ships' cats were named after the original Paco, including the one on the *Elon Musk*.

"You've met the ship's cat," the purser said. "How would you like to meet the ship's captain?"

Crater said he would like that very much, and CP Strickland led him to the bridge.

The bridge was gleaming steel and aluminum, utilitarian with the singular exception of the faux leather chairs for the captain and helmsmen. There were no view ports, although two wide holoscreens were programmed for a variety of views of both the exterior and interior of the spacecraft. Because of the electrical blackouts sometimes caused by solar flares and electromagnetic storms, the Cyclers used hardwired fiber optics, rather than wireless communications.

The ship's captain was a Cycler veteran of forty years' service named Captain George E. Fox. Fox was a broad-shouldered man with an air of authority. A smart blue uniform and a gold braided cap made him even more imposing. "Well, Crater, my crew tells me you have a few ideas regarding how to improve some of our hardware."

Crater had made some suggestions about the fuel cell designs in the engine room and was surprised the captain had heard about it. "Nothing important, sir," Crater answered. "This is a well-designed ship, from all that I can see."

"Still," the captain said, "it is good to see a young person with practical engineering knowledge."

Captain Fox went on to say that Crater was welcome to come on the bridge anytime he wanted, and that there was always a great deal of activity on a Cycler bridge that Crater might find of interest. "Cyclers are complex machines with components that have to be constantly monitored, adjusted, and maintained," Fox explained. "Perhaps someday you'd like to be a crewman on a Cycler. We could use smart lads such as yourself."

The next day, Crater was on the bridge when Captain

Fox noticed something wrong on the bank of controls, monitors, and status lights. "That pressure is unacceptable, Miss Clayton," he said to a harried-looking helmsman. "I don't care if the volumetrics are otherwise within limits. I have seen droppages like that which later caused a complete shutdown in those utilities. Get on the horn. Talk to Mr. Damson and tell him that an adjustment is required in his sensor pressures. Move smartly, Miss."

"Aye, sir," the crewman responded, reaching for a comm unit.

The captain called Crater over. "The news from Armstrong City has indicated you've had quite the adventure," he said.

Although he didn't like being cynical, Crater thought maybe now he understood why Chief Purser Strickland and Captain Fox had been so attentive to him. They knew something of his mission and wanted to know more. Captain Fox looked around his bridge with evident pride, although it did not keep him from noticing fault. "You there," he said to a member of the bridge crew who had briefly turned to glance at him. "Write yourself up for lethargy."

"Aye, aye, Captain," she said and turned back to her duties, which consisted mainly of staring at a single screen of data, searching the scrolling numbers for some minute discrepancy.

Crater took his leave, pulling his sticky boots from the floor and heading for the bridge hatch. Before he got there, Captain Fox detached his boots and drifted over to put his hand on the hatch cover. He studied Crater, then said, "We are to meet a ship after the scramferry. I presume it is for you."

Crater saw no harm in answering. "I think so, Captain,"

he said. "If so, it's bringing with it a package for Colonel Medaris. I am on board to receive it. What it is, I don't know."

"I trust there is no danger involved for my ship or crew."

"I wouldn't discount the possibility," Crater admitted.

Captain Fox looked disappointed, but said, "Thank you for your honesty."

Crater found Maria in the starboard lounge and sat across from her. "The captain knows," he said.

"Knows what?"

"About us. What we're here for. He's worried."

"He shouldn't be. It should just be a routine transfer."

"The crowhoppers attacked our convoy. Why not attack us here?"

"Crowhoppers are land troops."

"Are there sky troops?"

"Crater, stop it. There's nothing to be done. Everything is in motion. We know what we're doing."

Crater went back to his cabin, bothered by Maria's assertion that "we" knew what "we" were doing. By that, he was sure she meant the Medaris family. It was a family that was willing to risk people's lives for their own ends. Captain Teller was proof of that.

The next days passed until Earth filled the porthole in the observation lounge. "Lovely, isn't it?" Maria commented as Crater came up beside her.

The misty blue world *was* lovely, but Crater was thinking it was maybe too lovely because it was covered by people willing to fight wars to gain even a little part of it. Now maybe they were ready to fight one for the moon too.

Maria pondered Crater pondering the world. "Well, you're

the gloomy Gus. I told you to stop worrying. What's going to happen is going to happen. We might as well enjoy the view until then."

Crater wanted to discuss the Medaris family with Maria, wanted to hear from her that she had a greater allegiance to truth and honor and maybe just people than to the family business. But he lacked the courage to ask her, mainly because he thought he already knew the answer.

At last, the scramferry approached as the *Elon Musk* began its looping voyage around Earth. Crater's first view of it was a bright moving star that gradually grew until he could discern a white shape that was sleek and had wings. A scramferry took off from a runway utilizing a turbo jet, which then switched to a scramjet to streak out of the atmosphere. Rockets then maneuvered it to the Cycler. This meant it required an aerodynamic design, which Crater very much admired.

Crater went down to the entry hatch and positioned himself to watch the process of new passengers coming aboard and the disembarkation of the passengers returning from the moon. CP Strickland floated up, then righted himself by pressing the soles of his sticky boots on the deck. His duty was to release and open the hatch.

When the ferry docked, the Cycler shuddered as the big craft hugged it close. Since it took awhile to make certain of the mooring, the chief purser waited patiently beside the hatch while Betty and Tommy, the two tour guides who worked for Lunar Expeditions—Lunex as it was called—shepherded their tourists into the area. Crater had spent some time with B&T, as they liked to call themselves, and listened to their stories of their various adventures on the moon with their clients. He'd also received a job offer. "We think you'd be perfect for what we do," they said.

Tommy came over to Crater and remarked, "I hope none of the noogies are sick. Imagine you've spent your entire life in Earth gravity, then you're slung up here, pulling about three Gs on the scrams, then once the rockets stop firing, you're down to zero. Oh yeah, there'll be a few folks who won't be feeling all that well."

After CP Strickland finished checking the seal between the scramferry and the Cycler's airlocks, he announced, "Look alive, look alive! Passengers coming aboard!"

After some pulling of levers and twisting of knobs, the *Elon Musk* crew swung open the airlock, then got out of the way to let the Lunex tour guides do their jobs. The first passenger, a graying man in a suit and tie, pulled through the hatch and drifted out into the arrival area. Tommy floated over. "Welcome aboard, sir," he said. "I am Tommy and this is Betty. You can just call us B&T. We are your lunar adventure guides."

"I'm no tourist, B&T," the man said. "I'm a representative of the Unified Countries of the World. There are no other passengers."

B&T were astonished by this turn of events and turned to CP Strickland for an explanation. "Captain Fox's orders. No tourists on this swing-by."

"But we have contracts," Tommy said to Strickland's shrug.

Crater was pleased and sorry at the same time, pleased that if there was trouble, there would be no innocent tourists who might get hurt, and sorry for B&T who were going to lose some good money. Crater had no doubt that Captain Fox had used up more than a little of his company clout to cancel the tourists.

Betty and Tommy shook off their disappointment, not that they had much choice. Tommy crossed over to the inner hatch and swung it open to let their returning tourists go aboard the scramferry. Veteran space flyers now, they greeted B&T with grins, nods, handshakes, and cheerful asides, and slipped them envelopes that surely contained tips.

"Thank you, thank you, had a great time too, won't be the same up here without you," B&T said as they took the envelopes and helped their clients with their luggage.

Crater followed Tommy into the scramferry where he was giving his final speech to his clients. "Folks, you have been the best group Betty and I have ever had the privilege of leading on the moon. I will be bragging about you to my supervisors. If you enjoyed yourself, we wouldn't mind if you mentioned B&T to Lunex. On the puters on the back of each seat, you'll find all the information you need to write to the president of Lunex to let her know your opinion of your entire experience."

"We love you, B&T!" a young woman yelled. Cheering and applauding from the other tourists erupted, and Betty and Tommy made a great show of bowing and looking delighted— although they turned a bit grim as they made their way back into the *Musk*.

Crater watched the offloading of a variety of cargo from the scramferry including, he noticed with interest, crates bound for Moontown. Other items were personal in nature with the names of the recipients printed on the sides of the packages. It made him wonder why the Colonel had not sent his package up with those goods. Surely, whatever it was could have been hidden in one of the crates. The answer, after Crater gave it some thought, was obvious. The package was not yet in the hands of anyone within the Medaris empire.

A thump and a shudder announced the departure of the scramferry, and the Cycler was alone again. That was when Maria tracked Crater down. She was carrying one of the rail-gun rifles. "How did you get that on board?" he asked.

"We Medarises have our ways," she said with a smile. "I put your rifle in your cabin. Stop looking at me like that."

"Like what?"

"You know like what. You're thinking whatever's coming up couldn't be worth endangering the Cycler. Look, I don't know how else to say it. This is very important. Trust me."

"What is in the package?" Crater asked. He supposed it was time for him to know at least that.

Maria told him, and Crater's response was immediate. "But that's not worth anything!"

"It will get the monorail built."

"How?"

Maria told him how. "This is madness," Crater said.

"No, Crater, it's business. Family business."

Crater thought over her answer and came to a conclusion. "I don't think I want to be part of your family's business."

"Does that include me?"

Crater didn't know. All he knew was he couldn't stop what was about to happen. He went to his cabin to check on his rifle.

::: THIRTY-TWO

Up the freighter came a scramjet—small, sleek, with delta wings, and white as the Earthian clouds from which it appeared. It streaked up from somewhere in Asia. Crater saw its twinkling star rise and arc toward the Cycler, going through its turbo, scram, and rocket phases. It was a beautiful machine. Then he saw something, a flash like a rocket pulse, behind the freighter. The gillie stirred in his holster, then said, *They are under attack.*

Crater flew up to the bridge and told Captain Fox what the gillie had said. The gentleman rocked on his heels, then studied the gillie. "I've been wondering about that thing. Where did you get it?"

Crater quickly told him the story. "They are fiercely loyal, or so I've heard," the captain replied. "It was one of the reasons they were made illegal, then all were destroyed. They couldn't be sold, you see, because to remove them from their original owner made them sick. Often, they would just shut themselves down."

"The gillie is just a biological machine, Captain," Crater said.

Fox's bushy eyebrows went up. "Why, Crater, they're much more than that! They were introduced on Earth as a family pet. Over time, they were given more intelligence until . . . well, they had to be banned because they were taking on too many attributes of their owners. Some widows even claimed the ones owned by their deceased husbands *were* their husbands. Philosophically, morally, socially, scientifically, and every 'ly' you could name required their manufacturer to stop making them."

"Captain," Crater said, "this is interesting but . . ."

"But I should prepare myself for attack?" He shook his head. "I'm as ready as I can be. Something for you to know, Crater. A leader must be able to recognize when all that can be done has been done. If he is outnumbered or outgunned, then what is left is to look for a mistake by his opponent. If we find ourselves in a fight, that's what I will be doing."

The sleek freighter came in fast, braked, matched the *Musk*'s velocity, and initiated a call to the bridge. "Request permission to dock," a voice from the scramjet said.

"Your pass code, if you please," Captain Fox said, then listened as the same voice rattled back a complex series of numbers and letters.

"It matches what I have, sir," the helmsman said.

"Permission granted," the captain said. "But be apprised we believe another ship is following you."

"Thank you, Captain," the voice from the freighter said. "We will be brief." Immediately, vernier jets spouted from various points on the freighter and it eased over. There was scarcely a shudder on the bridge as it mated with the Cycler.

"The people following them are very patient," Maria said, coming on the bridge. "They likely waited for months to spot and follow that freighter when it rose up."

The captain and Crater turned toward Maria. "What kind of craft is after them?" Captain Fox asked.

"Likely a warpod, Captain."

A warpod! Crater had read about them. They were the most fearsome space machines any country had ever constructed. Such craft were first a development of the ISA, but the Russians and Chinese had built copies too. Warpods were fast, stealthy, and armed with a variety of killing mechanisms used in space warfare, including lasers and kinetic projectiles.

"And how do you know this, young lady?"

When she didn't answer, Crater said, "She's a Medaris, Captain," and while Maria fumed at the answer, the captain, with a small, sad smile, nodded that he understood.

He tipped his hat to her. "Your family is a great one, Miss. It took chances, and it built this frontier."

"That is correct, Captain," Maria replied, shooting an angry glance at Crater. "I appreciate your recognition of that fact. Shoving back the frontier is still our intention. I regret it has impacted your marvelous Cycler and possibly endangered your crew, but I assure you it is necessary."

Crater didn't understand how Maria could be so sure, and he didn't much like it that the captain had taken up her part. It told him at least one thing. Colonel Medaris was probably a shareholder of the Cycler company, or maybe someone in his family owned the entire enterprise, Cyclers and all.

Maria said, "Crater, it's time."

Crater had gone this far, so he'd go the rest of the way—not that he had any choice. He and Maria reached the airlock just as CP Strickland completed the steps necessary to equalize the pressure in the tunnel between the freighter and the *Musk*, then swung open the hatch. In floated a bag made of thick, stiff material—a duffel bag as such are called—followed by a man dressed in brown coveralls. Another man, carrying a reader, followed the first inside the Cycler. "Where is the boy named Crater?" he asked. He was thin, intense, and wore old-fashioned wire-rimmed glasses. His accent was Russian.

Crater presented himself. "Place your thumb on the screen," the man said, and Crater did. "Look at that spot on the reader," he said, and Crater did that too, allowing his eyes to be scanned. "Now, give me the secret password."

"I don't know any secret password," Crater replied.

"Then you are the one we seek. Twisted Toes, give him the package."

Twisted Toes, who Crater saw now was an Umlap, pushed the bag toward Crater. Then the two men, without another word, went back inside the tunnel. CP Strickland closed the airlock hatch behind them, waited until he got a green light on the panel that the hatches were satisfactorily sealed, and released pressure. Within moments, there was a shudder as the freighter detached itself.

"Crater," Captain Fox said over the speaker, "please come to the bridge."

Crater gave the duffel to Maria. "Would you like to see inside?" she asked.

"No," he said and meant it.

On the bridge, the captain pointed at the radarscope. "We're barely registering a signal, so whatever's coming at us is stealthy. If we hadn't been looking for it, we wouldn't have seen it. Your gillie is a wonder."

"Captain," the helmsman said, "there, over the Indian Ocean."

Crater strained his eyes to see what the sharp-eyed helmsman had seen, and then there it was: a black dot against the bright blue ocean and coming fast. The freighter was moving slowly away from the *Musk*. Whether its crew saw the warpod rising toward them didn't much matter, since a projectile that seemed to come from nowhere suddenly blasted through the freighter's port wing, narrowly missing the Cycler. The freighter fired its rockets and began to move away.

"They'll never be able to reenter the atmosphere with that hole in their wing," one of the bridge crew said. That did not turn out to be a problem, mainly because a flurry of projectiles crashed through the freighter's fuselage, turning it into a cloud of shredded lunasteel, aluminum, and plaston.

The Cycler shuddered as a wave of debris struck it. "Check for leaks and hull integrity, if you please," the captain said in a calm voice. "Steady as she goes."

"The warpod is within visual, sir," one of the lookouts said.

Crater studied the spacecraft as it came closer. He estimated it to be about a hundred feet long with a blended wing and body, two short vertical fins on its outer edge. It was solid black, with a large section forward of the cockpit shaped like a spade that gave the thing a sharklike appearance. Looking closer, Crater saw the warpod's belly was contoured with channels and ribs. When he remarked on this odd feature, the captain said, "The grooves conduct heat away from the surface. An efficient and effective solution for reentry into the atmosphere."

The warpod came up alongside and matched the Cycler's velocity, though it remained menacingly silent. The captain said, "They won't ride with us all the way to the moon. Pretty soon, they'll have to talk to us or attack." He turned to his signal officer. "Give them a shout, Lieutenant."

The signal officer lit up the channels, saying, "Warpod, warpod, this is the Cycler *Elon Musk*. We are a civilian passenger vessel engaged in the peaceful pursuit of enterprise. Please state your business."

There was no response, but Crater could sense the evil within its hull. "Gillie," he said. "Can you communicate with the warpod?"

Yes, it said. *They have received the message from the Cycler.*

"Can you hear them talking inside?"

No voices. Puter silence. Creatures moving within.

"Creatures? Crowhoppers?"

Demons.

"Demons are biological nightmares," Captain Fox said with a shudder. "Killers who love to kill. If they're moving around, I think they're preparing to board us."

Crater made a decision. "Gillie, tell the warpod if they are here for the package that the freighter delivered, they can have it. We will send it across."

Message delivered.

"Thank you," the captain said. "After all you've been through . . . the Colonel will not be pleased."

"Neither will his granddaughter," Crater replied. "Anything, gillie?"

Negative.

Then came a crackle of static and a harsh voice. "We are

coming aboard. Do not attempt to stop us. We will kill you all if you do."

"Does that mean they've accepted my offer?" Crater wondered, then recalled that he did not, in fact, have the duffel in his possession. "Captain, I'd best go get that bag and be prepared to hand it over."

Captain Fox did not reply. His jaw was set, his eyes gone hard. "I do not believe it will matter," he said.

Crater didn't hear him because he was already pulling himself as fast as he could to the main entry hatch. When he got there, CP Strickland was still on duty. "I've sent the others to the rim for safety," he said.

Then the Cycler shook violently and the chief purser said, "They're docking hard." It was the last thing he ever said because the hatch suddenly blew inward, striking CP Strickland and killing him instantly. The air howled as it streamed out of the receiving room through the open portal into the blackness of space. The warpod pushed a cylindrical tube through the hatch with a clawlike attachment. The claw spread open and clamped itself to the wall around the ruined hatch. Crater threw himself into the main corridor and slammed the hatch behind him, sealing off the entry, then headed to the bridge. As he entered, Captain Fox glanced in Crater's direction, then spoke into a comm unit. "Crew of the *Musk*. We are under attack by the warpod. Section chiefs, seal all hatches immediately and keep checking hull integrity."

The captain glanced at a map of the interior of the Cycler. "I believe the warpod troopers intend to depressurize us by destroying our interior hatches. Based on their entry at the main entry hatch, the likely sequence is hatch numbers 2B,

3B, 4B, and 5A. After that, they will have other choices. Section chiefs with those hatches, go to sections 6, 7, or 8. Then stand by for further orders."

Captain Fox and his crew exchanged glances. "That will buy us a few minutes at best," the captain said.

The gillie trembled on Crater's shoulder. *Moontown cargo*, it said. *Detpaks.*

Crater instantly grasped what the gillie was getting at. He turned to the captain. "Captain, the scramferry. Did it offload any detpaks for Moontown?"

The bridge supply officer looked up from his monitor. "They did, Captain. Two hundred of them."

Crater told the captain what he had in mind. "A long shot at best, but take Ensign Klibanoff," the captain said. "He's our hull expert. Get going and good luck."

The ensign, who had the easy grace of a natural athlete, introduced himself to Crater. "Jackson Klibanoff," he said, then led the way to the hold. Klibanoff cranked open a hatch in one of the cargo bays and led the way inside.

Crater spotted the crates bound for Moontown and found the one with the detpaks. Klibanoff used a pry bar on it, and Crater took two detpaks and handed two more to the ensign. "We need to get on the hull of the warpod to set these," Crater said.

"Only one way to do that without being spotted," Klibanoff said, then led the way to a hatch in the core marked Maintenance Hatch: Not a Passenger Exit. Klibanoff explained that the hatch led to a small airlock used by maintenance workers that opened on the outer skin of the core module. A red light glared on the control panel. "The outer hatch is already open," Klibanoff said.

"The demons?"

"No. The hatch is locked from the outside. They'd have to tear it loose, and that would show up on the control panel. It's been opened from the inside."

Crater thought he knew who had done it. "Gillie, call Maria. Tell her to close the hatch so we can come out."

Done.

"Why is she out there?" Klibanoff asked.

"Family business," Crater replied with a bitter smile. "She has her grandfather's package. I think she means to hide it in the hull."

The panel light turned green, and Klibanoff swung open the inner hatch. Inside the airlock were ECP suits. Klibanoff and Crater climbed into them, strapped on tool belts, pulled on helmets, depressurized the airlock, then pushed open the outer hatch and went through.

The Cycler hull was generously supplied with handrails that made movement easy. Careful to stay out of sight of the warpod, Crater and the ensign pulled themselves along the hull until they crossed the rail used by the toolbot. A squat module with a set of versatile arms and onboard toolboxes, it was designed for hull maintenance and repair of small meteorite punctures. The rail system allowed the toolbot to not only travel along both sides of the core but also, using rail switches, along the passenger tubes.

Crater found Maria and the duffel behind the toolbot.

"What's your plan?" she asked as Crater came up alongside her. When he showed her the detpaks, she said, "Nice."

"Here's a better plan," Crater said. "Hand over that bag to them, they'll leave, and we save the Cycler."

Maria looked at Crater in disbelief. "We are under attack by demons. Don't you understand what that means? They will not leave until they kill us all!"

Ensign Klibanoff interrupted. "They're coming out."

Crater peered around the toolbot and saw four creatures in red armor floating out of a warpod hatch. They were carrying short axes and grappling hooks. "What are the axes for?" he asked.

"It's their signature weapon," Klibanoff replied. "Demons hack their enemies to death."

"You see, Crater?" Maria said. "You might not think the contents of this bag are worth anything, but somebody does."

Crater had to admit somebody did, indeed, especially since they'd sent up a warpod filled with genetically tweaked ax murderers. "Take the bag, get inside the airlock," he told her. "Ensign Klibanoff and I will hold these fellows off."

When Maria hesitated, Crater said, "Look, if that bag is important to you, it's important to me. Now go."

She nodded gratefully, then headed for the hatch.

A grappling hook came flying in, catching on the toolbot. Klibanoff detached it and threw it off, the demon on the line helplessly drifting away. But three demons were already across and making their way toward the toolbot.

Klibanoff handed his two detpaks to Crater. "Get on the warpod. I'll hold them off."

Crater wanted to argue, to tell the brave ensign that they'd fight them off together, but he knew better. Klibanoff had no chance, but maybe if Crater was fast enough and lucky enough, he might be able to get aboard the warpod hull. He clipped the two detpaks to his belt with the two he already had, and using the toolbot rail, pulled himself around the core to emerge beneath the warpod.

A demon was waiting for him. It swung its ax, Crater dodged, then both he and the demon floated off into space—their only connection the tether attached to the creature's grappling hook. Crater desperately pulled on the demon's arm, trying to make it drop its ax. The demon retaliated by trying to tear Crater's helmet off. They tumbled and gyrated around the tether as they fought.

The demon was astonishingly strong, and Crater knew it was only a matter of time before he going to be worn down. That was when, out of the corner of his eye, Crater saw the gillie crawl onto the base of the demon's helmet. It disappeared, then reappeared inside the helmet. The demon became aware of it and began to scream, a scream that ended instantly when its helmet faceplate suddenly popped open. The gillie crawled out of the helmet and into its holster while Crater fought the gorge in his throat. Death in a vacuum was ugly.

Crater took the tether off the demon, hooked it to his belt, and after the gillie crawled back on his shoulder, pushed the creature away and pulled himself along the tether back to the core. There were no demons where he landed. He worked his way around to the Cycler entry hatch where the warpod was docked. He stuck two detpaks on the warpod near the hatch and set them to explode in three minutes, then crossed over to the warpod and placed two more near its engine nacelles, programming them to go off in five. He then headed back across to the Cycler to see if Ensign Klibanoff was still alive.

To his surprise, he was. Somehow he'd fought off the demons, but now a dozen more had appeared. They were howling a silent scream of rage and waving their axes as they came aboard. "This is it," Crater muttered, preparing himself for the final onslaught.

Toolbot can fight, the gillie said.

"Can you control it?" Crater asked, with sudden hope.

Yes, it said.

"Good old gillie!"

The gillie crawled down his arm and onto the squat machine, signaled a hatch to open, then disappeared inside. Lights glowed on the toolbot's control panel and it began to move along its rail, turning at the switch that took it toward the demons. The toolbot's arms came out and flicked the demons away, cutting their tethers and sending them spinning into space.

"Crater, we're going to win!"

It was Maria. She was back, armed with her rifle. She used it to pot away at the demons. "Don't worry, the bag is safe," she said, but Crater didn't care about the bag and what was inside it. He was just relieved to see her alive and well.

Eight more demons came out of the warpod, two of them heading for the detpaks Crater had stuck near the entry hatch. Maria shot one of them. The other one threw its ax at her. It flew end over end and struck her helmet. Her rifle went spinning away and she fell back.

Crater launched himself at the red-suited creature. He fell onto it and used the elk sticker on his tool belt to cut the demon's tether, then pushed it away. A quick look showed there were at least a dozen demons helplessly floating in space, flailing their arms as if trying to swim back to safety.

Thirty seconds, the gillie said, signaling Crater from the toolbot.

Thirty seconds before the first detpak exploded, Crater shouted to Maria and Klibanoff. "The first detpaks are about to blow. Get some cover."

Crater saw another demon had discovered the two detpaks he'd placed near the warpod engine covers. He went hand over hand across the warpod hull to stop it from pulling them loose. Before he got there, the first two detpaks exploded, severing the warpod from the Cycler. Crater knocked the demon off the warpod and cut its tether. The warpod began to drift away from the Cycler while the two remaining detpaks, not five feet away from Crater, were counting down to explode.

Jump, the gillie said. *Now.*

Crater threw himself off the warpod toward the Cycler and saw immediately he had misjudged it. When the two detpaks went off, he was sailing past the Cycler. That was when a metallic arm reached up and grabbed him by his boot. The gillie through the toolbot pulled Crater in while the remnants of the shattered warpod tumbled away, except for one piece: a ragged chunk of hull, which harmlessly ricocheted off the Cycler.

Crater hugged the toolbot. He knew it was ridiculous, but since the gillie wasn't likely to appreciate a hug, it was all he could think to do. Then a demon that had been hiding rose up with his great ax. He swiped at Crater, missed, then swung again. That was when Ensign Klibanoff appeared and finished the demon, using the creature's own ax to do the job.

The battle was over and Crater took a deep breath. "We did it," he said. "We beat them."

When Ensign Klibanoff didn't say anything, Crater—sensing something terrible—asked, "We won, right?"

"It's Maria," Klibanoff said, and Crater felt his glittering triumph turn into a darkness blacker than the farthest reaches of space.

::: THIRTY-THREE

octor Kelly Arnold was the name of the Cycler's surgeon. She was, according to Captain Fox, a young woman of great competence who'd served his crew and passengers well across a dozen cycles. "Severe trauma," she apprised Crater, "decompression sickness, frostbite, and skin burns. That's what happens when you're too close to an explosion and your ECP suit is compromised. I'm sorry."

It hurt Crater to see Maria in such an awful state. He wished more than anything that he could take her place, and his mind kept returning to when he told her to go inside. She had gone but then come back to fight. It was, he supposed, that awful Medaris family pride.

Maria's face was swollen and discolored, and her arms were mottled with frostbite and scabbed with burns. She was reduced to lying in bed with tubes leading in and out of her and an oxygen mask attached to her ravaged face.

"What she needs," Dr. Arnold said, "is microbe therapy to heal her liver and kidneys, plus DNA therapy to cure her skin lesions. I am not set up for such delicate work in my surgery, nor do I have the necessary equipment to prepare the microbial material."

Earth was receding, the Cycler gone too far for a scramferry to catch it. It would be another five days before Maria could be transported to the hospital at Armstrong City. "Will she make it, Doctor Arnold?"

Dr. Arnold was, by nature, honest and direct. "Understand," she said, "there is a great deal of damage inside Maria's body. Her liver is releasing poisons and her kidneys are not properly filtering. She also has a fever that I am having difficulty controlling. On top of that, she is developing pneumonia. I can take care of some of that with traditional medicine but not all."

Crater hadn't prepared himself for such bad news. He had, upon reflection, perhaps become used to escaping death and even expected it now that it had happened a number of times. He supposed maybe that was why wars were fought with young men, because as a group they never figured anything bad would happen to them, always the other fellow. Since the beginning of the trek across the wayback, Crater had never thought anything would happen to Maria because he was ready to lay down his life for her, as was Captain Teller. Now, Doctor Arnold had slapped him in the face with the truth although he rebelled against it. "She can't die. I told the Colonel I wouldn't let her."

Dr. Arnold studied him, then said, "Your promise to Colonel Medaris holds no weight with the unfolding of the universe, Mr. Trueblood, nor, for that matter, with Maria's liver function."

Ensign Klibanoff was with Crater. In an attempt to be kind, he said, "Don't feel so low, Crater. After all, you saved the Cycler and all of us aboard it, except poor CP Strickland."

Crater slumped into a chair beside Maria's bed and held his head. "You give me too much credit. In a way, this is all my fault."

Ensign Klibanoff didn't argue, mainly because he suspected Crater was right, although certainly the maimed girl in the bed bore some responsibility as well, not to mention Colonel Medaris and his extended family. To let such a young girl go out across the wayback and then into space for whatever was in that bag—well, their reputation for ruthlessness was apparently a correct one.

Captain Fox was thinking along the same lines when he called Crater to the bridge. Crater stood with his head bowed while the captain railed against the nations of Earth who, he said, "could not be trusted to keep the peace for more than a day." He also harangued Crater about Colonel Medaris and the other heel-3 company owners who "consider their own writ as holy as the words in the Bible."

"And you," he roared, pointing at Crater, "you come aboard my Cycler, knowing full well you are putting every manjack and womanjill aboard in jeopardy, and for what?"

Captain Fox ordered the duffel bag brought to the bridge. A crewman opened it to reveal a jumble of bones, including a skull. Crater peered at the yellowing, musty artifacts with the same fascination as the bridge crew.

"Are these bones worth death, misery, and the near-destruction of my ship?" Captain Fox demanded.

"No, sir."

"Whose bones are they?"

Crater told him and Captain Fox frowned in disbelief. "How is that possible?"

"It shouldn't be possible," Crater admitted. "But it is."

Captain Fox walked to one of the view ports and looked at the receding Earth. "Such evil yet occurs even when the good succeeds," he muttered, then ordered the bag closed and placed in Crater's cabin. "If there is a curse on those bones, let it descend on you, not my Cycler." And with that, he made the sign of the ancient cross and ordered Crater off his bridge.

When Crater returned to his cabin, the duffel was resting on the deck. He stared at it, then put the quilt from his bed over it so he wouldn't have to look at again. He was joined soon afterward by Paco—the cat had also survived the demons' attack—who settled on his lap as Crater looked out the cabin view port that was turned toward the cold, unblinking stars of deep space. Paco didn't stick around too long because he had other laps to grace, and Crater, growing restless, asked the gillie about his parents. The gillie complied, using holopix, their birth announcements, photos of them growing up, being married, and working in their laboratory flitting by in the air. "Could you show me their inventions?" Crater asked.

The gillie showed Crater the charts, graphs, pix, and text of more than a dozen new designs his parents had invented. One after one, Crater dismissed their designs as elegant but impractical. One design, patent pending, was the manufacturing methodology required to produce what they called "heavy air," or a mix of oxygen and nitrogen molecules made heavier by the addition of sticky neutrons to provide extra mass. *Heavy air,* their application for the patent claimed, *would revolutionize the colonization of the moon and Mars by covering these airless or near-airless orbs with breathable air of sufficient mass that the new atmosphere would not leak into space.* Crater instantly spotted a couple of problems with heavy air, not the least of which was the creation of the trillions of tons of the stuff needed to cover the surface of the moon and trillions more for Mars. The other flaw, of course, was that people weren't designed to breathe heavy air, nor were plants designed to make use of it. That would require the design of new humans and new plants, and Crater didn't even want to think how much that would cost both in money and souls.

"Nice try, folks," Crater said with a sigh. His perusal of the designs had informed him that he came from intelligent parents who were probably great scientists but, sadly, sometimes lacked practical engineering sense.

Some people dream, the gillie said. *Others believe only in reality. We turn dreams into reality. That was the motto of your father and mother.*

Crater absorbed the motto, then asked, "Did any of their dreams turn into reality?"

Yes. They made water from sand.

Nurse Soichi had mentioned this invention, and Crater watched the gillie's presentation of it with interest. His parents had built a device that gathered dispersed water, such as might be found under the driest desert, then caused it to rise to the surface.

We turn dreams into reality.

What was the dream of all who lived in the wayback of the moon? Abundant water. To get it, ice trucks had to make their way to the poles, there to harvest ice locked in permanent shadows within certain craters. The trek up and back was dangerous, and the amount of johncredits the icemen at the poles charged for their product was necessarily outrageous. Because it was so difficult and expensive, and the amount of water brought back was so small, the number of people the moon could support was limited.

How much water lay beneath the regolith rubble of the moon had been long studied, and the conclusion reached was startling. There was an enormous amount of water there, most of it probably brought over billions of years by crashing comets, but it was unusable because it was dispersed, almost molecule by molecule.

Crater sat back and dreamed. He dreamed of a lush moon, of real trees and plants in vast geodesic domes, and even broad savannahs where animals might roam free beneath the stars. He dreamed of lakes beneath the domes and people swimming and families on the beaches with picnic baskets. He dreamed of cool and peaceful forests with hiking paths and birds chittering in the branches.

We turn dreams into reality.

When Dr. Arnold would allow it, Crater sat with Maria and willed the monitors connected to her to click, buzz, and whir on, audible and visual demonstrations that she yet lived. He prayed for her when he was with her and he prayed for her when he wasn't. He went to the ship's chapel and there he prayed too. Before long, crew members heard he was in the chapel and joined him to add their prayers for Maria's recovery.

There was a great deal of work to be done on the Cycler,

and Crater signed up to work with the repair crews hoping that hard work and sweat would dissipate his pain. He helped scrub away the blood the demons had left behind as the crew fought back against them, corridor by corridor, hatch by hatch. The demons had proved to be fierce but inept warriors, and Crater wondered why anyone would use them. They were nearly mindless in their ferocity, leaving themselves open to thrusts of elk stickers taped to metal tubing, and their armor could not stop a bullet from a powder gun. Warriors might be bred in laboratories, but clearly their brains weren't always up to the task.

Cycler work crews sealed the battered hatches, welded shattered wall struts, and went out on the hull to remove the remnants of the battle, including one deceased demon who'd gotten tangled in a grapple line.

In the lounge was the only passenger aboard the Cycler. He wore a gray suit, had a square jaw, crisp blue eyes, and silver hair. When Crater went there, the passenger stuck out his hand and Crater shook it. "Todd Vanderheld," he said, then explained that he was a government official of the Unified Countries of the World, an organization of about thirty nations. Crater noticed that Vanderheld had a small case chained to his wrist. When he saw Crater looking at it, he said, "It holds fifty million johncredits."

Crater was stunned. "Are there really that many johncredits in the universe?"

"Oh, yes, indeed. It is to establish a UCW office in Armstrong City."

"Why?" Crater asked.

"Because the UCW has passed a law that regulates the

quality of Helium-3 that enters our various countries. The office I am going to establish will house a team of inspectors."

Crater pondered the answer, then asked, "Has the quality of heel-3 delivered to your countries been low?"

"Not that I know of," Vanderheld replied. "But this way we can assure it will always be high."

Crater pondered some more, then said, "The fusion companies that buy heel-3 would know right away whether it was good or bad. And there are lots of companies producing heel-3, so if one company produces a bad product, another will step in and take its place. It's a competition thing."

The UCW man smiled. "I'm sure that's true, Crater, but the inspectors will act in the interests of the public."

"The public?"

"The people, you see. The little people. Those people who can't fight the big heel-3 companies and the fusion companies."

"Why would they want to fight them if they provide good, cheap energy?"

Vanderheld had kept a smile during their conversation, though it had become more fixed than real. "Well, this way we make sure they continue to provide good, cheap energy. Everybody wins."

Crater was still confused. "But isn't that the business of the fusion companies? I mean, if they don't provide cheap energy, they go out of business."

"Oh, we intend to regulate the fusion companies too," Vanderheld said.

Crater just couldn't wrap his mind around it. "The heel-3 companies are mining and shipping their heel-3 and are happy, the fusion companies are getting their heel-3 and producing energy and are happy, and the public is getting its cheap energy and they're happy too. Why would you want to interfere with that?"

Vanderheld's smile vanished. "You clearly don't understand the delicate balance between government and business."

Crater felt like he was trying to put his arms around smoke, but somewhere in his mind there was a little truth knocking around. He nodded toward the briefcase. "Where did all that money come from?"

"The member nations gave it to me."

"Where did they get it?"

"From their people."

"The little people?" Crater scratched his head. "Is this why they stay little?"

Vanderheld's expression had by then turned sour. "I'm sorry I wasn't better able to explain to you my purpose," he said.

Crater's brain was worn-out, and he didn't want to talk to the UCW man anymore. Changes were coming to the moon, he could see that, changes that probably nobody was going to like, maybe not even the people who were bringing them. Crater was just too tired to think about it. He also had some more praying to do. So far, his prayers had not helped Maria. She kept getting weaker with every passing hour.

We turn dreams into reality.

Crater visited the Cycler's machine shop and began to develop a microwave device similar to the one his parents had designed to gather water beneath the Earthian deserts. If it was going to work on the moon, it would have to be far more powerful. He fiddled with it on the Cycler's puter by putting in variables such as the thickness of the lunar soil that had to be penetrated and the sparseness of the water. Using those results, he kept improving his design, then built a prototype. It was at least an interesting intellectual and physical exercise that kept him from going entirely crazy while Maria lay possibly dying and the Cycler flew in stately fashion to the moon.

Crater also built a neutron emitter to find water. Since water absorbed neutrons, Crater reasoned that sending out a constant stream of neutrons into the lunar rubble would find any water that was there. He attached micro-biofuel cells to both devices to power them.

At last, the Cycler came within distance of the elevator, and the rocket ferry came alongside. The captain came down to honor CP Strickland as his shrouded body was reverently carried aboard the ferry. With Dr. Arnold hovering over her, Maria was also transferred.

Crater carried both the awful bag with its moldering contents and the devices he'd built in the Cycler's machine shop. "Good-bye, Captain Fox," he said.

"Just get off my ship, Mister Trueblood," Captain Fox replied. But he then added, "You fought for the *Elon Musk* and for that, at least, I'm grateful."

Crater wanted to reply, to say again how sorry he was for what had happened, but the captain turned away and headed back to the bridge. At least Ensign Klibanoff shook hands with Crater. "Keep me apprised of her condition," he said, nodding toward Maria, and Crater promised he would.

The ferry ride to the elevator was uneventful, as was the long, slow ride down the ribbon to the surface where Crater and Maria were met by the sheriff and an ambulance. After

Maria was carried off, Crater handed the duffel to the sheriff, who was surrounded by three big men, presumably employees of the Medaris family. They climbed aboard the tram for the ride back to Armstrong City. Once there, they walked to the offices of the Medaris Mining Company. The sheriff put the duffel bag on a table and sat down. "A lot of trouble for this," he said.

Crater saw no reason to say anything. Of course it was a lot of trouble, not to mention people getting killed and Maria nearly so.

"Sadly, it's not going anywhere anytime soon," the sheriff went on. "Nobody and nothing is. A convoy coming up from New Bombay was attacked two days ago. A lot of drivers were killed and all the heel-3 cans were destroyed. The dustway is closed and all jumpcars grounded by order of the Helium-3 Producer's Council until further notice."

"The Helium-3 Producer's Council?"

"The Colonel organized it. He convinced the other heel-3 company owners they needed to come together to defend themselves. Unfortunately, General Nero and the Russians are holding out."

"Was it crowhoppers who attacked the New Bombay convoy?"

"Most likely. We're not sure where they're coming from. We're not sure who's hired them. We're not sure of anything. It's like we're in a war but we don't know who we're fighting."

Crater thought about that, then asked, "How can we fight a war? We're just a bunch of heel-3 miners."

"Exactly." The sheriff shifted in his chair, his hand unconsciously going to the powder gun on his hip.

"Have you seen Petro?" Crater asked.

"Saw him once or twice around town while you were gone. I'm not sure where he is now. Maybe he joined a convoy. If so, he's probably stuck somewhere in the wayback."

Crater could feel everything shifting beneath his feet. He'd done the Colonel's bidding, fought his way across half the moon, then flown nearly all the way to Earth for a bag of stupid bones and none of that mattered. The moon was being attacked for a reason nobody could figure.

The sheriff sensed what Crater was thinking. "I think those bones, placed in the Colonel's hands, could help the situation. It's a shame they're stuck here."

Crater left the worried sheriff sitting in the chair in the little office and walked to the hospital where at least he could be with Maria. When he got there, he first sought out Mr. Justice. Nurse Soichi came out to talk to him. "He isn't here," she said.

"Do you know if he's with Pegasus?" Crater asked.

Nurse Soichi touched his arm. "He's dead, Crater."

Crater's legs nearly gave way. "How is that possible?"

The gillie came out of its holster. It, too, seemed shocked.

"Someone came in the clinic and stabbed him to death," she said. "We have vidpix of the man we think did it. No one has identified him. Would you care to look at it?"

Gillie show.

That fast, the gillie had tapped into the hospital's puter and produced the vidpix. It showed a big man with legs the size of heel-3 cans striding into the entrance of the clinic, then another angle showed him leaving. He was wearing a tunic and leggings, dressed normally except for a dust mask on his face, but his size gave him away. "I know him," Crater said. "It isn't a man. I met it on the dustway. It's a crowhopper."

"Then it has likely already escaped."

Crater asked about Maria, and Nurse Soichi said, "I had her transferred to my ward. Our best doctors are on her case. It will be many days before the microbes can repair her liver. Give it time, Crater, and let her rest."

Crater nodded, then thought of Pegasus and wondered if the giant crowhopper had also taken his revenge on the horse. He was relieved when he found Pegasus being spoiled by the mechanics in the maintenance shed, which also gave him an idea. It was a crazy idea, an insane idea, but the more he thought about it, he realized that everything that had happened had somehow put into his hands everything he needed.

We turn dreams into reality.

If his idea worked, it would cause the fulfillment of the Colonel's purpose in dispatching Crater across the moon and into cislunar space. It might even justify the terrible pain that Maria was enduring. If Crater's idea didn't work, then there was a high probability he would die. And so would Pegasus.

Crater felt his heart fill with resolve. "We'll do it," he whispered to the great horse who, sensing something magnificent was about to happen, nickered conspiratorially, then stamped his great hooves on the deck of the maintenance shed.

::: THIRTY-FOUR

The airlock door to the maintenance shed slowly rose, and the moon's vacuum sucked out the air within and dispersed it into the nothingness. Crater, dressed in improvised padded armor with an elk sticker prominently strapped to his waist, stepped from the airlock into the dust leading Pegasus in his magnificent war suit. The long shadow was still on Armstrong City. At Crater's request, no lights shone from the airlock. All was darkness except for the bluish glow of the great star field overhead.

Crater, with the gillie in its arm holster, climbed aboard Pegasus, made certain both their helmet starlight scopes were switched on, then turned the horse to face in a northerly direction. "Now we fly, boy," Crater whispered, and the great horse responded, walking, then trotting, then galloping through the tortured field of small craters and hillocks that led away from the city.

Behind Pegasus's saddle was lashed the bag of bones and the neutron emitter and microwave transmitter Crater had constructed aboard the Cycler. Also slung off the saddle was a sack containing horse food pellets, food bars, and detpaks. There was also a holster for Crater's railgun rifle. They were as nothing to the big warhorse as Pegasus bounded across the rubble and craters. Crater leaned forward, his rump off the saddle, his hands clutching the bridle, letting Pegasus run on the rim of the moon beneath the vast, ebony, star-sparkled sky.

All day, boy and horse flew across the Ocean of Tranquility until they reached the Carrel way station. There they stopped to rest, replenish, and bed down in the maintenance shed. The small contingent of workers at the Carrel crater, which was used principally as a signal tower to serve Armstrong City, were delighted by Pegasus and were glad to provide shelter. The next morning, the trailing edge of the long shadow had advanced to the middle of the Tranquility basin, providing enough light for Crater and Pegasus to do without their star-light scopes. They pushed on in the strange, milky light of the lunar terminator, going farther into the vast emptiness.

Dawes crater, which provided an outpost for a contingent of Earthly scientists, was their next stop. There, Crater asked for shelter in their garage. "Where could you possibly be going with that poor animal?" the chief scientist demanded. He had a goatee as silver as the wig he also wore. It was clear to Crater that the man was given to putting on airs of scientific authority.

"North," Crater answered, and then held his peace.

The chief scientist peered at the gillie. "That thing is illegal!" he declared.

"It knows that," Crater replied.

"What are you doing with it?"

The gillie climbed out of its holster and eyed the chief scientist, or would have had it any eyes, then said, *Gillie is Crater's friend.*

"I guess that sums it up," Crater said.

The chief scientist leaned forward until his nose was just inches from the gillie, then sniffed it. "It has no odor. Intelli-activated slime mold cells, I recall. Might I study it? If you'll agree, you may spend the night here and we will provide water and food for both you and your animal. Does the gillie eat?"

This was a question that had never occurred to Crater. "I honestly don't know, sir, but as for studying it, I will have to respectfully decline. The gillie doesn't like anyone touching it."

Gillie is sensitive, the gillie said.

To Crater's surprise, this made the chief scientist laugh. He drew back and waved his hands to his research subordinates. "Give them whatever they need. I shall be in my laboratory if required."

After a night in the garage tube of Dawes, Crater rode Pegasus northerly until they reached the black lava barrier that marked the boundary between the Ocean of Tranquility and the great nothingness that was the Sea of Serenity. "We're on our own now, boy," Crater said. "One hundred miles of dust that no one has ever crossed from this approach. Out there lies Le Monnier crater and New St. Petersburg. We'll have to find water if we are to make it. Do you understand?"

If Pegasus understood, and Crater believed he did, he stamped his hooves and seemed to be girding himself for what lay ahead. Crater said, "Let's go." Twelve hours later, Pegasus began to slow, and finally began to falter. "We need water," Crater said, his mouth feeling as dry as the dust they were crossing. He had been using the neutron emitter but the read-outs had been consistently disappointing. Crater knew they were in trouble. No neutrons were being absorbed. Beneath them was just dry rubble and regolith.

Then, when he began to think dark thoughts about their chances, the digits on the readout began to move. Crater reined in Pegasus and climbed off to set up the microwave transmitter. If his theory was correct, exciting the dispersed water molecules below with microwaves would turn them into clusters. After that, the increased vapor pressure would cause them to rise. He ran the instrument for an hour, then unfolded a small shovel and dug.

Water—blessed, ancient, and pure—filled the resulting hole. Before the pool could evaporate, Crater used a hand pump to fill a collapsible container, then used it to fill Pegasus's water tank. The horse greedily drank as Crater used a straw in the port of his helmet to suck the refreshing liquid into his mouth, swallowing it with a great deal of satisfaction and relief. "You were right, Mom and Dad," he said, suddenly feeling very close to them. "We turn dreams into reality!"

The onrushing terminator chased the long shadow away as Crater and Pegasus ran along north. The sun then blasted the sky apart over the vast Serenity lava flow. They were only about twenty miles away from New St. Petersburg when the crowhoppers found them.

The silvery jumpcar flew in on a parallel track and attacked. When the first flechette flew past his nose, Pegasus swerved and began to gallop in a zigzag pattern, the way he had been taught to respond to aerial attack on Earth. Nudging the horse with the reins, Crater brought Pegasus beneath the jumpcar where its electric guns could not track them. Holding a det-pak, he reached up and pushed it into the belly of the jumpcar, but it wouldn't stick. The jumpcar was made of a slick, composite material.

Gillie fix, the gillie said.

The gillie jumped onto the detpak and spread itself across it, holding the explosive charge in place.

"No, gillie!" Crater cried, just as the crowhopper jumpcar swerved away. A few seconds later, the detpak detonated. Out of control, the jumpcar nosed upward, flew briefly, then pitched over and slammed into the dust.

Before Crater could register what had happened, he saw that the impact of the jumpcar had caused a lava tube to collapse. The tube was at least a hundred yards wide and the collapse was coming straight at them. "Go, boy!" he yelled, and Pegasus responded, racing away. Behind them, the giant lava tube fell in on itself, a massive trap at least three hundred feet deep. Crater looked over his shoulder and saw that the collapsing tube was coming too fast and was going to catch them. "Jump, Pegasus!" he cried.

Pegasus, with a strangled exhalation, made his leap. As they soared, Crater and Pegasus were wrapped in a cloud of frothy dust hurled up from the forming trench. When they burst into the clear, Crater saw they were not going to make it.

Pegasus, sensing the same thing, stretched out, his hooves just catching the edge of the trench. He dug desperately, got hold of the vertical wall with his rear hooves, gave a mighty shove, and fell forward, Crater flying out of the saddle. The warhorse took a wrenching tumble, turned beneath his neck, his legs flailing, and then fell onto his side where he lay still.

Crater crashed into the dust, bounced, and rolled until he stopped. When he was able to sit up, he said, "Gillie, check suit," but then he remembered the gillie couldn't answer.

Crater climbed to his feet and loped over to Pegasus. The great horse lay in a heap, his eyes rolled back in his head. Crater knelt beside him. "Pegasus," he moaned. "Please, please get up."

But Pegasus didn't get up.

That was when Crater sensed something behind him. When he turned, there stood a spiderwalker, and perched on it was the giant crowhopper he'd encountered so long ago at the Dustway Inn. "Would you like to know my name, child?" it asked.

Crater faced the doom riding on eight legs. "Why would I care to know the name of trash?" he demanded.

"It is always good to know the name of that which is going to kill you," it replied. "My given name is Volsokoff. I was once a Russian, or I should say my parents were, before the procedures were performed that produced me."

"You are a biological nightmare," Crater said while his eyes roved, looking for the protection of at least a small crater. There was nothing but a featureless plain.

"My creators made me far more powerful and intelligent than mere humans birthed the old way. I also lack fear. It makes me and others like me the most fierce creatures on Earth and its moon."

"But are you happy?" Crater asked, stalling for time. "Do you know joy? Do you know the sweetness of love?"

"I have no need of such emotions, but when I crush my enemies and see their blood flow, I feel something akin to happiness. Soon, I will know that feeling again."

"But I am not your enemy," Crater said.

Volsokoff pointed at Pegasus. "Strapped to your dead horse is what I seek. That you would deny it from me makes you my enemy."

Crater's shoulders drooped. "Take those old bones, then. They are nothing but death."

"I will take them," the crowhopper answered. "After I tear your arms off, then your legs, then crush your face into the rubble of this terrible little planet."

Crater started to run. It was all he could do. Over his shoulder, he saw the spiderwalker coming, its terrible legs striding across the dust. Crater ran to the edge of the collapsed lava tube and looked over its edge. Its walls were vertical, and there was nothing but vacuum for hundreds of feet. Just for a moment, he noticed something sparkling far below, and he realized the tube had collapsed to a depth where it revealed a layer of water, apparently collecting naturally. This was interesting but, since the spiderwalker was almost upon him, he had to dodge away. He kept running along the edge, hoping Volsokoff would make a mistake. But the crowhopper was in perfect control of the machine and kept its feet just far enough away from the edge to keep it safe.

Just as one of its feet nearly stomped on him, Crater abruptly turned and ran beneath the spiderwalker, swung up on its thorax, and pounced on Volsokoff's back. The crowhopper reached back with a giant hand, contemptuously plucked Crater off, and threw him into the dust.

But Crater's surprise move had been enough to cause a distraction. One of the spiderwalker's feet came stomping down and found nothing but vacuum. The eight-legged machine tipped over, its legs waving ineffectively. Then, as it arched its back, the ugly thing fell off into the nothingness of the lava tube.

Volsokoff did not go with it. Crater crawled to his knees and saw the crowhopper advancing toward him, an elk sticker in its hand. "I do not need a machine to get at you," it said. "I can run faster, jump farther, and endure much more than you. Give in now and make it an easier death."

Crater withdrew the elk sticker from the sheath on his waist. He recalled the advice of Doom and Headsplitter. *What your enemy least expects, that you must do.*

Crater threw the knife. He had practiced throwing it countless times at the Dust Palace with the two Indian assassins showing him how. His aim was true. It struck point-first into a gap in Volsokoff's armor at its right armpit, embedding to the hilt. The crowhopper stopped and roared out its pain and frustration. Crater waited and watched, hoping Volsokoff's suit would begin to unravel. Blood spurted and flowed, but the crowhopper reached over with its left hand and pulled out the elk sticker and threw it down. Wordlessly, it advanced.

Crater leapt, fell, and ran and leapt some more, but still the giant crowhopper relentlessly came after him. Crater staggered and fell, then rolled on his back.

The crowhopper screamed out its triumph and reached down for Crater, but then something huge suddenly appeared, and the monster was lifted off its feet and sent flying.

"Pegasus!" Crater cried with joy.

The warhorse flew after the giant crowhopper. It only managed three steps before Pegasus was upon it, the horse's great hooves pounding, striking, pummeling the black-suited warrior into the dust. Pegasus's last kick caught its helmet and tore it away. The mutant's face swelled and turned a bright red before blood flowed from its ears, nose, and mouth. It rolled facedown into the dust, the length of its body quivering as if rejecting its situation, then went still forever.

::: **THIRTY-FIVE**

They were found by a Russian patrol. Crater was leading Pegasus, but they were both staggering, exhausted and injured. When Crater saw the Russians, he first assumed they were crowhoppers and knew it was all over for him and the Peg. But they were gathered up and given water and food. Crater was invited to sit in a fastbug and, somehow, they made room for the warhorse on a truck.

Crater went in and out of consciousness. When he woke, he found himself sleeping on silken sheets. When he switched on a light, he saw it was the most ornate tube he'd ever seen. The baroque, filigreed furniture seemed to belong in a nineteenth-century historical romance. He lapsed back into a deep sleep until finally he woke once more, found a tunic, leggings, and boots laid out for him on a settee, dressed, and pushed open the tube hatch. There he discovered a guard dressed in the fanciest uniform Crater had ever seen, all scarlet and black with gold braid, buttons, and epaulets. The guard ordered him back inside. "Food and drink will come," he said in Russian.

"What about Pegasus?" Crater asked. "What about my horse?"

"Your horse is quite healthy," the guard answered.

Relieved, Crater went back inside the tube. A few minutes later, a woman, dressed in a green tunic with a high collar, appeared carrying a tray of food. It was a thick strip of beef with a side of fluffy potatoes and a bowl of green beans. There was also a bottle of vodka, a bottle of mineral water, and two glasses. Crater skipped the vodka but dug into the excellent food and drank the entire bottle of water. He felt immediately better and began itching to explore. Before he could figure out how to escape his ornate prison, the woman in the green tunic returned. "The Czarina will see you now," she said.

Crater followed the woman through the corridors of New St. Petersburg, which were sumptuously decorated with statues of Russian heroes and paintings of the mother country. The people in the corridor looked well-fed and content. The shopping area was filled with many stores, selling fine consumer goods. They reached a hatch that had the seal of the old Russian czars, a double-headed eagle. The woman in the green tunic said, "This is the Czarina's palace."

Crater followed the woman through more ornate tubes until they reached one that had a throne of gold-painted mooncrete with cushions of red and black velvet. A big guard walked up and shoved Crater to his knees on the scarlet carpet that led to the throne. From behind thick curtains, Czarina Zorna—dressed in regal robes of red, white, and black—emerged and sat on the throne. "State your business," she said.

Daring to lift his head, Crater said, "I have brought you something that belongs to you and your people. It was in the bag tied to my horse."

Czarina Zorna nodded to a guard who pitched the bag to the floor in front of Crater. "Do you mean this one?"

"Yes, ma'am. Have you looked inside?"

"Do you think we are thieves? No, we have not gone through your personal things. So, tell me, what in this bag is so precious that you would dare cross the Sea of Serenity to bring it to me and my people?"

"Bones."

Crater's answer startled the Czarina. She drew in a quick breath, and a guard was moved to draw his elk sticker from its sheath. The Czarina raised her hand to the guard, who reluctantly lowered the knife. "And whose bones might they be?" she asked.

Crater opened the bag, then unfolded a purple cloth within to reveal the yellow bones and the skull. Reverently, he placed the skull on the carpet. "These are the remains of Yuri Gagarin, ma'am," Crater said. "The first man in space."

The Czarina's eyes widened. She stood and, with a hesitating step, walked down onto the carpet, then knelt before the skull and the bag of bones. "The bravest Russian," she whispered.

"Yes," a deep voice boomed, "and he is my gift to you, my dear."

Crater looked toward the voice and there stood Colonel Medaris, splendid in a bemedaled military uniform and cavalry boots. He walked up alongside Crater. "You were supposed to deliver this package to me, Crater," he said in a severe tone. "But I will forgive you if you'll tell me how you got here."

"I rode a horse, sir."

The Colonel lifted a single eyebrow. "You are an interesting young man," he said.

"My gillie was killed along the way," Crater added.

"Is that so? I am sorry to hear that. It was an interesting artifact although illegal."

"It knew that, sir."

"We also found some odd devices with this boy, their purposes unknown," the Czarina said as she rose. "What was most intriguing was a container of water that my chemists tell me is perfectly pure, even purer than the melted water ice of the lunar poles. Where did you get it?"

"From the dust of the Sea of Serenity."

"Impossible," she scoffed.

"I can find water there," Crater said. "And I know how to bring it to the surface."

The Colonel and the Czarina traded glances. The Colonel said, "It seems I've underestimated you from the start, my boy."

The Colonel noticed the Czarina was frowning and said, "You are not pleased, my dear?"

"Are these bones a bribe to convince me to let your monorail cross my land?"

"No, my lady," he said. "It is an engagement gift. I have come to ask your hand in marriage."

The Czarina's frown deepened. She nodded to the guards, who reverently picked up the skull and restored it to the duffel bag, then carried the bones away. She turned back to the Colonel, saying, "We will create a fine memorial for the man who led the way for all of us into space. I thank you, Colonel." Then a small smile replaced her frown and she said, "I shall consider your proposal, although marriage of royalty to a commoner is a delicate proposition."

"Yet we would make a great team," the Colonel answered. "The future would be ours."

"Perhaps," she replied with a regal tilt of her head.

The Czarina climbed the steps to her throne, gesturing for the Colonel to sit before her on the steps. He did so.

"Sir," Crater said, "if I may ask, how did you get here? I thought your jumpcar was in need of repair."

"So it was," the Colonel replied, "but the sheriff dispatched the part by a rental jumpcar."

"Did the sheriff tell you I was headed to New St. Petersburg? I didn't think he knew. I didn't tell anyone. I just stole the bones and took off."

The Colonel shrugged. "There are many spies everywhere. If there is a thing that needs to be known, I usually know it."

"Do you know Maria's condition?"

"Of course. I have been in constant contact with her doctors. She is a Medaris, Crater. None so tough in the universe. She will be fine."

Crater knew his part in the Colonel's plan was done. He started to leave but the Colonel's voice stopped him. "Crater, thank you. I suppose now you will want your old job back on the scrapes, but I intend to do better. Your ambition, so I've heard, is to be a foreman. Consider it done. You are now a blue banger."

Crater wanted to be happy. He knew the Colonel expected him to be, and he knew Q-Bess and probably even Petro would be happy for him. But he just couldn't be happy. He was no longer certain he wanted to be a Moontown blue banger. He wasn't even certain he wanted to go back to Moontown at all. So much had happened. He wasn't the same Crater who'd joined the convoy. Maybe his future was to be a convoy scout. He'd liked doing it well enough. "I will think about it, sir," he said.

"That's fine," the Colonel said.

"What happens now?" Crater asked.

"I suppose now things will really get interesting. We're going to build that monorail, assuming the Czarina accepts my idea, and then we may have to fight a little war."

The Colonel's answer, at least the last part of it, confirmed Crater's worst fear. "But who is the enemy, sir? Who are we fighting and why?"

The Colonel allowed a gentle smile. "We fight the ones who lurk in the darkness, Crater, those who would take away our freedom to live our lives the way we choose. Can we count on you to fight with us?"

Crater didn't know if he could be counted on or not. He still felt it important to know who the enemy was. "If you could give me and Pegasus a ride back to Armstrong City, sir, I would appreciate it."

"Of course," the Colonel replied.

Crater left the throne tube and headed to an airlock. There he donned a suit, pulled on a helmet, and went out into the big suck. He needed to get outside where at least he might think and maybe even reach some conclusions.

The sun blazed down, obliterating the stars and casting a golden glow on the dust. Crater looked across the emptiness and thought of his gillie and how it had sacrificed itself. He swore to himself that someday he would go back to where the crowhopper jumpcar had exploded. The gillie had been his friend and deserved at least a prayer said over where it had last breathed, that is if it had any lungs, which, of course, it didn't.

Crater thought about the journey he'd just made and the dangers he'd managed to live through. From the start, the crowhoppers had known too much, had always seemed a step ahead. Were there traitors in the Colonel's circle or on the convoy? If so, who were they? Or was Crater always meant to be a sacrificial lamb, his mission deliberately leaked, so that the sheriff or somebody else could catch the Cycler?

And where was Petro? Had he joined a convoy as the sheriff had suggested? Or did the sheriff know something he wasn't telling?

Crater also thought of Maria, what she had come to mean to him, and also her family. He didn't know if there was any chance of a future with her, but he hoped there might be. Maybe he could be a scout in her company. He just didn't know.

Everywhere Crater looked, there was dust and more dust and the endless expanse of his little planet that Earthians dismissed as the moon. It was a serious little planet, that's what it really was, and also the blessed home for anyone willing to brave its harsh beauty.

Crater was willing. He was willing because of the kindness the people of Moontown had shown him over the years. He was willing because of Q-Bess, Petro, and all the residents of the Dust Palace. He was willing because of the gillie, and the convoy drivers, and poor, brave Captain Teller who'd given everything just to deliver heel-3 to a desperate Earth that depended on his homeland, the moon.

And, to keep his homeland safe, if it meant fighting in a war—even though he knew deep in his heart that there was something very peculiar, perhaps even wrong, with the conflict that was about to be fought—Crater was willing to do even that. He reached for the courage that had always been there, even as he yet doubted its existence. *Let war come if it must*, he thought. He was a boy of the moon. He would fight.

Return to the Moon
for the Next
Helium-3 Novel

∞

≪ TAKING OFF IN 2013 ≫

::: **Notes and Acknowledgments**

The eighth continent of Earth, commonly called the moon but more appropriately Luna, is the least explored of all our land masses, perhaps because it lies approximately 239,000 miles away from the other seven. The continent of Luna—many scientists believe it was torn from the Earth by a little understood but clearly gigantic impact with perhaps another planet—was first visited in 1969 by two Earthians, then followed by ten more on five excursions, bringing back a treasure trove of unique minerals for further study. At the time, it appeared the expansion of our civilization onto the moon was imminent. Lunar facilities were on the drawing boards and a vast new frontier seemed to be open for business. But then it all stopped. Although there are many explanations as to why, none of them are rational or good. As a nation and a world, we've suffered ever since and our eyes and minds have turned inexorably inward. The new frontier, the new continent, remains closed.

Humankind will, of course, eventually sweep back to the moon. It's just a matter of time and circumstances. Luna is too close, too rich, to be ignored forever. Some people will go for scientific purposes and others will go as tourists, but I believe most of them by the thousands will go into that extremely harsh environment to dig, process, containerize, and transport a magical but very real isotope called Helium-3. In other words, they're going to be miners, convoy truckers, and bush pilots, which describe some of my favorite people. As someone who grew up in a mining town and was a coal miner, I am pleased that the future citizens of the moon and I will share a natural bond. It also means that anything I write about the way they act and think, even before it happens, is probably going to be fairly close to reality. Miners and mine owners don't change that much just because a century or two passes by. As for bush pilots and convoy truckers, I know them pretty well too. They're actually a lot alike. They'll get their rigs from point A to point B one way or the other—and do it with some flair.

These days there is much fretting about the kind of energy we use to run our civilization. It is too dirty, some say, and it causes bad things to happen to our climate. That may be so, or it may not, but the fretting will continue either way, and eventually we'll decide to do something about it. No matter what the claims of the green energy industry are, the truth is there is only one clean energy source that has any hope of ever replacing the fossil fuels and nuclear reactors that keep our modern civilization going, and that is the process called fusion. The fusion of two hydrogen atoms to make one helium atom, thus releasing energy, is how the sun works. One of its byproducts, an isotope called Helium-3, turns out to be the best fuel possible for earthly fusion reactors. In a way, that is unfortunate, since it's rare on Earth. This is because the solar wind, that gigantic river of energetic particles (including Helium-3) that flows from the sun, is repelled by our atmosphere and magnetic field.

For those of us who think people should live on the moon, however, this is a good thing. The moon has neither an atmosphere or a magnetic field and therefore the solar wind washes over it like a constant gale, loading it up with lots of Helium-3. When we need it, all we'll have to do is go get it. To accomplish that, surface mining operations on Luna will have to be organized, and miners will be sent to do the work. Robots, however clever and dexterous, will never be able to replace human miners. If they could, they would have already done so on Earth. No, it will take those special men and women who bring with them not only their muscle, but supple minds to solve the myriad and constant problems inherent to all mining.

This novel is my vision of what life will be like on our eighth continent during its raw, frontier mining days before everything gets civilized. It is derived somewhat from an earlier novel of mine, *Back to the Moon*, and is based on my knowledge and biases of the moon, the space business, the mining profession, war, and history. To help fill in, I also interviewed Dr. Barbara Cohen, a NASA planetary scientist and geologist who is often called the "Moon Goddess," for a couple of reasons, one of them because she believes, as I do, the moon will ultimately be settled by Earthians. Dr. Cohen also perused an earlier draft of Crater's fine adventure, making a few suggestions to improve its accuracy, which I appreciated very much. Of course, any scientific or technical errors in this tale are entirely my own.

Further thanks are extended to my most excellent editor, Ami McConnell, whose encouragement almost singlehandedly caused me to write this, the first in a planned trilogy of Helium-3 novels. That's why I dedicated this book to her. She and publisher Allen Arnold and all the folks at Thomas Nelson are truly prodigious. Thanks are also extended to my first editor and wife, Linda Terry Hickam, and her helpmate Mango, our beloved orange tabby, who usually graces her lap while she peruses my scribblings. Of course, I thank all the true rocket boys and rocket girls who are still out there in the space business constructing the machines that will eventually carry us back to the moon, this time to stay, build, dig, sweat, and prosper.

::: Reading Group Guide

1. At the beginning of the novel, Crater is very happy just working the Scrapes, collecting Helium-3. But Petro has bigger plans for both of them. Why do you think Crater was happy doing the same job every day, and why is Petro so eager to get out? Which character do you relate to the most?

2. What would be the best part about living on the moon? What would be the hardest to adjust to? What would you miss most about Earth?

3. The gillie has been with Crater his whole life, but it is illegal, as everyone keeps telling him. Why do you think he never got rid of it? In what ways does it help him in the course of the novel?

4. If you had a gillie, what would you get it to do?

5. When you imagine life on the moon in the years to come, in what ways is it similar to the way life is described in *Crater*? What do you think will be different?

6. What are Crater's greatest strengths? What are his greatest weaknesses?

7. If you lived on the moon, which profession would you be most interested in?

8. Describe life on Earth as Crater sees it. What is different than the way it is now? What is similar? Do you think the Earth in the book is how Earth truly will be in the future?

9. How would you describe the relationship between Crater and Petro? How does it change over the course of the novel?

10. Why did the Colonel choose Crater for his mission? Why did he have second thoughts?

11. On the Colonel's desk is a placard with the phrase "Do not wish ill for your enemy; plan it" engraved on it. What does that let you know about the Colonel as a leader? Do you think Crater thought the same things?

12. On the convoy, the truckers seem to have little respect for Crater, yet Captain Teller expects him to control the truckers. Do you think there is anything Crater could have done early on to gain their respect? Do you think they gained respect for him by the end of the convoy?

13. What do you think is the hardest obstacle Crater encountered on the road to completing his mission? How do you think he managed to survive it all?

14. What do you think will happen next for Crater and his friends?

::: About the Author

HOMER HICKAM is the author of the #1 *New York Times* bestseller *Rocket Boys*, which was made into the acclaimed movie *October Sky*. He is also the author of the bestseller *Torpedo Junction*, *The Keeper's Son*, *The Ambassador's Son*, the award-winning memoir *Sky of Stone*, and the bestseller *Back to the Moon*. He is married to Linda Terry Hickam. See www.homerhickam.com for more information.